DON'T BOTHER KNOCKING. WE ALREADY KNOW YOU'RE HERE.

DEAR ABBEY

DO COME IN, ACOLYTES! NO NEED TO FEAR THE DOG. INDY IS EVER VIGILANT HERE AT THE ABBEY—BUT I KEEP THE BEAST WELL FED. HIS DIET CONSISTS OF BLOODY MEAT... AND THE OCASSIONAL MORSEL HE MANAGES TO UNCOVER WHILE PROWLING THE GRAVES BEYOND THE ABBEY WALLS. He gets plenty of exercise, too. In fact, Indy particularly enjoys a rousing chase. However, with each passing day, our Amazon deliveries become fewer—and I can't understand why: the Abbey is always ready to "entertain" visitors, and Indy just adores having his way with them. Oh well, we'll always have FedEx.

INCIDENTALLY, Indy continues to "have his way" with my much-maligned caretaker, my dear Abbey. Just the other day I watched as that hound from hell dragged the poor fellow through the cemetery, slamming the Keeper of the Crypt against several headstones. Not a bad way to spend a dreary autumn day; I myself rather fancy a scenic stroll among the tombs. And, after all, I did adopt Indy to encourage my dear Abbey to get more exercise—for my cowled caretaker had become a regular lazybones! (Um, a whole bag of 'em, in fact.) But I can now safely write that, thanks to our heavy-duty husky, and after numerous trips and tumbles resulting in a hyperextended knee, a broken finger (which made work on this publication a bit more challenging), several cracked ribs, and a concussive collision with an ancient oak, we're all a lot... "healthier" here at Nightmare Abbey!

In other news, my dear Abbey recently sold two articles to *Better Haunts & Torture Gardens* ("How to Operate a Bloody Dungeon on a Budget!" and "Five Fabulous Decorating Projects Using Shrunken Heads"); and, not to be bested, Indy just made the cover of *Time Magazine*. (Hey, seeing is believing, so turn the page.)

DOG of the YEAR

TIME

THE 100 MOST INFLUENTIAL HUSKIES

INDY ENGLISH

MORE THAN A BEST FRIEND

JUNE 2025

I toil away in the dark recesses of this decaying pile (define the word as "ancient edifice"), wearing out a particularly uncomfortable chair while editing my guts out on this wretched publication, until I...uh, have piles. (I'll leave it to the curious reader to look up this sense of the word. A good medical dictionary may be of some assistance.) With, I might add, little critical recognition.

Face it, we all enjoy an ocassional moment or two of celebrity. Such occasions, no matter how brief, make us feel special: birthdays, anniversaries, funerals even—like the time the local historical society paid me tribute for my outstanding involvement in the community. I was so honored! Yes indeed, I *really* felt special! The Society had constructed a unique chair especially for their guest of honor, and enthroned me upon it, shouting my name with raised fists and great emotion! It was all so touching! Below is the official Society photograph commemorating the event. *Ah, memories!*

I'm exceedingly proud of my Nightmare Abbey roommates and their current accomplishments—if not more than a trifle suspicious of these unusual claims to fame—but I must confess to being rather jealous, as well.

Until next time, faithless readers. (By the way, you guys are sooo crazy!)

Tom English
New Kent, VA

THE BRIDE OF FRANKENSTEIN
(1935, Universal Studios)

NIGHTMARE ABBEY

GHOST STORIES AND OTHER WEIRD TALES

9

COVER AND INTERIOR ILLUSTRATIONS: ALLEN KOSZOWSKI
INTERIOR PHOTO ART: NATU SHABBEY
EDITOR AND PUBLISHER: TOM ENGLISH

GREGORY L. NORRIS (MAY 12, 1965 – MAY 4, 2025) • REQUIESCAT IN PACE

Nightmare Abbey 9 is published by Dead Letter Press and copyright © 2025 by Tom English and Dead Letter Press, PO Box 134, New Kent, VA 23124-0134. All rights reserved, including the right to reproduce this book, or portions thereof, in any form including but not limited to electronic and print media, without written permission from the publisher. Dead Letter Press has endeavored to source and credit the copyright of all stories, photos, and artworks used in this volume but would be glad to right any omissions in the next available issue. All stories, art, and film and television images are copyright © the relevant writers, artists, producers, studios, or publishers, etc. The publisher adheres to the "fair use" policy of using photographic imagery, artworks, and other material for critiquing purposes.
www.DeadLetterPress.com   ISBN-13: 979-8-9927092-2-3

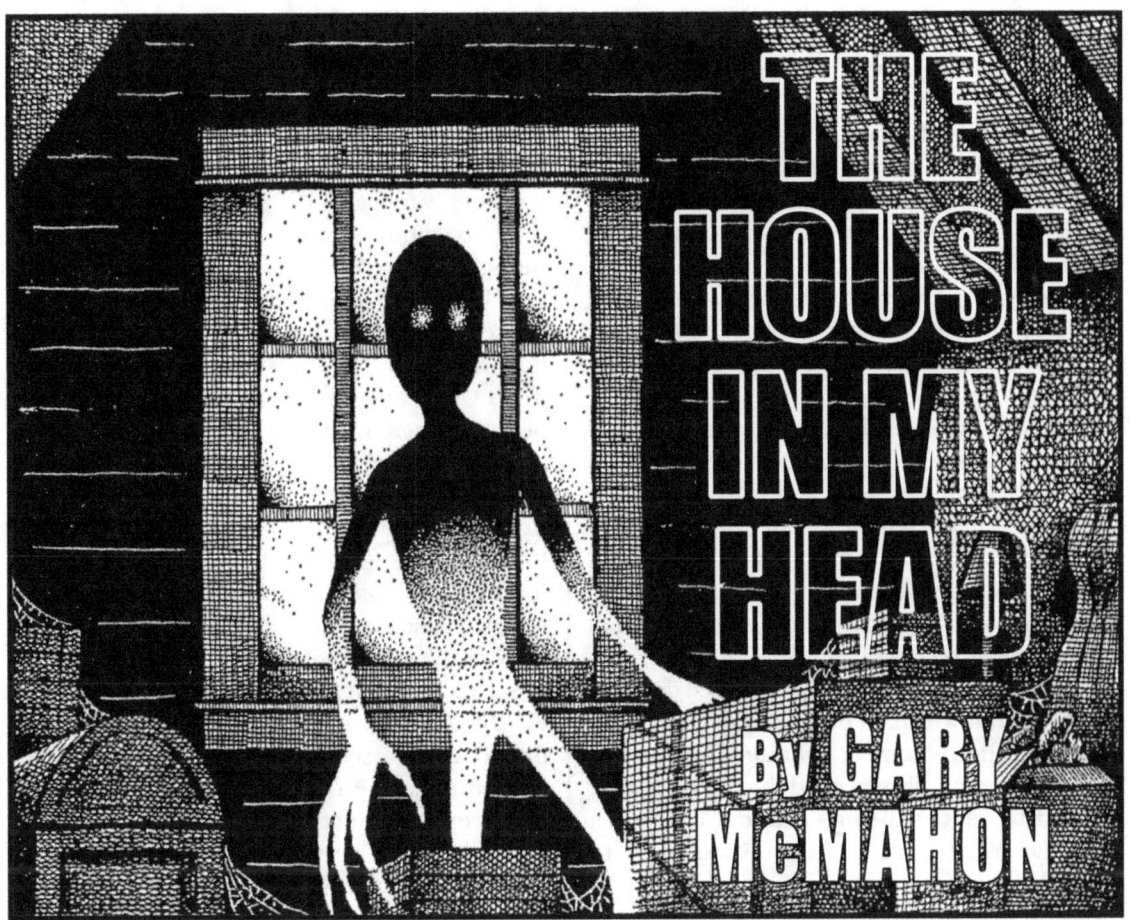

THE HOUSE IN MY HEAD

By GARY McMAHON

THERE'S A HOUSE IN MY HEAD. I KNOW IT'S THERE; I CAN FEEL IT. IF I SIT QUIETLY, WITH NO DISTRACTIONS, I AM AWARE OF THE FOUNDATIONS BURIED IN THE MATTER OF MY BRAIN, the masonry walls as they subtly shift and settle, the roof timbers creaking under the weight of the old slate tiles. Nobody lives in the house. It is unoccupied. I used to reside there once, a long time ago when it was the only place I knew where I could escape the rest of the world. It was my bolt hole. My safe space.

Now that it's empty, I can hear things moving around in there. Late at night, I sense footfalls on the worn floorboards. When I can't sleep, I am aware of something drifting through the dark rooms like a light mist. Even though the house is now un-inhabited, there's something in there. I can feel it, hear it, even smell it—a subtle aroma of lilies.

There's a house in my head, and I think it might be haunted.

LAST NIGHT I called Iris. We hadn't spoken since we split up and I was initially afraid she might hang up on me. I shouldn't have worried: we fell back easily into our usual conversational rhythm.

"How are you?" she said.

"I guess I'm okay. I think."

There was a pause, then she said, "Are you really?"

"No," I said. "No, I'm not okay."

"That's why you called me, right? Because you think I might be able to make you feel better?"

"You always did."

"Ouch."

"Sorry. I didn't mean it that way. Not as a dig. What I mean is, you were the only one who ever made me feel...in balance, I guess."

"That's over now, Paul. *We're* over. I'm not sure what you think I can do for you."

"Just talk to me," I said, fighting back tears. "That's all I ask."

Once she relented, we discussed her new job, my most recent paintings, her mother's failing health. We talked about the weather and pensions and holidays. Food and drink and television. We pretended we were normal people, having a normal conversation."

"I think I'm being haunted," I said, surprising myself.

"Wow. Where did that come from?" There was amusement in her tone, but also a note of concern. "One minute I'm telling you about my neighbour's cat taking a dump on the lawn, and the next you're leaning into the supernatural."

"I'm sorry," I said. It was the truth. I wish I'd not been so hasty.

"Don't be. You were always weird. If I'm honest, that was part of the appeal. Can you explain what you mean, though?"

I'd known this would happen, that I would be required to go into details, and I felt awkward, like a child telling tales to an adult.

"Well, can you?" She was always so damned patient.

"Okay. I'll try." I paused for a couple of seconds, just to clear my mind, before continuing: "You know I told you ages ago about the big anxiety meltdown I had when I was in my early twenties? The time when I was in and out of hospital and dosed up on all kinds of meds."

"Sure. You never kept any secrets from me."

I smiled. She was right. "So back then, when it got really bad, I built a house inside my head."

"A house?"

"Yeah. A house. Or the concept of one, anyway. I used it when I needed to get away, to shut out the noise of the world. When even my art couldn't offer me any refuge. I'd close my eyes, and I'd go deep inside my head, and then into the house. It was nice in there. Clean and minimal. White walls. Tiled floors. No mess. No fuss. Just a peaceful place—a quiet little retreat when things got nasty."

"I think I understand. It's like some kind of psychological trick. You shut yourself up inside your head and wait for the world to quiet down, yeah?"

"That's right. As near to the truth as we'll get, anyway."

"So, what has all this got to do with being haunted?"

"The house has lain empty for years. Since I got better. It's all boarded up, derelict. I even put up a sign saying "Danger! Keep Out!" and I left it to rot. But like a lot of old houses, I think it's got a ghost."

I waited for her to say something—anything—but all I could hear was her breathing on the line. I used to listen to her breathing as she slept. It comforted me, made me feel safe and secure in a way that nothing else could.

"Are you still with me?"

"Yes. Yes, I'm here. Just trying to process all this. If I have it correct, you think the imaginary house you built inside your head is haunted, yes? Your conceptual house has a conceptual ghost."

I nodded. "Sorry. Yes. That's right. Except for one thing: the house might be imaginary, but I think the ghost is real."

"Why now?"

"What do you mean?"

"Well, why has this not happened before? What's suddenly caused this supposed haunting? I watch a lot of those paranormal investigation shows on TV, and there's always a reason for those TV hauntings—a wronged widow, a vengeful lord, a kid who was locked away in a basement to die. There's always a back story."

It was a good question. "I have no idea. It just started happening."

The conversation petered out after that, and eventually she said she had to feed her cat, so we said goodbye and she hung up. She didn't tell me not to call her again, which I took as a good sign. She didn't ask me to keep her in the loop, or let me know if anything else happened either, so I wasn't holding out much hope for some kind of intervention from her. I was going to have to deal with this alone.

That night, things started getting freaky again.

I was sitting on the sofa watching some boring documentary about a failing hotel in Quebec, when I heard a soft, distant moaning sound. I reached out and grabbed the remote, muted the television. I heard the sound again. I stood and walked to the window, looked out into the street to see if there was anyone there. We have a problem with homeless people in this part of the city: they roam around, going through bins and sleeping in gardens and parking spaces. I thought it might be one of those poor people causing a scene.

The street was empty. It usually was, on a Sunday. The road surface and footpaths were wet from the rain we'd had earlier. The little off licence over the road had the shutters pulled down over its windows but the door was open. A tall, thin figure—probably the owner, Ali—stood just inside the doorway, holding a lit cigarette and blowing smoke out into street.

I realised the sound was not in fact coming from outside; it was coming from inside my head. I heard it again, followed by the slamming of a door. Footsteps on wooden boards, a swishing noise, like the wind through trees. Then my nostrils were filled with the smell of lilies, strong enough to almost make me choke.

I stepped back from the window, coughing and sputtering, and went through to the kitchen for a glass of water. I chugged it down, trying to clear my throat. Seconds later, the smell was gone. The sounds inside my head had ceased.

Later, as I lay in bed, I wondered why this was happening to me? What had I done to draw the attention of whatever entity was roaming around inside the house in my head? I picked up my phone to type Iris a text message: *It's happened again. I'm scared now.* I deleted it without sending; I didn't want to burden her with my worries, not after the lukewarm reception she'd given me when I'd called her.

It struck me then how selfish I'd been, calling her like that. I hadn't even asked how she was, simply blurted out my own problems, expecting her to run to my aid.

"Idiot," I said. Somewhere inside my head, a door slammed shut.

The next day I called in sick from work. I had a headache and couldn't face being around my colleagues. Most of them were nice enough people, but I struggled to fit in. All my life I'd felt like an outsider, a "black sheep." It was even worse at work, where the subjects of conversation tended to be football, families, dull little office affairs... none of it mattered to me. All I really cared about was my painting, and that didn't make me enough money to enable me to quit the day job, so I dragged myself through the days, praying for something better. Wishing for a miracle.

I went into my little studio and looked at the canvas that was currently taking up space on my easel. It was a mess: lines and slashes, obscure clusters of colour and dots of black that refused to take shape. I had no idea what I was trying to do; the whole thing was a bad joke.

I sat at my desk and grabbed a pencil, started doodling in a pad. It was a habit I'd picked up in my childhood, and it often helped me relax when I was feeling anxious, almost like a form of meditation. I let the pencil wander across the page, drawing from instinct. A sheeted ghost, a bowl of noodles, a car with a tent on top of it. Mindless stuff, quick sketches to distract myself from more important matters.

I started to draw the floor plan of a house. *The* house. The one in my head. It was a small dwelling, with not much of a footprint. The ground floor consisted of a short hallway, a living room, a kitchen, and a tiny toilet under the stairs. I filled in the gaps, drawing furniture and kitchen appliances. Before long, I'd outlined the entire floor plan.

I tore the sheet out of my sketch pad and did the same for the first floor: a narrow landing two double bedrooms, an upstairs bathroom, the stairs to the roof space.

I tore out that sheet and sketched the roof plan. It was a simple layout: one large empty room divided down the middle by the head of the stairs.

I laid out the sheets on my desk, examining them. On the ground floor, behind the sofa I'd drawn, was a smudge of grey, as if I'd dragged the ball of my hand across the page and smeared graphite from the pencil. I looked at my hand: it was clean. I looked again at the smudge. It seemed slightly larger than it had a second before, and more defined.

The smudge now resembled a figure, balled up on the floor behind the sofa with its legs bent under and its arms curled over its head. It lay in what seemed to me a crude foetal position.

Was this my ghost? The entity that was haunting the house?

I tapped my fingertips on the desktop, thinking. Then, slowly, I reached for an eraser and held it above the smudge.

Could it really be this simple? Could I erase the ghost and never be bothered by it again?

I rubbed out the smudge, clearing that part of the paper. It stayed blank; the form did not slowly leech back onto the sheet or come crawling out of another corner, inching across the page towards my hand like some relentless Jamesian phantom.

Something caught my eye—one of the other pages, the one upon which I'd sketched the first-floor layout. In the bathroom, curled up in the bathtub, was the smudged figure. This time It was lying flat, face down, with its arms held stiff at its sides. My mouth was dry; my eyes ached. I could smell the aroma of lilies.

I screwed up the sheets of paper and tossed them into the litter bin under my desk. If I'd had a fire in the room, I'd have burned them. Purified them. And maybe scattered salt over the ashes just to be safe.

It was never going to be that easy. Of course it wasn't. I needed to work harder for my freedom, put in a lot of effort to exorcise this sketchy spirit. I thought about all the ghost stories I'd read, the horror films I'd seen. There was always a quirky medium, or a friend who had a friend who owned an occult bookshop with books full of answers. But real life is rarely so neat and tidy.

I picked up my phone and thought about calling Iris. The phone rang, shocking me into dropping it onto the floor. I crawled around on my hands and knees under the desk to retrieve it and frantically pushed the button to answer the call.

"Hi. I had a sudden urge to speak to you."

"Iris? I...I was only just thinking about you."

"Is it still happening? Your haunting."

"I'm sorry, I shouldn't have told you about it. That was so selfish of me—I was always selfish, which is probably why you wanted to leave me."

"I never *wanted* to leave you; I just felt that it was better for both of us if I did. We're not good for each other, and you know it. All we do is stroke each other's wounds, making them worse under the pretence of making them better. I couldn't see any future in it, that's all. I...I'm still your friend. We were always that: friends."

"Yes, we were. Thanks. I need a friend right now."

"Have you thought about what you might do, how to solve this thing? I had an idea last night—a silly one, but I think I'm going to tell you anyway."

"Right now, any idea might help. I don't care how silly it sounds."

I imagined her smiling. My heart was breaking all over again.

"Maybe if you thought about demolishing the house. I mean, really thought about it. Visualisation, you know? Manifestation. The same method you used to create it in the first place. Just turn that energy around on itself and imagine a demolition crew—trucks and diggers and one of those huge metal balls on a chain. Tear the house down... trash it so that there's nothing left but a pile of rubble."

Under the circumstances, it seemed like a decent plan.

"I don't think that's as silly as it sounds, you know. I remember when I first thought about the house. I drew it, visualised every detail, and then it appeared in my head. This time, I could try a similar thing and draw it as a ruin, a wreck: all torn down and ripped apart, or burnt to ash."

"It might be worth a try."

"Would you come over and help me. I could use the moral support, just someone being here in case—I don't know, in case something bad happens."

"I'll be there in half an hour."

When I opened the door, she was wearing a little summer dress with big work boots and a denim jacket covered in patches for obscure bands I'd never heard of. Her dark hair was wet from the rain. Her mascara had run down her cheeks like black tears. I'd never seen her look so lovely.

"The lift was out of order," she said, breathing heavily and wiping her face with the sleeve of her jacket. "Those stairs are a killer."

"Sorry. It's the local kids. They're a menace, vandalising everything."

She pushed past me, took off her jacket, and sat down heavily on the sofa. For a small girl, she was incredibly heavy on her feet. It never ceased to amuse me.

"I think it might be better to try this in my studio," I said. "That's where all my art stuff is, and where I feel most creative."

She followed me into the spare room, which served as my creative hub. I grabbed a hand towel and threw it to her. She caught it deftly and rubbed the rest of the watery makeup off her face.

It was growing dark outside, so I switched on the light. Her cheeks shone. Rain pattered at the windows. Inside my head, something stirred. Footsteps lightly tapping up or down the stairs, fingernails scratching the walls, a strangely familiar low humming sound, like the beginning of an almost forgotten children's song.

"I've already made a start." I showed her the large sheet of paper where I'd drawn the front elevation of the house and the outline of a bulky hydraulic excavator.

"You were always so good at this. I still can't believe you're not a famous artist by now." She winked. I smiled. I couldn't believe how excited she was, and it started to rub off on me. This plan, I thought, might just work.

Leaning over the desk, I started to fill in the background. Slashes of rain, a grey sky, workmen with sledgehammers and pickaxes, a digger on caterpillar tracks. I heard Iris dragging over a stool and felt a light pressure as she sat right next to me, her body touching mine.

"Close your eyes," she said. "Let your imagination guide your hand."

I closed my eyes but kept on drawing, trusting myself to express what I felt. The pencil seemed to move across the paper on its own. I was barely pushing it. I saw the workmen, heard them shouting, felt the rain on my face, tasted the dust in the air. Engines. Hammering. Drilling. The house began to break apart, piece by piece: the walls fell away, the timbers snapped, the floors and roof caved in. It all fell to earth, demolished by the power of my imagination—the same way it had been built in the first place.

When I opened my eyes, it was dark. Iris was staring at me, her eyes wide. I could smell lilies.

"The lights went out," she whispered. "I was shaking you, shouting your name, but you were in some kind of trance."

Slowly, I shook my head. It felt heavy, filled with debris. "Did it work?"

"I don't know," she said. "But look." She motioned with her head towards the desktop, where the sheet of paper still lay. The pencil was in my hand, but at some point, it had snapped. The end was splintered; the graphite point had turned to powder under what must have been immense pressure.

The drawing was terrifying. It had been done in a rage, conceived by an angry hand and a tortured mind. The workmen either lay or knelt on the ground, most of them covering their faces with their hands or forearms. The machinery was smoking, the wheels broken, the windshields shattered. The crane tower was bent at an angle of ninety degrees, the metal cross braces twisted and snapped.

The house was a pile of rubble. It looked as if it had sunk partially into the ground as it was demolished, forming a crater. Within that crater were strange things—deformed creatures I could barely make out, all torn and twisted and impaled on the exposed rebar from the house's foundations.

"Can you turn on the lights?" Iris was still whispering.

I stood, steadying myself against the desk, and then made my way towards the light switch on the wall. When I flicked it, nothing happened, so I did it again, several times. Finally, the spotlight bulbs in the ceiling flickered, then brightened.

That was when I saw it. On the wall behind the desk, not far from where Iris was still sitting, rubbing her arms as if she were cold. A huge grey smudge on the wall, as if someone had taken a giant pencil and shaded the area directly behind my chair. It was the shape of a figure, but bloated and elongated, and with what seemed to be far too many limbs. It looked to me like a flattened representation of a person, a body upon which a massive amount of pressure had been applied, squashing it against the wall.

The smudge had spread.

It was out of the house in my head and in the real world. A virus infecting my reality.

"Come here," I said, looking only at Iris. "Now, please."

Behind her, the smudge shifted, pulsing gently.

Iris stood.

"Don't look anywhere except at me," I said, holding out a hand.

She walked stiffly towards me, stumbling a little as her hip caught against the edge of the desk.

The lights flickered. The smudge seemed to leap silently from its spot on the wall and attach itself to the ceiling, where it hung like a wispy spider before starting to drop towards the floor in a strange liquid motion.

"What's happening?" Iris grabbed me.

"I don't know...just be calm. Stand here with me and don't panic."

The lights flickered again. The smell of lilies intensified, becoming a stench.

In the centre of the room, something was taking shape. It formed between the flickers of the lightbulbs, growing in those tiny interstices of darkness between the flashes of light. It was a house. A small house whose layout I knew only too well.

"Stay there." I walked towards the house, watching as it emerged clumsily into the world in a series of painful tics and twitches, like something reluctant to be born. It grew to a height where the roof was level with my waist, and then it stopped. I touched the roof tiles, the chimney, the gutters. They were solid. They were real.

Bending down, I opened the front door. I stared along the little hallway, looking at the open internal doors. The doorframes held only blackness. I was dimly aware of movement behind me, and I felt the ghost of the house move across me, like a shadow over water, and watched as it rippled over the front elevation of the house before oozing inside.

The door handle began to vibrate in my hand, rattling as if it were alive, and then the door slammed shut, almost breaking my fingers with its sudden burst of violence. Inside the house, the lights went on. In the larger room where I stood, the bulbs popped, one by one, letting the darkness in.

"Paul, I'm scared..." Iris was still behind me, where I'd left her, safe at least for now.

"Hush," I said. "It's all going to be okay."

Something was running up and down the stairs, excited and energetic, strips of it peeling away like ribbons to drift away and begin to birth new tenants for the house. These additional forms took up residence in the dusty corners of rooms, inside canted doorways, inside and on top of the broken kitchen counters...anywhere they could find a space to occupy. The lights in the house flashed on and off wildly, a tiny display of eagerness. For so long, this house had existed only inside my head, and now it was here, it was real—and it was miraculous.

"Paul!" I'm sure she screamed my name, but I was so far away now that it sounded like a hushed whisper. I was in another place, at another point in time, and her fear was nothing but a distant echo from a place to which I could never return. My only regret was that I'd never got to say goodbye.

I sat down on the floor outside the house and peeked in through the windows. The movement inside was becoming frantic. There was a celebration going on.

Misshapen figures danced and careened silently across the rooms, along the hallway, up the stairs, and finally gathered in the attic, where they began to sing a wordless melody, something that sounded a little bit like a child's nursery rhyme—one I'd not heard for such a long time and was only just starting to remember.

The one ghost had become a crowd.

These were all the ghosts I'd ever known, the personal phantoms I'd created since childhood. The hopes and fears, the joy, the pain, the heartache; the good days and the bad, the gains and the losses, every tiny victory or defeat I'd ever experienced. My ghosts; my houseguests, finally inhabiting the space I'd made for them. They were hosting a homecoming party just for me.

I knew at some point I would be invited inside to join them.

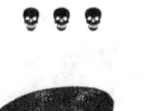

Gary McMahon writes intensely personal horror stories. His short fiction has appeared in countless anthologies and magazines and has been reprinted in The Best Horror of the Year, The Year's Best Fantasy & Horror *and* Best New Horror. *He's been nominated for several awards and even won a couple of obscure ones. He is the author of the* Thomas Usher *novels,* The Concrete Grove *trilogy.* The End, The Bones of You, *and his novella* The Grieving Stones *was recently adapted into a feature film. He lives with his family in Yorkshire, UK, where he reads, writes, watches far too many films, lifts weights, and trains in Shotokan karate.*

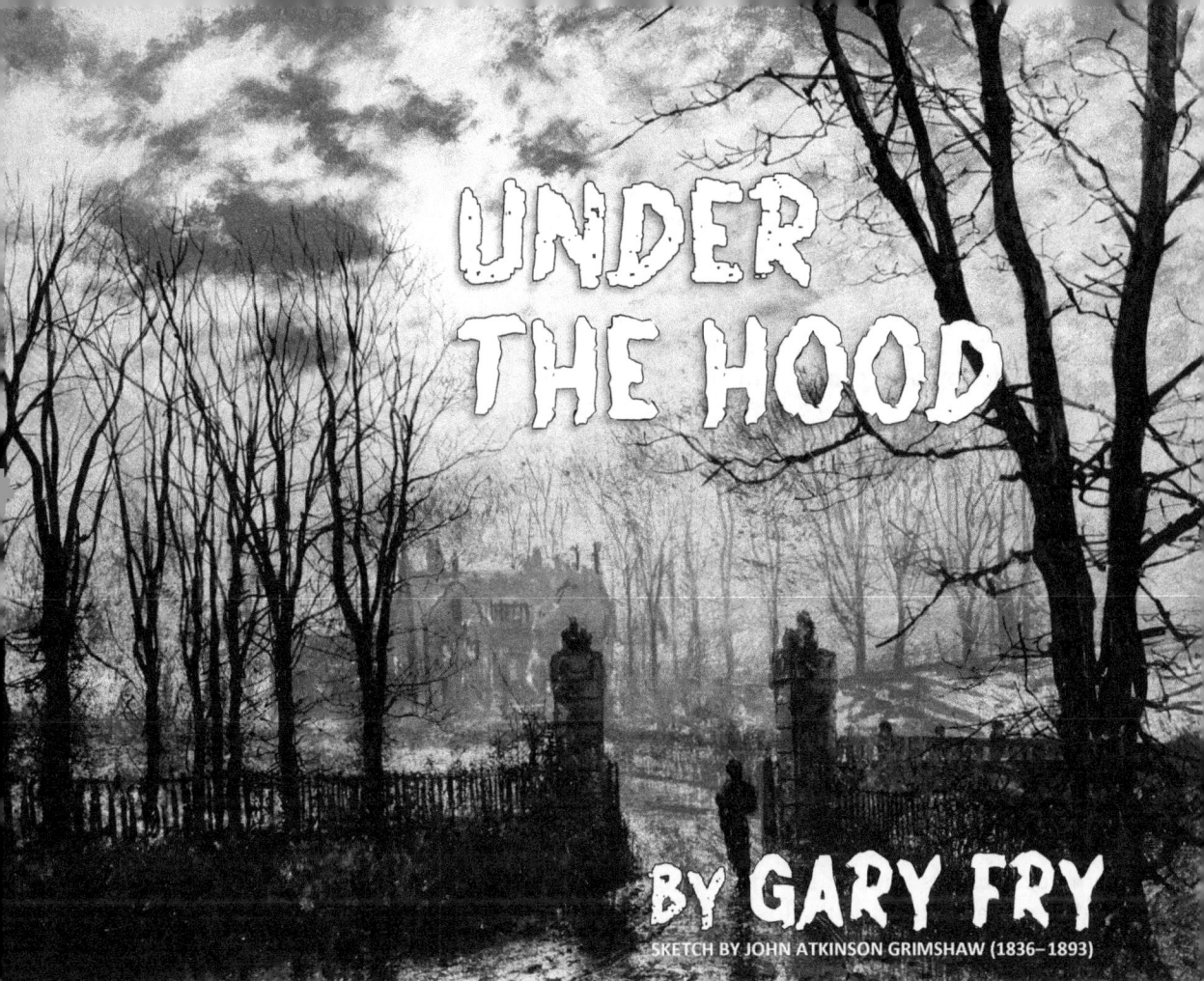

UNDER THE HOOD

BY GARY FRY

SKETCH BY JOHN ATKINSON GRIMSHAW (1836–1893)

"SINCE MY HUSBAND DIED LAST YEAR, THE PLACE HASN'T HAD MUCH ATTENTION," said Josephine, a spiderweb of wrinkles rippling across her face. "So I'm afraid you're likely to have your work cut out."

After being unemployed for over a year—much of that time spent under the influence of one substance or another—Lauren was just glad of the opportunity. The cleaning job was well paid and involved working only one day a week, which meant it wouldn't affect her welfare support arrangements.

"I reckon I'll be all right," she said, slightly embarrassed by her coarse accent in the company of such a well-spoken older woman. "It's a lot bigger than me own little pad, like. But I manage to keep that tidy nowadays."

It was true. Her flat back in the city was maybe only an eighth of the size of this house out in the country. She'd read about the job on a card placed in a local shop window, and after calling the number last week,

she'd been invited for an interview. But the owner, clearly living alone, had hardly made that an interrogation; it had been more like getting to know each other, as if they might even become friends.

"I'll make a start then, shall I?" said Lauren, who'd just finished a cup of tea the woman had made after she'd arrived.

"Take it at your own pace, my dear." At that moment, however, Josephine's smile seemed to lose a little of its charm. "I've never been one to crack the whip, not like my... ah, but *he's* gone now. So let's not worry about that."

If the woman had once had a difficult partner, Lauren could understand that well enough. Her own boyfriend, Kieran, had always been hard to live with. In fact, she might have got herself straight a lot sooner without him.

Smiling as she exited the kitchen, Lauren took herself off to a cupboard under the grand staircase, where she removed a vacuum cleaner to join the various cloths and sprays she'd brought along in a bag. Deciding to start at the top of the building and work down, she headed up the stairs, a hose slithering along in pursuit like some stealthy python.

It was a beautiful house, spread across three levels, but it had sadly been neglected. The carpets were thick and the walls elegantly papered. Robust sticks of antique-looking furniture occupied each of the twelve rooms she'd examined during her one previous visit. The windows surely remained in their original form, lead-hatched with fragile panes of glass. It must get cold here in winter, thought Lauren, feeling grateful it was only October.

She vacuumed and dusted the top-floor bedrooms, whose ceilings sloped to accommodate the slate roof she'd observed from outside. Spiders had left the spaces behind thick curtains filled with dusty tangles of web, but she managed to dispatch them all at arms' length with a nozzle attachment. She didn't like anything that crept or crawled, nor any insects that flitted around on wings.

Returning to the first floor, she observed artefacts mounted on the walls or perched on shelves. Most of them—bizarre sculptures or weird sorts of symbols—looked like stuff that appeared in the films Kieran liked to watch. Lauren always preferred a good romance to any grisly horror. If not for all the strange stuff in this house, she might have thought Josephine would, too. Perhaps some of the items were religious in nature.

The next room Lauren entered seemed to have been reserved for storage. Amid more strange bric-a-brac, she was struck by a number of framed paintings clustered in one corner, at least twenty-five standing vertically in a row—certainly more than could be hung in even such a large house. Had Josphine's money originally come from art dealing? As Lauren flipped through them, she made a mental note to ask the homeowner about that later.

She thought her boyfriend would like some of the pictures. He'd taken a painting class while serving a latest sentence for possession and knew a little bit about art. All the canvases were dark in nature—creepy old people with unsmiling faces, vast landscapes bathed in moonlight, and houses even more gothic than the one in which Lauren stood. She removed her phone and took photos of each image. It would be something to discuss when Kieran came over tonight, keeping their minds off drugs they no longer used.

LATER, AFTER LEAVING the property much cleaner, Lauren headed home, clutching the £60 Josephine had given her. "See you next week, I hope," the older woman had said in a tremulous voice, and Lauren had nodded. She wondered if Josephine was lonely; it couldn't be easy living so remotely, in a house big enough for more than just one person.

Before dense roadside foliage fully concealed the building, Lauren turned to observe it again in the gloom. Its redbrick façade glared back, the upper-storey windows on this side resembling watchful eyes, unblinking as some dead body's. She thought (but couldn't be certain) one of them belonged to the room containing the paintings, and if she saw a figure beyond the window—however smudged with shadow it appeared—that was far from a mystery. Perhaps Josephine was wandering around the place, inspecting her new cleaner's work.

An edgy breeze pursued Lauren all the way to the main road, ruffling the hedges to each side of her. But she was soon on the bus and heading towards her familiar manmade environment. Once her ride had grumbled to a halt in a high street, she got off and hurried along a number of dark alleys. When she reached her tenement building, she spotted a figure loitering in its doorway, but it was only Kieran, swathed in the hoodie he'd taken to wearing, which helped him handle his paranoia. He didn't even remove it after she'd led him inside, and she'd warmed them both a processed meal before she saw his face for the first time today.

He didn't look well, the bones of his skull worryingly angular amid so much pasty flesh. He needed feeding up, as Lauren's mum might have said, before she'd succumbed to cancer in Lauren's mid-teens. Lauren's vulnerability at the time had left her susceptible to the older boy's coping habits, but in such mutual adversity (he'd also lost a parent early in life), they'd forged a strong bond.

Later, while watching TV and smoking skinny rollups, she showed him the photos she'd taken earlier on her phone. He was immediately engaged; a teacher running his art course had suggested that his need to take drugs might be an attempt to stifle a creative instinct which had never been allowed to flower.

"Are they all originals?" said Kieran, leaning forwards on the worn couch they shared.

"I forgot to ask the woman anything about them." Lauren used her thumb to sidesweep through several more of the images. "But they all looked quite—"

"Hey, wait a minute," said Kieran, jabbing a skeletal hand at the screen. "Scan back a few."

She did as she'd been asked, and her boyfriend soon stopped her, nudging aside her forefinger with one even thinner.

"Christ, I don't believe it," he said, voice quavering, the way he'd used to sound whenever he was in need of a fix. "That's an *Atkins Shaw*."

"That's a *who*?" she said, getting her grammar confused, not least because she'd messed up her final year at school.

"Oh, he's a *great* painter. I learned all about him in my class. His style is hugely recognisable." He glanced again at the picture. "And *that's* definitely one of his."

What was Kieran suggesting—that Josephine, back at that isolated house, was in possession of one or even more valuable paintings? When her boyfriend went on with some eagerness, Lauren sensed her anxiety levels rise just a little.

"Shaw is not, like, *world* famous. But he's known well enough to be highly sought after on the UK art circuit." He pointed again at the painting, which was of countryside crowned by starlight and with a property lurking in the distance, its features hardly distinguishable. "I bet this one is worth at least fifteen or twenty K."

Her eyes widened; she knew she'd have to work a lifetime to save anything like the sum. Kieran, registering her expression, smiled for the first time since his arrival this evening. He didn't need to put into words what he was thinking, and on this occasion, Lauren was unable to assign the unbidden voice in her head to any drug.

"Oh *no*, Kieran. I'm trying to do things *proper* now," she protested, still feeling ashamed of the shoplifting to which she'd resorted the previous year. "I want to cut out all the bad stuff. Earn an honest living, like."

"I'm only saying you should make some enquiries. Who knows, maybe the old biddy—"

"She's *not* an old biddy. She's *nice*."

"Okay, okay. So maybe the nice old lady doesn't even know what she has in her house."

Lauren thought for a moment, struggling to get two meddlesome figures out of her head: fifteen-thousand pounds…twenty-thousand pounds…A moment later, she said, "Well, she did mention her husband, who apparently died recently."

"There you go, then. Perhaps the pictures were his."

"Yeah. But that only means they're *hers* now."

"That's true, I suppose. But come on, Lauren, from the way you've described her house, it hardly sounds like she's short of a few bob."

She hated the way he always did this—made bad behaviour sound reasonable, even justifiable. How many times lately had she considered chucking him? But she also knew he needed her. He hadn't worked in years—in fact, with his mental condition, he *couldn't* work. If she abandoned him, he'd go straight back on the gear, she just knew it.

Observing his gaunt face, she let out a sigh. "Okay, I'm not promising anything," she said, putting away her phone and staring once again at the TV they had quietly running. "But I guess there's no harm in merely asking, is there?"

• • •

WHEN SHE ARRIVED for work at Josephine's house the following week, Lauren felt hugely apprehensive. She'd been unable to get Kieran to shut up about the painting for days. He'd disturbed her by mentioning some dodgy contacts in the underworld, including a guy who could apparently fence any kind of goods. Lauren wished she'd never agreed to get involved in such a racket. Was anything lower than conning a single, elderly woman?

Even so, after cleaning the property's upper levels, Lauren found herself back inside the room containing what might be a treasure trove of unknown art. The painting she'd come to look at again was about half-way along the row. It was quite small, about eight inches square, and now, with a better view of it than the bleary image on her phone, she noticed two initials in its bottom-right corner: "A. S."

That surely meant that Kieran couldn't be wrong about the artist, but what to make of the picture itself? Lauren drew it closer to her face and grew immediately puzzled. Was the house, lurking just below the horizon, much larger than she'd originally believed?

She pulled away, stupidly using a cloth to wipe her fingerprints off the frame as she replaced the painting. If she did end up stealing it—a thought that made her heart rate accelerate—she'd be in much more trouble than merely touching things that didn't belong to her. Exiting the room, she suddenly spotted, hanging on the wall above the door, a photograph of a dour older man, eyes staring madly. She felt observed, found out, but then went hurriedly downstairs.

It was time for her break, and Josephine had prepared a pot of tea and put a plate of biscuits on the kitchen table. Lauren appreciated the hospitality, especially as she hadn't eaten that morning, as much a result of anxiety as lack of funds.

"Your house is full of such wonderful stuff," she said a few minutes later, shielding her face behind a steaming cup. "I guess most of it means a lot to you."

Josephine shrugged, her usual warm expression becoming neutral. "Most of it was my late husband's. He travelled a lot, pursuing his interests, and used to bring back plenty of garish things."

Lauren wondered whether the older woman's dismissive attitude extended to the art stored upstairs. But it would be unwise to concede such thoughts so soon. Anyway, something else Josephine had said had piqued her curiosity.

"You mentioned he had interests—uh, what *were* they?"

"Oh, just rather obscure religions, my dear," the older woman said, taking up a biscuit and snapping it in two, which sounded like a bone breaking. "But it was more than mere scholarship. In later life, he also engaged in certain practices."

That would account for the many weird symbols scattered around the house, thought Lauren, thinking again of her boyfriend's scary films. But spooking herself would only add to her unease.

"I, uh, take it you didn't share any of his beliefs?"

"Not when they turned him into the person he became at the end."

It would be unkind to ask more about that, so Lauren switched to a new method of getting the information she needed. "Is that why you're not fond of all the gear, then—because it puts you in mind of him?"

Josephine nodded, glancing out of the window, where a tidy garden shimmered in a silent breeze. "I keep meaning to get rid of it all," she said, flicking rheumy eyes back towards Lauren. "But you know how it is. *Tempus fugit.*"

Lauren had no idea what this meant—a phrase from the dead man's peculiar studies, perhaps—but it wasn't important right now. All she knew was that, should she choose to act upon it, the woman had just approved Lauren's boyfriend's devious plan.

DESPITE FEELING WATCHED later that day, it was easy to remove the painting from the centre of the pile and transfer it to the bag in which she carried all her cleaning products. At that very moment, she sensed a presence behind her, but when she whirled to look, there was nothing: just the window with its fragile pane of glass, presumably letting in an autumnal chill. Steadying her shaking hands, Lauren told herself not to be stupid. What kind of a ghost would possess the ability to exhale against the nape of her neck?

The idea disturbed her, so she hurriedly left the room and descended the staircase. Suddenly she seemed even more aware of the artefacts placed around the property. One framed photograph, so smudged it might even be a work of art, showed several monk-like figures clustered outside a dilapidated church. It was hard to detect a face beneath the voluminous garments each wore, but Lauren nonetheless wondered which of the figures might be the late homeowner, whose watchful eyes she'd surely observed in that photo back in the room.

But she managed to suppress her panic. After collecting her usual cash payment and bidding goodbye to foolishly trustworthy Josephine, Lauren left the building, rushed down the garden path and out into the country lane, and finally started advancing for the main road.

It was getting dark already, and when she turned without slowing to look again at the house, she struggled to distinguish its features. Feeling certain this time that she could see nobody through that second-floor window—no sign of Josephine checking if anything had been stolen—Lauren snapped her head forwards, the bag shuffling at her side like some prowling animal.

Whatever lurked in the hedge alongside her seemed restless, seeming to pace her as she moved…But she wouldn't allow that thought any room in her head. She was simply feeling paranoid, like the addict she'd once been. That must also account for her impression that, after she'd boarded the bus, a figure was seated behind her on the lower deck, despite none having been there when she'd sat down. Putting trust in her sobriety, Lauren refused to turn and check. And when she finally reached her stop, she felt relieved, even though there was still the short, moonlit walk through the city's backstreets to endure.

Someone up ahead was chanting as she rounded a corner, but it turned out to be only a football fan emerging from a rundown pub. Wishing the man might mimic someone nobler, taking a vow of silence perhaps, Lauren approached her tenements. She prayed God had no further plans to draw her attention to the bag she carried, one packed so full of sin.

Then she was inside, throwing off her jacket, grabbing a beer from the fridge, slumping on the couch, and at last, once she'd drunk enough to settle her brain, texting her boyfriend to say she'd done what he'd so thoughtlessly proposed.

THEY BOTH SPENT most of the evening looking at the painting. Its landscape had been rendered aggressively in thick oils, the effect of nightlight vivid and suggestive. Most of the environment it depicted was rural, though a hint of human intervention was present in the form of the house at its centre, as thoroughly secluded as the one from which Lauren had stolen the canvas.

"It's beautiful" said Kieran, revealing a sensitivity she'd often detected, possibly the only reason she hadn't moved on from him.

"Does that mean you don't intend to sell it?" she said, perhaps even hoping he'd say yes, despite the nerve-wracking risk she'd taken to boost their finances.

"I'm a big fan of Atkins Shaw, but not *that* much of one." He pushed back his hoodie, revealing his cadaverous face. "Besides, I need…I mean, *we* need the money."

For what, Lauren reflected with sudden unease? She'd been sharp enough to pick up on her boyfriend's verbal slip just now and wondered whether drugs still spoke through him, controlling his brain, operating his tongue. Possession could take many forms, as she knew all too well; it wasn't always as silly as it appeared in the horror films Kieran liked to watch.

The canvas was perched on her coffee table, propped up by a beercan neither of them had yet to open. Kieran leaned forward from the couch, reaching out to touch the painting with one febrile hand. The instant he made contact, his face creased into a scowl as he snatched away his spindly fingertips.

Lauren told herself that the chill she suddenly experienced arose only from the lack of heating in the room. But then she glanced at her boyfriend, his face appearing so frightened that she immediately grabbed the beer, letting the canvas fall over as she offered it to him. When he turned the drink down, she grew all the more troubled.

"I've gotta go," he said, rising from the couch and dragging the hood back across his head. When he spoke again, looking pointedly away from the toppled painting, he sounded almost fearful. "I'll get in touch with my contact. Set forces in motion. We need to...we need to get rid of that *thing*."

He was right to want the canvas gone, but maybe his reasons were different from hers. Suffering memories of all the derangements they'd endured during the last few years, Lauren stubbed out her inadequate cigarette and saw her boyfriend to the exit. He went eagerly, body looking frailer than usual, as if something clung to him, weighing him down. And when she finally shut him out, she couldn't decide whether the real trouble in their lives right now was on this or the other side of the door.

IN THE MIDDLE of the night, Lauren awoke with a start and got up to investigate a sound she thought she'd heard in her flat. She'd been burgled twice since moving here a year ago, which had bemused her, as she had nothing much to steal. Even so, she felt fiercely protective of her territory; it was really all she had.

There was nothing amiss in the lounge. The only difference from the previous day was the presence of *that* painting, still laid out on her coffee table. She flicked on a light to dispel the flat's spectral gloom and then paced towards the picture, shoving aside an overpopulated ashtray and several crushed tincans. That was when the image astonished her.

It had *changed*. Yes, the house at the centre, previously so lacking in size that it had been impossible to see it properly, was much larger now, boasting a number of moonlit features that, in Lauren's half-awake state, caused her even more anxiety. For one thing, the place was made of red brick, and for quite another it possessed three floors...

But no, she wouldn't speculate recklessly. Instead, she went to fetch her phone from the bedroom and accessed its photos. When she returned, she sat on the couch and held her back-turned device next to the canvas. Although the image onscreen was small, there was no question that in the newer version beside it, the artist who'd created this work—Atkins Shaw, had Kieran called him?—must have been stationed a few hundred yards *closer* to the property. The landscape around the building had also altered, reflecting such a spatial shift forwards. It was as if the viewer were zeroing in on the house.

Lauren felt herself shudder, but then, with a strength arising from many negative recent experiences, she accessed the internet on her phone. At first, her fingertips fumbled on the screen, but she eventually managed to type the name of the artist into a search engine. Several frustrating seconds later, a page of results appeared, allowing her to select the first link in the list.

It turned out that Atkins Shaw was a cult British artist who'd lived in the late twentieth century and was known for a spectral style. He'd been drawn to dark subject matter, particularly nocturnal landscapes, or people occupying that tenuous borderland between life and death. At the end of his career—he'd succumbed to cancer in his late forties—he'd explored various arcane religions, seeking a chaste existence in contrast with one previously bedevilled by substance abuse. Rumours that he'd also been involved in occult practices were unsubstantiated, though a journalist claimed to have strong evidence in favour of such nefarious activities on the part of Shaw and several unnamed associates.

Lauren let her hand fall away, revealing the canvas once more. Was it possible, she wondered with mounting fretfulness, that the artist had known the painting's owner, Jacqueline's late husband? It had been the reference to obscure religious practices that made Lauren think this likely. Her body beginning to tremble, she glanced again at the starlit building stationed amid what suddenly struck her as familiar countryside.

Now she'd had time to reflect, there could be little doubt about it. Although she had no reason to suppose the picture had changed once more as she'd explored the internet—shifting incrementally like a clock hand, moving nearer still to the viewer—the house at its heart was almost certainly the one from which Lauren had stolen the canvas.

SHE DIDN'T SLEEP again that night, just sat up in the lounge as dawn rose at her curtained window. She'd called Kieran early, knowing he'd be asleep in bed in his own flat but not caring about that. He'd got her into this weird situation and must now do what he'd pledged to do the previous evening: get rid of the painting. At once.

By noon, Lauren, who'd frantically checked the canvas at least every half-hour, felt as if she'd moved closer still to that property. She could see the place's hatched windows, its erect chimney, its sprawling garden. To judge by the modest height of trees around it, the painting must have been executed a few generations ago, back when Shaw had lived and practised his peculiar art. Lauren spotted the familiar lane running through hedge-lined fields, the one she'd walked to and from the house. If not for all the alarming hallucinations she'd experienced in the last few years, she thought she might shriek with terror.

In the event, she held herself together, at least until her boyfriend arrived early in the afternoon. By this time, the canvas's paint had altered even further, transporting its viewers right up close to the house. The scene's darkness prevented Lauren from observing much more—for instance, she was unable to see through the windows—but this did little to reassure her. That slow zoom towards the place was definitely getting faster.

"Look!" she said, after gulping from her fourth beer can in as many hours and drawing on yet another bulging roll-up. "I'm scared, Kieran."

Her boyfriend, whose hooded eyes looked doped with more than recent sleep, stepped forwards to examine the painting, stooping on legs so thin Lauren feared they might snap.

"I don't understand," he said, turning to look her way and yet refusing to remove the baggy cowl hanging around his face.

"Where's the other picture? Where did you get this one from?"

Despite sounding mad, what choice did she have but to say it? "It's the same one," she cried, lurching Kieran's way, beer sloshing and smoke billowing. "It's changing."

Kieran glanced down at Lauren's trembling hands. Raising his spindly arms—each enshrouded by his hoodie, as if he was swathed in too much skin—he said, "Just give that stuff to me, my child."

She hadn't cared for his fatherly tone—it resembled the pastoral support she'd received from several drug dependency groups she'd attended the previous year—but she nonetheless handed over her drink and the smouldering butt. Lauren assumed Kieran would do what he always did with such substances—consume them at once—but was surprised when, with a gentleness unlike his usual self, he placed both on the coffee table. A moment later, like someone much older than his twenty troubled years, he twisted frailly back to observe her.

"This is what we're trying to get beyond, isn't it?" he said, again displaying a tolerance and patience Lauren struggled to recognise. "I'm just sorry that you've lapsed first."

She found it hard to believe what she'd heard. She certainly wasn't about to let him get away with it.

"This has nothing to do with bloody drugs! I haven't used anything other than booze 'n fags."

"Lord, such profanity."

Had the shock of all these new developments left Kieran oversensitive? Whatever the truth was, Lauren ignored his comment. Pointing once more at the canvas, she added, "It's the sodding painting! I tell you, it's alive. Just watch!"

"But, Lau—"

"Watch, I said!"

And for the rest of that day, that was what they did. By early evening, as darkness drew in at the flat's window, they were almost in the grounds of the house. By this time, the transformations had become so rapid that all the oils had begun to visibly twitch, churning and settling to reconjure the scene in the artist's unmistakable style. Before long, that once distant property almost filled the picture's frame. Not only was it made of red brick and spread across three levels, but also one of its windows gave on to that first-floor storage room, the original home of this haunted work of art.

"Do you *see* now?" she said to her boyfriend beside her on the couch. "Do you *believe* me?"

When Kieran didn't respond, she grew angered, even though she was unable to take her eyes off the shifting canvas. She had an impression that he was squirming inside his hooded garment, but without turning to check, she couldn't decide whether his response was embarrassment, fear, or some other emotion. Whatever the truth proved to be, it was impossible to deny what continued to unfold in front of them.

All the paint rippling with liquid haste, the house advanced quickly, as if someone were walking towards it. The view remained elevated somewhere above ground level, steadily encroaching upon that tell-tale window, whose glass eventually lost its sheen of starlight to reveal the contents of the room beyond.

"There! *Surely* you see!" cried Lauren, leaning forwards to observe. Her heart beat hard; her whole body shook. And yet she was still unable to remove her gaze from the rapidly mutating image.

Now she was *inside* the building and in the presence of objects she recognised: all the bizarre sculptures lurking in dark corners and weird symbols mounted on shelves. That same imposing photograph hung above the door, its elderly subject's eyes watching and watching, while the row of upright paintings remained huddled against one wall. Worst yet was the figure bent over them, also skilfully rendered in oils. It was *herself*, maybe at the point of stealing the smallest of the available canvases.

"There!" she screamed, so loudly it sounded like an alarm. "It's *me*!"

As if he'd taken a vow of silence, Kieran again failed to engage. All the while, the painting continued to change. Lauren leapt up from the couch, aware of only dimness in her peripheral vision. Her pseudo self up ahead, dressed exactly as she'd been on that regrettable day, reached out to tug the

smallest frame from its refined brethren.

Just as she did so, a *second* figure appeared in the painted room.

Lauren's mouth was suddenly so dry, she was unable to speak. She could only hope that her boyfriend would register her distress and use his enfeebled body to comfort her. Because whoever now crept stealthily towards her alter ego hardly appeared human at all.

The figure shambled rather than strolled. Its entire body was encased in a monk's outfit stretching from ankle to head. As all the painting's distortions progressed further still, it was just possible to perceive the entity's bare hands and feet, though none seemed to possess sufficient flesh to cover their constituent bones. It was a mercy that Lauren was unable to observe the newcomer's face, a baggy cowl sparing her such horror.

"*Kieran!*" she cried, at last finding some volume, though the husky croak she produced had hardly been worth the effort. Instead, she leaned forwards to snatch up the canvas—just as that grisly entity in the picture reached for her sinful sister—and finally turned to her boyfriend.

He stood there, his patience palpable.

Or at least *something* did.

And when his hands—diminished not only by age but also death—rose to reveal whatever was left of the withered entity that must have emerged from the painting to possess him, Lauren finally got to see the face under the hood.

Gary Fry is a semi-retired academic who lives in coastal countryside in the northeast of England. He has had published around 100 short stories, a bunch of novellas, and several novels. He was the first author in PS Publishing's Showcase range, and none other than Ramsey Campbell has described him as a "master of philosophical horror." He plays piano, loves dogs, and reads a frightening number of books each year. His web presence can be found at:
https://garyfrytalks.blogspot.com

MATT COWAN'S HORROR DELVE:

A TRICK OF TERRIFYING TREATS—
13 HORRIFYING HALLOWEEN TALES

DO YOU EVER WONDER WHAT INSPIRED YOUR INITIAL LOVE FOR THE HORROR GENRE? For me, its exact origins stretch beyond my earliest childhood memories, but I strongly suspect Halloween had a lot to do with it. I was nearly six years old in October of 1977 when my parents gifted me a *Gilroy the Ghost* finger puppet as a Halloween present. Molded from some sort of glow-in-the-dark vinyl plastic, Gilroy was a sheeted phantom with long, sorrowful, amorphous eyes. Looking at him filled my mind with ideas about ghosts—what they might be and what mysteries they may hold. It was an early step towards what would become a lifelong journey for me. Following this intro-

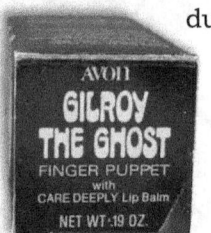

duction to ghosts, Halloween further tempted me by offering up more of its treasure trove of creepy delights. It was during that singular time of year that grinning skulls, sinister jack-o-lanterns, and cackling witches all skittered forth from their shadowy hovels to loom proudly in department store windows or beckon to walkers from neighborhood front lawns.

I was only slightly older when I started listening to a couple of records we had in our house around Halloween time. The first was an LP (Long Play vinyl album) published by Disneyland Records and titled *Chilling, Thrilling Sounds of the Haunted House*. It contained the loose suggestion of a storyline crafted primarily as a setup for its spooky sound effects, some of which were pretty inventive. The sounds emanating from my record player inspired more ideas involving the terrors they suggested. The other record was a "45" (a seven-inch vinyl record which played at 45 revolutions per minute) which I bought from the Scholastic Book Catalog in elementary school. It also had sound

effects, but its reverse side contained readings of magnificent classic horror stories and poems. I especially remember "The Erl-King" (1782) by Johann Wolfgang von Goethe and "The Woman with the Velvet Collar" (1929) by Gaston Leroux. Those stories will forever remain cemented in my mind as Halloween-adjacent tales.

Back when I was a young and there were only a handful of television station choices, a few kid-friendly Halloween horrors were broadcasted to coax soon-to-be horror mongers like myself to dip our toes into its frigid depths—cartoons such as *It's the Great Pumpkin, Charlie Brown* (1966) and *The Legend of Sleepy Halloween* (1980), for example. As I grew a bit older, I experienced the terrifying television movie *Dark Night of the Scarecrow* (1981), in which a mentally

Halloween 3:
Season of the Witch
(1982) Universal Pictures

challenged man nicknamed Bubba is falsely accused of harming a young girl. An angry mob forms to go after him, forcing him to flee. Attempting to hide her son from them, his mother dresses Bubba like a scarecrow and has him hide out in the field. When he's ultimately discovered, the mob exacts their misplaced justice, but that isn't the end of the story. Bubba returns from the grave to track down the men who murdered him. Set at Halloween and airing during the season, this film had a major impact on me and was a great ambassador for the holiday.

Our friends across the pond in the UK were treated to an even bigger hit in the form of *Ghostwatch*. Airing on Halloween night, 1992, this 90-minute BBC1 movie was filmed as a documentary investigating a haunted house. Written and produced by Stephen Volk (whom I interviewed here last issue), it cast actual television newscasters to play themselves, lending the fictional documentary such an illusion of reality the station was flooded with calls from concerned viewers. Television isn't the only medium to invoke the haunted season for our viewing pleasure, however.

Regarding Halloween horror films, John Carpenter's *Halloween* franchise is the forerunner, and while I enjoyed the relentless killing sprees of Michael Myers well enough, he isn't even glimpsed in my favorite offering from this series. *Halloween 3: Season of the Witch* (1982) abandoned the knife-wielding, un-killable murder-man storyline entirely in favor of a stand-alone tale set during the season. In it, The Silver Shamrock Novelty Company plans to broadcast a television signal on Halloween night which will activate a

Lady in White (1988)
New Sky Commiunications

Sleepy Hollow (1999) Paramount Pictures

curse via the masks they produce. It's a fun, campy flick, and I loved the creepy-looking masks they employed.

As an adult I've found several more Halloween horror films to love. There's a good one from 2007 titled *Trick 'r Treat*, in which Sam, a child-sized demon wearing orange pajamas and a bulbous burlap sack over its head, intersects throughout four stories of terrors that take place in a small town at Halloween. *Lady In White* (1988) is an excellent ghost story film set in a small town in 1962. When a boy gets locked inside his classroom alone on Halloween, he witnesses the spectral murder of a young girl in the coat closet. This sets him on a path to try and solve the mystery of what happened to the girl years before. If I had to pick a personal favorite Halloween movie, however, it would have to be director Tim Burton's *Sleepy Hollow* (1999). It's a live-action version of Washington Irving's classic 1820 tale *The Legend of Sleepy Hollow*. Steeped in rich, seasonal atmosphere and with a storyline that presents us with witches, curses, jack-o-lanterns and, of course, the Headless Horseman himself, the film exudes Halloween greatness in all its majesty.

Literature-wise, there are several iconic novels and novel series set during the season, *A Night in Lonesome October* (1993) by Roger Zelazny and *The Manse* (1987) by Lisa Cantrell, to name a few, but as I'll be referencing others in the list below, we'll hold off for now.

As a final quick note, Jim Moon has covered the history of Halloween extensively through the years over at his *Hypnogoria* podcast, which helps set the seasonal mood for me every year.

Now, on to the list (chronological by publication date):

1. **"Randall's Round"**
Eleanor Scott (1929)

During a brief stay at a remote town in the Cotswolds on All Hallow's Eve, a man witnesses people engaged in an odd dance ritual full of disturbing iconography. He determines to learn more about its origins, only to find it harkens back to ancient sacrificial ceremonies centered around some nearby burial mounds. This is a quintessential example of the folk horror genre and Halloween provides the perfect backdrop for it.

2. **"All Souls'"**
Edith Wharton (1937)

Sara Clayburn encounters a woman she doesn't recognize walking towards her house one cold October evening. When she asks the woman what she wants, the lady says, "Only to see one of the girls." Shortly afterwards, Sara injures her ankle in a fall and is subsequently confined to bed. To her dismay, the next morning none of her servants come to attend to her and she's forced to hobble on her damaged ankle through the house in search of assistance but finds the place mysteriously deserted. Time drags on with no one around and no clue to their whereabouts. A year later, when she again encounters the strange woman, she begins to piece together the meaning of those strange days of solitude endured in the house. If you haven't read any of Edith Wharton's brilliant ghost stories yet, you should definitely treat yourself. She wrote quite a few—"The Eyes" (1910), "Afterwards" (1910), "The Triumph of the Night" (1914), and "Pomegranate Seed" (1928) are all particularly fantastic.

3. "The October Game"
Ray Bradbury (1948)

A man who hates his wife, as well as the fact their daughter looks nothing like him but very much like her mother, devises a way to take revenge on his partner in a most horrible fashion. This dark Halloween story isn't supernatural but remains unsettling to the end. Ray Bradbury is a Halloween icon in-and-of-himself. Having published the autumnal novels *Something Wicked This Way Comes* (1962) and *The Halloween Tree* ('72) as well as the story collection *The October Country*, he placed his distinctive stamp upon the season forevermore.

4. "Pumpkin Head"
Al Sarrantonio (1982)

Raylee is the new girl in her elementary school class. She's shy and mistreated by cruel classmates but manages to win them over by telling them a scary story during a Halloween party. It's about a boy with a bloated, pumpkin-shaped head who was similarly mistreated before going on a murderous rampage. Everyone is so impressed with her story that she's invited to another student's party that evening. Al Sarrantonio is masterful as ever at infusing his holiday tales with superb sights and sounds of the season. His love of Halloween led him to produce a number of classics, including his highly regarded Orangefield trilogy of novels (2002–2009) and various short stories, particularly "The Big House" (1999) which, although light-hearted in nature, really encapsulates the themes of Halloween night.

5. "Apples"
Ramsey Campbell (1984)

After they accidentally cause a cantankerous old man to have a heart attack around Halloween, a group of kids become the target of something undead stalking them. The old man had been upset at the kids for stealing apples from his trees. That anger ran far deeper than they ever imagined. Ramsey has several more excellent Halloween-centric tales I could include here—"The Trick" (1980) and "Her Face" (2018), for example, but this is my favorite of them.

6. "Ceremony"
William F. Nolan (1985)

A hitman who suffers from triskaidekaphobia (tris·kai·dek·a·pho·bi·a), the fear of the number 13, takes a long bus ride to Providence, Rhode Island to eliminate a target. The bus is forced to stop early in the small town of Doour's Mill due to engine trouble. The town is inhabited by a handful of skeletally thin locals who keep wishing him "Happy Holidays" in reference to it being Halloween night. Each person he meets tells him he's invited to a ceremony later that night. They seem to indicate his attendance is mandatory.

7. "Hallowe'en's Child"
James Herbert (1988)

After a couple struggles for years to have a child, the day finally arrives. The soon-to-be father is sent home from the hospital to await their call as his wife's labor looks to be several hours away. It's late on Halloween night when he gets the call to head back for the delivery. On his frantic drive there, he has a terrifying encounter on the road with a hideous goblinoid creature that threatens dire things to come to him. Herbert was a best-selling author of several tremendous horror novels, including *The Fog* (1975), *Haunted* ('88), and *The Secret of Crickley Hall* (2006), just to name a few.

8. "The Autumn Man"
Mark Justice (2011)

This harrowing tale follows a young boy, growing up in the 70s, dealing with a brutal bully and a dangerous supernatural force in the nearby woods. "The Autumn Man" is a riveting page-turner with a strong setting that harkens to the likes of Bradbury at evoking nostalgia and the eerie atmosphere of the season. It's a shame Mark's work isn't better known these days. He was a phenomenal writer and his 2011 collection *Looking at the World with Broken Glass in My Eye* is an undiscovered masterpiece. Sadly, Mark passed away in 2016, and I'm certain if he'd had more time, he'd be counted amongst the greats today.

9. "10/31: Bloody Mary"
Norman Partridge (2013)

A teenage boy, struggling to survive in a world overtaken by Jack-O-Lantern creatures, witches, and all sorts of Halloween

beasties, meets another, more aggressive survivor who calls herself *Bloody Mary*. Partridge is one of the premier masters of the Halloween tale, in both short and long forms. He's written a number of them, and his Halloween novel *Dark Harvest* won a 2006 Bram Stoker Award and was adapted to film in 2023.

10. "White Mare"
Thana Niveau (2018)

After being forced to move from her hometown in America to a remote village in England with her father, Heather struggles to gain acceptance from the locals. She and her father, who's been raising her alone following the disappearance of her mother, are only going there for a few months to sell an old farmhouse full of antiques they inherited from a recently departed aunt. Heather's misgivings about the move are eased once she discovers the place contains a beautiful horse she instantly falls in love with. When she asks around about Halloween, she's mocked by the local kids and told that what they have is much different than what she's used to and that she'll find out for herself soon enough. When Halloween night does arrive, it brings a terrifying horde to their door, and a bizarre ritual takes place. This is a great story which involves an impressively eerie play-on-words. Thana has had two story collections nominated for the British Fantasy Award, *From Hell to Eternity* (2013) and *Octoberland* (2019), and much like the main character in this story, she herself is an American now living in England.

11. "Offerings"
Joe Koch (2018)

While preparing to celebrate Halloween in her new home after having worked her way up enough to move out of her previous, rough neighborhood, Blaine notices Amelia, the local pariah, stalking down the street with her three rambunctious children in tow. Blaine makes the

mistake of reaching out to her, only to discover the depths of Amelia's oddness. Amelia claims the children are not hers but accepts Blaine's panicked offer for them all to stop by for trick or treating the following night. When Amelia and her children do arrive late on Halloween night, the children's masks are bizarre, elaborate, and horrifying. This is an excellent weird, horror tale for Halloween.

12. "The Phénakisticope of Decay"
James Ebersole (2018)

When, as children, a group of friends enter a house rumored to be haunted on Halloween night, they are greeted by a strange man. This man gives each of them a Phénakisticope, a pinwheel-style device with drawings on it which appear to animate when it's spun and viewed in a mirror. These particular drawings, however, depict extremely dark cartoons involving horrific deaths. Years later,

after they are older, the trinkets take on a new meaning. This is an excellent, unique Halloween tale.

13. "Screen Haunt"
Orrin Grey (2020)

A filmmaker screens his new horror movie which is set during Halloween in the '80s. It's about three trick-or-treaters wearing old Ben Cooper masks who aren't what they seem. There turns out to be some unnatural guests in attendance at this screening. Orrin has penned quite a few Halloween tales and has proven to be a master of them.

And with that, we close this suggested reading list to brighten your darkest Halloween nights. May all your treats be tasty and your tricks terrifying!

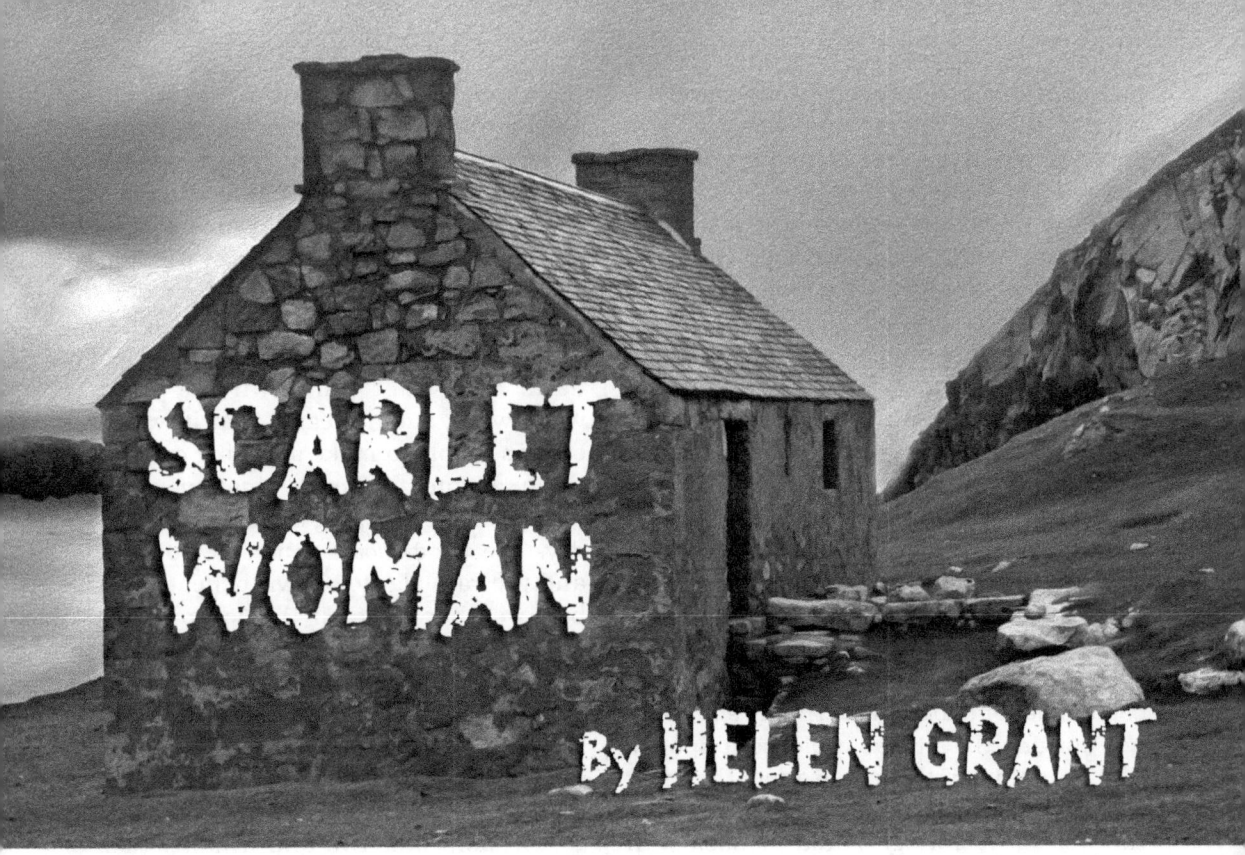

SCARLET WOMAN

By HELEN GRANT

When Raymond Dalgleish was killed in action in January 1945, his wife's main reaction was that of relief, although she would not have admitted this to anyone.

Verity Dalgleish was a slender woman with abundant light brown hair usually worn in a neat chignon, and soft blue eyes hidden behind sober-looking spectacles. She was some fifteen years younger than Raymond had been; she had married him chiefly to get out of a bad situation at home, and it had been a little while before she realised that she had got herself into a very much worse one. However, the Germans obligingly killed Raymond a few months before the Armistice, and Verity found herself in the novel position of being free.

Her immediate concern was how to support herself respectably, and to this end she took up a post as amanuensis to a retired professor who was writing a book. Once a week she travelled down to collect new bundles of papers for deciphering and typing, and to drop off the old ones. At the beginning she intended to move into lodgings in the city where the professor lived, but somehow this never came about, partly because she realised that she enjoyed the train journey, which took several hours.

Verity would board the train early in the morning, when there was still a nip in the air, even in summer. She liked to see the great black bulk of the locomotive standing at the platform, steam drifting about it like breath on a freezing day. Whenever possible she would take a seat on the left facing the direction of travel, because the unfurling views were particularly charming from that side. Sometimes she would lay out pieces of work she wanted to go over again, but more often than not she would end up with her chin on her hand, gazing out of the window.

The line passed through mountainous country, where the hills were capped with snow as late as April, and also through sections of forest where streams tumbled along little rocky gorges. There were several fine country houses along the route, and a crumbling castle with a crenelated tower, as well as a lone standing stone in the middle of a field. Verity sometimes saw deer, pheasants, and rabbits, and for a while a snowy swan on her nest amongst a patch of reeds. All of it lifted her heart.

All of it? No; there was one spot she was not so pleased to see, and ironically the train always slowed on the approach to it, because the track curved a little, and there was a station not quite a mile ahead.

It was a dank place with a narrow stretch of river overhung with stunted trees. There was a rickety wooden footbridge across the water, and close by stood a squalid-looking stone cottage with a slate roof. It was clearly not derelict, because the roof and windows were intact, and sometimes the door stood open. Still, it made an unpleasant impression upon her; she had a vague sense of grubbiness, even contamination, about it. Certainly she could not imagine that it was a pleasant spot to live: in summer the air around the river would be thick with midges, and in winter the wooden footbridge would be slick with ice. She tended to look away from it, at her work, or the windows on the other side of the carriage.

Some months after she had started travelling the line, she saw something that reinforced her opinion of the place rather than altering it. The inhabitant of the cottage was outside, chopping logs for firewood. Verity thought he was in his thirties, with an unkempt mop of dark hair shot through with white and the lines of ill temper already deeply graven in his face. His shirt and trousers were both filthy, the shirt also having big dark patches of sweat under the arms. Afterwards she wondered how she had noticed these things at a distance of some hundreds of yards, but then she concluded that he must have very strong features, and the light, too, had been good. Verity felt instinctively that he was a brute. She had developed a keen awareness of such men during her brief marriage to Raymond; she took care to evade them, as she would have avoided a vicious dog.

After this brief glimpse of the cottage and its owner, Verity was borne onwards and very soon forgot about it. The station was reached with a long squeal of brakes, and there was a little bustle as people got on and off the train. When the journey resumed it ran through such a pretty stretch of countryside that she became absorbed in watching the morning sunshine sparkling on the river, and looking out for rabbits.

The next time she took the train, and the time after that, it was raining heavily. Low, purplish clouds made the day unseasonably dark, and water ran down the carriage windows in such streams that it was nigh on impossible to make anything out. When Verity alighted at her destination, she had some difficulty keeping her bundle of papers dry. The wind *would* buffet her umbrella, and the rain slanted down beneath it. The bad weather took all the joy out of the environment, and when she picked her way home through the puddles in the evening she found herself thinking that perhaps living in the city would not have been so bad after all; there would have been cinemas and warm, well lit tea rooms.

At last, after two and a half weeks of rain, the weather abruptly cleared up. Verity took the train again, and this time the unfolding landscape was drenched with glorious sunshine. Everything conspired to look perfectly idyllic; sturdy little lambs gambolled in the fields, flowers were springing up everywhere, and the gorse was vibrantly yellow. She felt splendidly content, right up until the moment when the train began to slow as it went into the curve before the station.

He was there again, not wielding the axe this time but crossing the open space in front of the cottage with a gait that was half slouch and half swagger. His sleeves were rolled up to the elbow, revealing thick, muscular arms, and his hands were curled into fists, as though he were looking for a fight. The sight of those fists made Verity shudder involuntarily.

She sat back, and the next instant he was gone; she was looking at a swiftly passing series of tree trunks. The mood had changed, however; for the rest of the journey she was listless and introspective.

None of her fellow passengers seemed disturbed. A stout man diagonally opposite was tucking into a sandwich, and an older woman a few seats behind him was knitting with determined concentration. Probably they had not seen the man, Verity thought, or if they had, they thought nothing of it. That was the depressing truth: people *didn't* see, sometimes wilfully. People had undoubtedly thought that Raymond was a fine, upstanding man and model husband. She rubbed automatically at her wrist, soothing vanished pain.

It was a relief to leave the train and walk to the professor's home. He was kindly in an absent-minded way, and physically rather feeble; Verity could have knocked him down quite easily. She listened to his longwinded explanations with a gentle smile on her lips, but the memory of that glimpse from the train was a fish hook in her mind.

For several weeks after that, she saw no sign of the man at the cottage. The first time, she sat on the other side of the train quite deliberately; the second time, she looked the other way as they passed that spot. On the third occasion, she couldn't help herself; she looked, but the cottage was shut up tight and there was nobody around.

Verity reflected that in all the time she had travelled this line, she had only seen the man twice; it was not something to be expected, or indeed concerned about in some irrational way. And yet, it had become the grimy window that no passing child dared glance at, for fear of seeing something wrong peeping out, or the page in a book that they always skipped over because the illustration frightened them in some indefinable manner. She felt the vague, turbid stirring of anxiety whenever the train approached that spot, and a small thrill of relief when they were past it, and the tree trunks were flickering by.

On the journey back up to her home town, she had never paid as much attention to that spot. Even if she were sitting on the right of the train as it headed north, it burst out of the trees at such an angle that the cottage and the wooden bridge were past in the blink of an eye; it was barely possible to take them in unless you actively turned your head. Now Verity found herself actually avoiding the sight. Somehow she could not bear the thought of seeing the cottage and its slovenly occupant and the ramshackle bridge at that time of day when the shadows were beginning to lengthen. When the autumn came, and then the winter, it would be even worse; the place would be suffused with darkness. She sat on the other side of the carriage, and occupied herself with looking over her work for the week.

Further weeks passed without Verity seeing the man again. When the train slowed at the curve she often looked up without thinking, but there was never anyone there. At the gable end of the cottage the stack of cut firewood never seemed to diminish nor grow any bigger. Perhaps the man had gone; perhaps he only ever visited the place intermittently. He might be a hunter, or a fisherman. Eventually Verity relaxed. Her strange dread of the spot began to fade, to feel ludicrous even: a baseless extrapolation of her own sorry experiences. She reminded herself that the man she had seen was not Raymond; indeed not all men were like Raymond.

In between her trips to the city, she worked at home with the window open to hear the birds. She cooked frugally and eked out her meagre tea ration as best she could. Eventually she took out Raymond's things and considered what to do with them. The knitted pullover could be unravelled and reknitted into something else, but she spent a long time considering whether she wanted to do that. It seemed wasteful not to, since her own things were becoming threadbare, but somehow she hesitated to carry Raymond with her in any way. In the end, she deferred the decision and put the pullover away again.

Then one morning in July, when she was travelling south in sunshine so bright and strong that it seemed to etch every detail of the landscape into the consciousness like acid, she looked up as the train slowed and felt a terrible jolt of shock. The man was there again, and this time he was not chopping wood nor occupying himself about the cottage. He was standing much closer to the line, perhaps only fifty yards away, arms folded, legs apart, staring at the train. There was a challenge in his stance—a deliberate defiance of the observer.

Verity found herself unable to hold his gaze, even in the few moments it took for the train to pass him. She glanced away, and in that last fraction of a second before the stripes of tree trunks blotted out the scene she saw something else. There was someone else there—someone thin and pale, standing timidly in the recess of the doorway. The glimpse she had of them was so momentary that she barely took anything in, but a flutter of fabric suggested that it might be a woman.

As the train continued swaying and clacking through the trees, Verity looked at her fellow passengers, her heart thumping wildly as she scanned each placid face. Had nobody seen anything? They all looked as docile as cows: the man in the slouch hat scanning a newspaper, the young woman idly filing her nails. She drew breath sharply, impelled to say something, but no words came out. A few eyes turned her way, incuriously, but when she said nothing any faint interest evaporated. Verity took out her handkerchief and pressed it to her mouth, pretending to suppress a cough. It took her until the next station and beyond to fully regain her composure.

Not a woman, she thought. *Please, not a woman. Or at least, not—*

She couldn't finish the sentence, even in her own head. She could think of no happy reason for a woman to be there, in that lonely place, with that man. The cottage was not big enough to demand a house-keeper. And then there was the way the person had hung back, as though afraid to cross the threshold. Hired help would not be so browbeaten, surely, or if they were, they would leave.

Verity asked herself: *how can you be sure what you saw?* and she also told herself again: *not all men are like Raymond.*

She felt a little sick, however. Enough of them were like that. She wondered whether she ought to keep looking out for the cottage, or stop looking altogether. If she sat on the other side of the train, she need never see it; and after all, if she did see something (something *bad*, a voice at the back of her mind supplied), what could she possibly do?

I could know, she thought. It was a small thing, but it was something. Nobody had known about what was happening to her.

The next week, and the week after that, she saw nothing. The cottage door was closed; there was no movement anywhere. It was high summer and vegetation had sprung up everywhere, but still that particular spot, with the cottage and the bridge, had an unhealthy look to it. Most of the growth was weeds, and the trees overhanging the river were damp and mossy. The air above the water had a faint, hazy look to it, which Verity suspected was a cloud of insects. The bridge looked more rickety than ever; she would not have trusted herself on it.

Perhaps, she thought, they had gone away, the man and his companion. Not-withstanding her personal history, it was strange how the matter had seized her attention. But then, when she considered her own life, it was for the most part pleasant but undramatic, and sometimes a little lonely. She visited the professor once a week, she went on with her work and shopping and cooking at home, and at weekends she walked in the countryside. She had friends, but they had their own preoccupations, and besides, there were oceans between herself and a young mother bouncing a baby on her lap and grousing good naturedly about her husband. Verity would listen to them com-plaining about socks needing darning and neglected jobs about the house, and she would rub her wrist over and over again, compulsively.

Another week passed, and there she was on the train again, her bundle of papers on the table in front of her. The carriage was rather busier than usual that morning and she soon gave up trying to concentrate on anything other than the view. One of the country houses the line passed was situated in a sunny position at the top of a slope, and it was still surrounded by vivid pink rhododendrons. Later, she saw the nesting swan with a bevy of grey cygnets, and still later the standing stone, now surrounded by tufts of long grass. All of it was very peaceful; combined with the rhythmic motion of the train Verity was almost lulled into a doze.

Then the train began to slow, and she felt that faint flare of apprehension she always did when it approached the spot with the cottage. Her eyes had been sliding closed, but now she opened them wide.

The next instant she was struggling to get to her feet. Papers cascaded to the floor.

"No!" she shouted. "No, no!" She struck the window wildly with her hands. "Stop it! Stop it!"

People were leaning away from her, startled. Verity looked from face to face and saw nothing but alarm and disapproval: pursed lips and furrowed brows.

"We have to pull the communication cord!" she said desperately, turning to look for it.

This produced a chorus of shocked denials.

"Hang on a minute," said a man at the table opposite, and he got to his feet too. He was taller than Verity, with a pencil moustache, and superficially smart in a seedy chalk striped suit. "We all have places to be, Miss. Why do you want to pull the cord?"

"Because he's killing her!" Verity burst out. She tried to dodge past him, but he blocked the way.

"Who's killing who?"

"That man!" Verity was almost screaming. She flung out an arm, pointing at the window. "Out there!"

All heads turned, but by now they were in the trees.

"She's drunk," said a female voice, sotto voce. "Disgusting."

"I don't see anyone," said the man in the suit, eyeing Verity a little too frankly. "What did you think you saw?"

"Of course we can't—not now!" Verity forced herself to calm down. She took a deep breath. "I saw it from the window, before we got into the trees. There's a cottage down there, by a bridge."

All this elicited were a few shrugs.

"I've seen it lots of times," she insisted. "There's a man there—a horrible man. He was beating her. A young woman. Someone must have seen?"

Now heads were shaking.

"Please," begged Verity. "We have to stop the train. We have to *help* her."

The man in the suit still didn't move. "If we stop the train we'll all be late. There's a station coming up, so if you're that worried, you can get off and report it there."

"But that won't... oh, what's the use?" Verity looked from one unsympathetic face to the next. Abruptly she sat down again, and put her head in her hands.

After a while the man in the suit bent and gathered up her strewn papers, crumpling them together in no particular order.

"Here," he said, putting them down in front of Verity.

She looked at him with red-rimmed eyes.

"You know," he said, "beating her or not, that's not our business. Maybe she asked for it."

Verity said nothing. She stared at him with venom in her eyes until at last he gave a contemptuous little snort and turned away.

She didn't get off at the station. For the rest of the journey she sat in silence, remembering that harsh face made terrifying by anger, the handful of hair clenched in a fist, the slim body twisting in a vain attempt at escape.

That evening when she travelled back, she did try to see, but the brief glimpse she had of the place from that direction showed nothing; the cottage might as well have been abandoned.

OVER THE DAYS that followed, Verity was restless; try as she might to concentrate on her work, her thoughts kept creeping back to that incident on the train.

None of our business, the man in the suit had said. *Maybe she asked for it.*

The memory of his words made her flush with anger, and then she felt a terrible helplessness, because she didn't know what she could have done differently, not with everyone against her. And what could she do *next* time? She imagined getting up without a word and pulling the communication cord to stop the train. That would work, certainly, but there were regulars on that train; somebody would be sure to stand up when the ticket collector came round, and say: *it's that mad woman, that drunk woman. She has some obsession about stopping here.* And Verity would have to explain, and people would be getting angry because of missed appointments and meetings, and besides, would she ever be able to persuade them to get off the train and investigate? She feared not.

The morning came when she had to catch the train again and still she had no answers. When she stood on the platform with her bundle of papers she felt terribly tempted to turn away, to walk out of the station without boarding. Threadbare reasons stopped her: she would be letting the professor down; she needed the money, meagre though it was. Then she thought that she would sit on the right-hand side, where she could look at a different view, and not see the cottage and the broken-down bridge at all. But when she boarded the train, there was a family group blocking the aisle, fussing with a large collection of bags and a gaggle of small children. The nearest free seat was on the left, so she took it with a sense of inevitability. After the whistle had blown and the train had moved off, she didn't change seats. There was a tight little knot of tension in her stomach.

Perhaps I won't see anything today, she said to herself, but even in her own head her voice lacked conviction.

The train squealed into motion, the sound of smoke issuing from the chimney quickening into a panting sound as the station slid backwards out of sight. Verity's papers lay on the table in front of her, un-examined. In her lap, her hands were curled tightly, so that her fingernails dug into her palms. The train swayed and clacked.

I could close my eyes, she thought. She knew the route very well now; she would know when the train was approaching the spot in question. *I don't have to see anything*. She told herself that, but of course, when the time came, she looked.

The train passed a clump of trees close to an overgrown hedge, and then the spot with the cottage and the bridge began to come into view.

Verity sat forward, her heart thumping. She stared, and stared, and her eyes widened with burgeoning shock. She grasped the edge of the table with white fingers, her lips quivering.

One, two, three... Just a few seconds and the train had plunged into the trees, blotting the scene from sight. Verity sank back into her seat.

"Excuse me, dear," said an older woman sitting opposite her. "Are you alright? You look a bit peaky."

Verity looked at her, her face blank with horror.

"No," she heard herself say, and then, "Yes. I mean, I don't know."

The sound of the woman opposite plain-tively asking if there was anything she could do faded in her ears. All she could think of was what she had just seen.

It was a woman. She was standing in front of the squalid little cottage, her faltering posture suggesting someone at the very limit of physical endurance, someone remaining upright only through the last shreds of self-will. From head to foot she was scarlet; she was *drenched* with it. Her clothes clung to her body; her hair was slick to her scalp. Her skin gleamed with red. In all that scene of dank grey and brown, of dull and rotting green, she was a solid pillar of vivid colour. She put out two trembling hands dyed deep with carmine as if to prevent herself from falling, and the next instant she was gone, replaced by passing forest.

As the train slowed, Verity got to her feet, moving as if in some terrible dream. She left the professor's work on the table, not hearing someone calling after her, telling her she had forgotten her papers. She went to the door and waited, watching the trees and then gardens and finally the beginning of the plat-form slide into view with agonising slowness. With the scream of brakes in her ears she struggled with the latch and then she was on the platform, hurrying through billowing steam. Behind her there was a click as some-one opened a window and shouted some-thing about the abandoned papers again, but Verity barely registered it. Nor did she listen to the ticket inspector into whose hands she thrust her train ticket, when he started to tell her that it was the wrong station, she had alighted too soon and ought to retain it for the onward section...

Outside the station she saw with grim inevitability that there were no taxi cabs;

the place was probably too small to have them. Nor was there anybody on the street to whom she could have applied for help: no friendly constable, not even a lone stroller. Verity glanced back into the station at the ticket inspector, who was old, stout, and self-important; a lost cause, she decided, and so she set off on her own, her rapid footsteps echoing on the deserted street. She was wearing low-heeled Derby shoes and she was fairly sure she could cover the mile or so in about a quarter of an hour. Whether that would be quick enough was another question, one she did not dare examine in detail.

The houses ran out pretty quickly and still she did not see anyone. After that it was just road, and not a wide one at that, the sides verdant and overgrown with summer vegetation. The railway line lay to her left and Verity thought that she must find the place without much difficulty so long as she did not veer too far from it. As she hurried along, she saw the down train go past not a hundred yards away, and knew that she was heading in the right direction.

When she had been going for a little under the fifteen minutes, she came to a left-hand turn, down towards the line. Verity paused, looking at it. It ran under trees; she couldn't see what lay beyond them. It wasn't metalled; it was really just a track, and it didn't look as if any vehicle had gone down it in recent memory. The earth was barely visible through the grass and weeds, and thick vegetation overhung it on both sides.

Verity glanced up the road and couldn't see any other turning. The seconds and minutes were beating like frantic wings; she had to make a decision. She followed the track. After twenty yards she looked back towards the road; with so much overhanging growth it almost looked as if the gap might seal up behind her. She shivered, and then went on, picking her way carefully around weeds and brambles. The sound of running water became audible, and Verity remembered the narrow stretch of river that passed the cottage.

Soon she saw a dark shape up ahead, something square and solid amongst the slender trunks and shifting patterns of leaves.

The cottage.

Verity thought she detected an odour on the air: damp stone and timber, something rotting. The enormity of what she was doing flooded in on her; conditioning and simple common sense urged her to go back, and yet she didn't. Nobody had ever come to save *her*; now she couldn't turn her back. She kept moving, but more slowly than before, conscious of every whisper of grass around her ankles, every small twig snapping underfoot.

When she was close to the window-less back of the cottage, Verity paused and listened carefully. She heard the gurgle of water over stones, and the rustle of a faint breeze through the trees. Otherwise, nothing.

She went around the right-hand side of the building and now the wooden bridge came into view. It was far more ramshackle than it had seemed in her previous glimpses of it; the centre had collapsed completely. Boards hung here and there like loose teeth.

Verity went to the corner of the cottage and peered around it, keeping very close to the wall. There was no sign of the woman drenched in scarlet, nor of anybody else. Verity let her gaze scan everything from where she stood up to the railway line itself. In the open area in front of the cottage there was a chopping block with an axe buried in it, and by the front door there were a tin pail and a shovel, but in spite of this evidence of activity there was no sign of the person who used them. Verity's gaze rested uneasily on the shovel, unwelcome associations running through her head.

Eventually she had to trust herself, or else go back, so she stepped out from the corner and walked along the front of the cottage. She forced herself to walk boldly, trying not to look like a target.

The first window was shuttered; Verity passed it without the possibility of seeing in or being seen. Then she came to the door, and found that it was ajar. She swallowed, and then she knocked firmly.

"Hello?"

Silence.

"Hello?" she repeated, raising her voice.

There was still no response, so she pushed at the door and it swung inwards with a long creak. The cottage exhaled a scent of dust and damp, overlaid with that rotten smell, and she heard an insect buzzing somewhere inside.

Verity looked down at the threshold, thinking that if anyone had passed over it soaked in that terrible redness there would be some sign of it: gelatinous scarlet globules or sticky streaks on the grey stone. There was nothing.

She thought: *he has taken her somewhere else.*

Eventually she put her head around the door. The interior of the cottage was dim and cool and seemingly empty; there were apparently only two rooms and although she could not see much of the further one from where she stood, the silence made her ears ring. With brisk nervous steps she crossed the space to the internal doorway and looked through into the far room. This was the one with the shutters up, and she had to stand there and let her eyes adjust to the gloom. There was a single bed made up with rough blankets and a battered chest of drawers with a jug and basin on it, the jug bearing a deep chip on the neck. Verity went over and looked into it; there was water in it, but so far as she could tell in the dim light it was clear. If the owner of the cottage had had to wash anything from his hands, she did not think he had done it here.

She went back into the other room, the larger one, and looked about her. There was an open fireplace, cold and ash filled, a deal table and a single chair. A couple of blackened pots hung from the wall, and a mug and a ceramic tankard stood on a little shelf. There was also a heavy wooden chopping board, of the kind used by butchers, at one end of the table, and on it a carving knife with a large triangular blade. Like the threshold and the water in the jug, the knife was perfectly innocent of any sinister red dye; it gleamed dully in the low light.

Verity pressed a hand to her forehead. She could feel herself perspiring slightly, in spite of the coolness of the room. She thought about the woman she had seen, scarlet from head to foot. It was not possible to make someone like that without leaving any trace on the things around them, nor was it possible to remove every sign of it in the space of perhaps half an hour. Was the man so brazen that he had done it outside, knowing that he risked the gaze of strangers' eyes? The thought of such arrogant brutality made her feel sick and faint. Suddenly she urgently wanted to get out of the cottage.

She turned, but with a jolt of shock that was so savage it was like being stabbed she realised it was too late. A flicker of movement at the doorway coalesced into a tall, broad-shouldered figure filling the door frame.

"What're you doing here?" he growled at her, halving the distance between them with a few long strides.

Verity took a step back. She groped for an excuse, for anything plausible to say, but her mind was an utter blank. All she could do was shake her head, her eyes wide and panicked.

"Well? You'd better have a good reason, Missis."

Without taking her eyes off him, Verity took another step back, and then darted behind the table, so that its scarred wooden expanse was between him and her. She was breathing hard, her chest so tight that she was afraid she would suffocate.

"So that's it, is it?" he said grimly.

He lunged after her, and Verity scuttled to the other side. She eyed the distance between herself and the door but she was afraid she wouldn't make it—and what then? Then she looked back at the man, and gasped.

"You're *old.*"

The light from the doorway was full on him now and she saw that he was at least sixty, perhaps far older; his hair was almost white and his face was deeply seamed with wrinkles. She had thought he was the man she had seen from the train, but now she realised he couldn't be.

A measure of courage returned to her.

"Where's your son?" she demanded, her voice almost level.

"Son? I have no son." He began to sidle around the table, and Verity moved to the other side, keeping it between them.

"Just me," he said.

"I saw him from the train," insisted Verity. "And I saw what he did to that woman. If you hide him, you're just as bad."

He stopped, his brow furrowed. "Woman? There's no woman here."

"Don't lie. I *saw* her."

He commenced his furtive movement again, and Verity moved too.

"What did you see?" he said insolently.

"She was right outside, covered in—in *blood.*" Her heart was thumping: the word was out. "And I know he did it, because I've seen him beating her."

"There's no woman here," he repeated stubbornly.

Verity stared at him.

"He's killed her, hasn't he?"

She saw him flinch at that. She said, "I suppose he's buried her—somewhere out there. I'll have the police in. They'll find her."

This time the man lunged around the table, and Verity had to leap back to stay out of reach. Both of them were breathing hard now.

"Stop hiding him," snapped Verity, strands of hair hanging over her eyes.

"I'm not. I told you—I have no son."

"But I've *seen* him!" she cried, beside herself.

The man began his slow prowl around the table again, and Verity moved too. It was ludicrous; she could almost have laughed, except the expression on his face was terrifying.

"When did you see him?" he growled.

"Last week! And I saw her today, from the train. Not an hour ago."

"Liar."

"I'm not! How can you say that?"

The man smiled then, a sly smile that was far, far worse than the scowl. Verity knew then that he wasn't going to let her leave.

He said, "Because it wasn't my son you saw. I have no son; I told you. I killed her, and you're right, she's buried out there, under the trees. But the devil only knows how you saw that, because I did it thirty years ago."

Shock spilled across Verity's face, and in that instant he went for her.

Verity snatched up the nearest thing she could to defend herself—the carving knife with its terrible triangular blade. As the man leapt at her, she grasped the handle with white knuckles and saw the steel slide into his flank.

The man grunted as though he had been punched, and looked down at himself. Verity yanked the knife out, and a gout of scarlet came with it. The man put a hand to the wound, and tried to grab at Verity with the other, but she was faster. She struck again, and again, and the man fell to his knees. As he slumped to the floor her arm rose and fell, rose and fell, and now the floorboards were slick with red and her shoes were sliding in it, but she kept on. With each blow she screamed raggedly, furiously, until the screams were not simply cries but a name: *Raymond.*

At last Verity realised that the man had stopped moving. It was hard to grasp the knife; the handle was wet. She opened her fist and the knife fell onto the floorboards with a clatter. She was kneeling in a great pool of scarlet, the effluent of the man's dying. It was on her hands and her legs and knees; it had soaked into her skirt and blouse and jacket. Even the skin of her face and her dishevelled hair had been spattered with hot, wet spray; she blinked it out of her eyes.

She was no longer screaming. She swallowed convulsively, as if trying to sob, but no sound came out. There was a coppery taste on her lips.

Verity stood up, unsteadily. The doorway was a rectangle of bright light; she stumbled slowly towards it, leaving sticky footprints. She went outside.

Sounds filled her ears: a rhythmic clattering, the panting of smoke from a chimney. Verity staggered towards them, and held out her scarlet hands to the train.

Helen Grant writes Gothic novels, the latest of which is Jump Cut (2023), and short super- natural fiction. Her new short story collection Atmospheric Disturbances was published late in 2024 by Dublin's Swan River Press. Joyce Carol Oates has described her as "a brilliant chronicler of the uncanny as only

those who dwell in places of dripping, graylit beauty can be."

According to Grant, "The germ of the idea for 'Scarlet Woman' came from Steve Duffy," whose work also appears in this volume. "I was casting about for inspiration, and he mentioned a recent train journey from Inverness to Perth that I had been raving about. 'There you go,' he said. 'I challenge you to turn something from that journey into a story.' And I have."

THE EMPTY VESSEL

BY RHYS HUGHES

I WAS COMING OUT OF THE ENTRANCE WHEN THE SHOT RANG OUT. TO BE HONEST IT DIDN'T RING LIKE A BELL, it was a thin sound like breaking ice, like the release of bubbles of nitrogen gas in the synovial fluid between my knuckles when I crack them. I have learned a lot about biology since I began attending the institute. But I was still unfamiliar with gunshots. I frowned, not knowing why my left side felt so much heavier than usual, and I paused.

The murderer could have hit me again, I was a static target, but he was of a timid disposition, I guess, because he was already running away. I heard his feet pounding the icy slabs of a nearby alleyway, diminishing into vague silence. But when I turned to face the direction the shot had come from, I finally understood what had happened. Ronald was dying.

The bullet had struck him in the chest and his heart was damaged. That is why he was slumping and dragging me down. I had to lean the opposite way to remain upright.

He said, "I'm tired. Lay me down on the ground, I want to sleep forever," and then he coughed up blood.

I compromised and sat on one of the steps leading to the institute doors. He remained coherent until the end, but he didn't say too much. I wanted to ask him to cling on to life, to resist the dimming of the light and all that sort of thing, not just for his own sake but for mine too. He said, "Arnold, just find out who did it, and why, and swear vengeance on them."

Well, it's easy to swear, to make a vow

concerning anything, but we rarely have the means to follow through. We scheme retaliation just to make ourselves feel a little better, it doesn't help. But Ronald was serious, dead serious, dead, it was clear I would be driven by a terrible obligation from now on, and I made up my mind to accept it fully. So I replied:

"I'll get them, I promise, but it won't be simple. I don't have any clues. Do you have enemies I don't know about?"

"How could you *not* know about them, Arnold? You are me, and I am you. I did nothing wrong, offended nobody."

His voice was weak, he sputtered as he spoke. Those were the words that I truly thought he'd said. He had given me a mystery. Once again I wanted to tell him to hold on, but he had already let go. His body trembled once, then was still. I seemed to feel his soul brush my cheek as it came out of him and flew off, but maybe it was a belated snowflake from a passing cloud. Most of the snowdrifts had melted in the afternoon, the few that remained didn't shine in the moonlight but resembled surgically removed tumours of a vast size. They were grubby and compressed by their own weight.

I said to myself and to him, because we were the same, "Rest well, brother, and don't trouble your mind anymore. I'm going to drag you back inside. There will be answers eventually. They might take time to come, sure, but any puzzle can be solved with determination."

With a tortuous effort I climbed the remaining steps to the doors, dragging my cooling burden, and pushed my way through into the corridor beyond. Then I tried standing and lurching along. The noise I made alerted one of the wardens and he came to assist me. He took me to a room with a chair, sat me down, then he hurried off to fetch a researcher.

It was Doctor Wallace who turned up. His first words were, "Back again? I feel honoured," but then he realised something was wrong. He came to my side, looked me over and said, "Damn."

"An attempted assassination, I don't know why."

My voice was feeble now.

He stepped back into the corridor, called for assistance. Men in white coats came, many of whom I didn't recognise, and somebody gave me brandy to sip. I think it was laced with a sedative.

"We'll have to summon the police. But first we need to cut him away from you. An emergency procedure."

I shook my head, finding a new strength from deep within. I said, "No, that is something I won't allow. Ronald stays with me. I have a task to complete and I want him there when it's done."

"Don't be a fool, Arnold. If we don't perform the amputations, you will be infected with gangrene in just a few days. You can't hobble around attached to a rotting corpse. This is an ethical issue as well as a medical obligation. What sort of a doctor would I be if I didn't take immediate action? We'll rush you into the operating theatre and save you."

I smiled but my smile was a rictus grin. Doctor Wallace recoiled when he saw it, and he was a hardened specialist, difficult to intimidate. I spoke with all the robust wisdom of my existence, a life spent outside the casual normality of society, toughened by constant mockery and the horrified reactions of people in the streets. I began nodding too.

"We are twins and more than twins. Arnold and Ronald, anagrams of each other, avatars of the same individual. He stays with me until I find his killer. He is my conscience, I won't abandon him. Don't call the police, not yet. Just give me a chance to find the culprit."

Doctor Wallace threw up his hands in resignation. He knew how stubborn I could be. And there was another thing: he owed me a lot. Every week I allowed him to examine me, test me. I provided the raw data for the scientific papers he wrote and published in the most respected journals. I had made his reputation, I was his ticket to fame and glory.

Conjoined twins aren't really so rare in this world, but I was very unusual, two bodies fused together side by side but with three working legs. That middle leg was shared equally by Ronald and myself, we both controlled it, we had to be synchronised to make it work.

And now it belonged only to me and it was awkward, difficult to operate, a hindrance rather than a benefit. But I would learn, I would practice and become the useless thing's master, it would propel me towards my destiny. I would find the assassin and keep my promise to my brother. I shook myself. The sedative in the brandy was fuddling my mind.

Doctor Wallace said, "I will give you a day."

His frown was a seal on the deal, I knew he wouldn't change his mind, his sense of honour was too evolved. The other medics cleared out, only two others remained, Hopkins and Gruber. I recognised them, blinked at them, they smiled back, looking concerned at the same time. Wallace was superior to them in rank and renown. They wouldn't protest.

Hopkins said, "But you need to rest, that's the important thing. You ought to sleep before trying to walk."

Gruber added, "Take more brandy."

I lurched to my feet. Ronald slumped on my left side. I had to lean a little to the right to counterbalance him. I stamped forward. My right leg was fine, it held firm, the knee bent correctly. But the shared leg was like an ache, stiff one moment, spongy the next, dead but alive with prickles and burns. I clenched my fists and my mind, refusing to be defeated. I staggered to the end of the room. I leaned against the wall, turned myself and walked back, picking up speed as my confidence increased. Then I said:

"I need nothing. There are no problems at all."

Wallace exhaled noisily.

Hopkins and Gruber exchanged glances. What did I know about this pair? Hopkins was a microbiologist, growing germs on Petri dishes and killing them with new types of mould. Gruber worked in a lab at the rear of the building and I had no clear idea what his area of expertise was. My interaction with them had been minimal. Hopkins dealt with protoplasm and Gruber with what precisely? Something that sounded similar but I couldn't remember the word. Wallace was my contact, he was the only one I cared about, despite the fact he had stuck me with syringes, bathed me in X-Rays. That was his job, the deal I had signed up for, my contribution to science.

I turned to face the door. "I'm going out now. I don't intend to waste time. Don't try to stop me." Then I added, "Stop *us*." That was more effective, to let them think I hadn't accepted the death of my brother yet. They parted to allow me through. But Wallace called:

"At least let me remove the bullet first."

"What's the point?"

"It might work its way through his system and enter yours. Arnold, this is very reckless of you. I suggest—"

I laughed a dry laugh, cutting and brutal. He fell silent. Doctor Wallace is a good person, so reasonable deep down that he can be manipulated with relative ease. I passed out of the door. He followed me into the corridor and to the main entrance, but he didn't press too close to me. I went down the steps to the street, my gait erratic, my brother swinging at my side, unbalancing me. But I kept my wits about me and descended safely.

Wallace tried one last time to dissuade me from the course of action that I had chosen. He coughed and said:

"Arnold, just one day. Seriously. Do you know what will happen to Ronald as the hours pass? He's dead. He will start to decay, you know this, but maybe it is news to you *how* the process will unfold. Like this, I'll tell you. His blood has stopped circulating, it is clotting fast and it will gravitate into his legs as long as you remain upright, thicker than gruel. His muscles will stiffen and his guts and torso will bloat. He will smell bad."

"The whole business stinks already," I said.

"Arnold, I am serious. Please consider the matter. It gets more unpleasant. The tissues will liquefy and the skin will blacken and insects will be attracted to the stench and lay eggs in the rotting flesh. Do you know what adipocere is? It's a waxy substance formed by the hydrolysis of fat. Putrefaction isn't symmetrical and Ronald might end up as a formless patchwork of slimy segments and a firm but crumbling crust of fatty acids."

Just the same tone of voice as if we were in a lecture theatre. I waited until he had finished, then I raised my hand in a farewell gesture, lurched off into the cold night. He must have lingered in the entrance because I didn't hear the main doors close. I propelled myself to the mouth of the alley. This is where the shot had come from, where I had heard footsteps. The assassin had fled down here. I would investigate, search for clues.

I will reveal a secret to you now, one that even Ronald didn't know, which is that I had often fantasised about solving crimes. I daydreamed about a career as a detective, a private sleuth, clever, calm and collected. At night I would lie awake on our uncomfortable bed while Ronald snored next to me and think of myself as a genius, a puzzle solver.

That's right, a crimefighter of astounding ability. And turning my head to gaze at my brother, I would toy with the notion that he was the supreme villain, a master of crime, my deadly opponent. We would set traps for each other, play lethal games, taunt each other and lay false trails. We would engage in cerebral warfare, full of mutual respect as well as hostility, new versions of Holmes and Moriarty, forced to act in one body.

But Ronald in real life was a gentle soul, kinder than I was, far less likely to be a criminal mastermind than almost anyone. My fantasy was absurd. Yet here I was, a detective at long last, pushing myself into the darkness of a chilly alley, working on his behalf as well as my own. Part of the daydream had come true, and that's always the way, isn't it? Our visions come to pass but never in the precise way we imagine them.

I was a sleuth but the real villain was unknown. His motive was a mystery and his whereabouts impossible to determine. But that's the fundamental reason detectives exist. And now I had full control over the shared leg, my balance was improving all the time. Just like riding a bicycle, having a dead brother attached to your side by tangled nerves and decaying flesh, stiffened muscles, veins and arteries full of sluggish blood like cold magma. It takes practice, that's all. Into the alley mouth I went, a swallowed morsel plunging into the throat of my own despair. I was strong, I kept going.

It was dark here, almost completely lightless, a very narrow alley indeed. I slipped once or twice on a patch of unmelted ice, I lurched first against the wall on my right side, feeling the scrape of decaying bricks, then against the wall of the institute on my left side, Ronald's side, feeling nothing of the texture of that windowless barrier, but hearing a faint clang. I had knocked against an unseen door, made from steel and sealed tight. I straightened myself, groping onwards, and abruptly I reached a dead end.

The alley went nowhere. This fact baffled me. I turned and made my slow way back, but I only went a few paces before I saw the break in the brick wall, now on my left side, Ronald's side again. I had somehow missed it earlier. Half the height of the wall was gone, broken down, leaving a narrow passage, a tight squeeze. There was a small pile of bricks at the base. This is where the assassin had made his escape, through here.

I followed with great difficulty. I had to ease myself sideways into the gap and struggle against panic, scraping my elbows, and fearing we would be stuck permanently, entombed like the accidental pharaohs of a freak Egypt. This was too fanciful a thought, unworthy of me, an insult to my brother. As I gritted my teeth and stretched my body, I suddenly burst through, emerging on the far side in a cascade of powdered bricks.

The wall was old, it hadn't been repaired for decades. We sprawled, limbs flung out, my knees in pain. I tasted bitter weeds. Raising my head, I saw that I was in a wasteland, one of those curiously neglected parts of the city that exist because no one thinks it worthwhile to construct anything new. There had been warehouses long ago, the foundations were still visible in the starlight. It had an awfully lonely atmosphere, this zone, but it was still better than the constricted darkness of the alley. I muttered:

"Ronald, we have arrived on the outskirts of the answer. Your killer came this way, he fled through the rusty maze of collapsed roofs and twisted girders, and we will track him to his lair."

It was too theatrical, that little speech, but Ronald wouldn't mock me for it, and that's all that mattered. I knew his mind, his nature, I had felt his soul brush my cheek on its way to the next world. I pushed myself to my feet and stumbled over rotten joists and other obstacles hidden in the undergrowth. Down below in the distance, the lights of the city blazed. Wooden fences sagged at the limits of the wasteland. Beyond them was an overpass on which traffic rumbled. I studied the ground for clues, marks that would indicate that the assassin had hurried this way, but I saw nothing unusual.

How would I know what I was looking for anyway? I wasn't a professional tracker, I was just a man. My mission was futile. I must acknowledge defeat and return to the institute, ask Doctor Wallace to surgically sever the fibres that held me enmeshed with my brother, give me the chance to live an independent life. I wasn't even confident an operation was feasible. I felt that I would die under the scalpel, end up as nothing more than data for his next scientific paper, a footnote in half a dozen medical textbooks.

But there was no need to abandon hope yet. A proper effort had to be made first. That's always the best way, the only acceptable course to take, as midnight agitated distant city clocks into hurling echoes into the air. I listened sadly to the chimes, issued by churches in the old quarter, where the buildings were elegant and the centuries had mummified.

It was one part of the city I rarely ventured into, where the aroma of strong coffee drifted down the cobbled streets, past theatre entrances, over quaint stone bridges, the quarter where men with more money and fewer worries idled away the long hours of their evenings. A place where you could buy excitement or the peace of release in the gala gardens.

I didn't feel the killer would have taken refuge there. It just didn't feel too plausible to me. I hadn't glimpsed his face but there had been something furtive about his actions, a quality the very opposite of sophisticated. The echoes of the chimes decayed to nothing and I returned my focus to my predicament. Unseen rodents scurried into tangled grass.

"We have all night," I told myself, as I stumbled down the incline towards the perimeter of the wasteland.

The fence was remarkably flimsy, easy to push over. Now I was in private property, the overgrown garden of an abandoned house. This suburb had quietly experienced an economic death a generation ago. The back door was wide open, the hinges having rusted away.

I passed through the house, which was completely empty inside, unbolted and opened the sturdier front door, emerging onto a deserted street. The silence was unsettling or restful, I couldn't decide which. The streetlamps lacked bulbs, all the fittings had been looted.

I navigated with the aid of starlight on frost, turned a corner and progressed down another street. I was heading into the heart of the city but choosing a route that would avoid casual contact with citizens. Ronald was a liability as well as a brother, a livewire, a dead twin. But it's not so easy to make quips when you are grieving. My mantra: keep going. More corners, more streets, a few houses that seemed to be occupied now. Then under the overpass, among wrecked cars and constellations of shattered glass.

I smelled the river and made my way towards it. I think I had forgotten my intention to track the assassin. I had given up a task unsuited to my abilities. But I was compelled to move, toe stumble, lurch, stagger, speeding up and slowing down, tripping over the uneven surfaces on which I travelled. Something drove me that wasn't rational, simply the urge to be a scalar force, with magnitude but no fixed direction. I knew how Wallace would describe me. A loose cannon, he would say, stuffed with an orb of putrid emotions and wounded flesh rather than a stone or iron cannonball, rolling on the pitching deck of the vessel of his own misfortune, a self-pitying monster.

The path that followed the river snaked me deep into the city and served to keep me safe from the scrutiny of pedestrians. It was too lonely and rough here to entice walkers in the deep night.

The active city, the contemporary metropolis, pulsed on both sides, hidden by the trees and the thickness of their gloom. It was a world of steel and glass, a forest of tall buildings, office blocks, bridges. The roads were busy, the citizens always in a hurry. That commercial nexus had little connection to the artery that I was moving along like a mutated blood vessel. It was still throbbing, cooling after a day of frantic business, and I felt the pulsation, the exclusion, a reminder of my status as a pariah, a freak.

I passed one sleeping tramp, a bundle of rags that might have been another further along, but no one awake, nobody who called to me, approached me. The solitude was welcome but painful.

I seemed to sense the migration of souls, a fluttering upwards, parcels of mist ascending, only seen from the corners of my eyes. Since Ronald's death I had acquired the ability to glimpse ghosts, that's what it felt like. I shuddered, I resisted the urge to run, to slip and roll and drown in the murky water, dragged under by my manifested mirror image. The wisps streamed into the sky, racing each other, an inverted blizzard.

The river widened, I heard the lapping of gentle waves ahead. I walked for another ten minutes, then I reached the sea, the rotting boardwalks and elevated platforms of an old amusement park, a little frequented area that had once been filled with visitors, a facility that had been crammed with laughter and games, carousels and roller-coasters, toffee apples, candy floss, and carnival sideshows, including the sorts of sideshows in which people like me were displayed for the amusement of an astounded public.

But I had no resentment, none at all. All those humiliations, if that is what they really were, had gone out of fashion before my birth. The place sagged, it seemed ready to sink into the mud of the shoreline. The collapsed rollercoaster was like the skeleton of a dinosaur in a bankrupt museum. Rotting seaweed and damp sand softened my footfalls.

I said with a smile, "Ronald, we have arrived," and I answered the question he hadn't even asked: "That's right, the funfair, our destination. Fun is never fair and you know this, dear brother."

I wanted to sit and contemplate the tide.

But first I wandered over the decaying planks of an unstable pier. A barrier had been erected to block trespassers: it had rotted away. Nothing prevented me from lurching to the end of the structure. I found the shell of an arcade, the sea spitting froth at me through narrow gaps in the boards below. Pinball machines lay on their sides, ruptured. A booth caught my eye, still intact, standing upright in the darkest corner of the room.

It was a genie machine, an automaton in a glass cage. Antiquated, peeling, grotesque, the figure was a wooden puppet sitting behind a crystal ball, a pearly orb like a dead man's eye magnified, just like one of Ronald's eyes. I lingered, I found myself reaching into my pocket for a coin, and finding one unexpectedly. I pushed it into the slot, expecting nothing. I blinked as the apparatus swallowed the coin and groaned into motion.

The turbaned sage in the cage came to life, creaking and squeaking. As the mouth of the puppet opened, I shook my head. The wooden tongue clattered and I heard words. The speech of the figure was distinct and intelligible but it didn't issue from the puppet itself. It came from a flared tube on the roof of the cage. I listened, drinking the inhuman sounds like a lost explorer in a desert lapping the bed of an evaporated oasis pool.

The voice said, "I am the Urban Turban, the sage, the teller of fortunes, the seer, the predictor, the prophet."

I waited as it paused and then continued, "I am the prognosticator, the truth teller, sadhu, fakir and magus."

"Who killed my brother? Who was it?"

The puppet turned to look at me: the wooden eyes swivelled, fixed me with a disturbing stare, sightless pupils converging on a point between my own eyes. I resisted the urge to turn and leave. The penny arcade boomed as waves struck the pilings of the pier below us.

The puppet bent forward and peered deep into the crystal ball. I could see the reflection of its face in the nacreous surface of the sphere. I asked myself if this experience was a product of delirium, a fever occasioned by my proximity to a corpse. The puppet jerked.

"The bullet was poisoned," it declared.

"What do you mean?"

"Your brother is decaying faster than he should. The bullet was coated with a toxic substance. The assassin wasn't experienced, he doubted his ability to aim accurately. He couldn't be certain he would inflict a fatal wound, nor did he care which one of you he shot."

I felt weak, I wanted to sink to my knees, but I had to remain upright, keep the shared leg under my control. These atrocious words had told me everything I needed to know. The mystery was solved, it had hardly been a mystery at all. I realised how blind I had been, how naive. The puppet smiled sadly at me, paint flaking from its golden lips.

The wooden eyelids closed with an audible clap, opened again, waited for a few moments before repeating the process. The puppet was blinking at me, it wanted to give me sufficient time to formulate a response. My mind was a whirl of simple truths spun into a vortex of complex power. A killer with easy access to poisons, to chemicals that worked havoc in the human body. The answer was obvious. But I blurted out:

"How can an automaton know so much? How can a puppet in a box be so wise? What is your secret?"

"I am not mechanical, I am not organic. I am a spirit, the soul of a sailor. I died at sea long ago, my ghost drifted on the wind. I was free, ready to find the empty vessel that would receive me. Buffeted by eddies of air, I was delighted to skim the crests of the waves. But I needed a new home, an empty vessel, the sanctuary of solid boundaries."

"Is that what happens to dead people?"

"Yes, it is. The empty vessel for most released spirits is the universe itself, the vastness beyond the atmosphere of this planet, intergalactic space, limitless and cascading with peculiar energies. Most ghosts rise up and keep rising. That is their desire and their destiny."

"Not yours? You found sanctuary here?"

"I passed over the fairground, over the penny arcade on the sagging pier, I was beginning to ascend, to rise in a gentle gradient. There was a storm, clouds clashed and lightning ripped the sky. A bolt struck the arcade, passed through a skylight, connected with the glass cage. The puppet inside moved, electrocuted, cogwheels turning and burning."

"And you were drawn to it? Sucked in?"

"Irresistibly. The voltage was high. I altered my direction, rushed into the cage. My spirit fused with the mechanism, and I waited for a customer. I waited in silence. The electric current was responsible. Then you came. Time is short for you. I can tell you this. Men and women die. Their souls depart their bodies and seek new vessels in which to experience the afterlife. Desirable vessels. But voltage confuses them, disrupts the natural process, the supernatural cycle. The bullet was poisoned. That is all."

His head drooped, his mouth closed, the speaking tube fell silent, and even the crystal ball lost its lustre. I delved in my pocket for another coin but found nothing. I attempted to turn but Ronald's foot had glued itself to the floor. Fluid was leaking from his pores. His decay was accelerating. I wrenched him free of this appalling adhesive, stumbled out of the arcade, back along the pier. I knew exactly what I was obliged to do.

My journey in reverse was more tortuous, slower, mentally painful. The flesh of Ronald was undergoing a rapid transformation. The night was nearly over, the stars were fading. My brother was melting, features distorting into an abstraction, his nose came loose and dribbled down his face, his fingers were charred, burned by some catalyst of malice. His leg stiffened, relaxed, warped itself until his damaged foot was pointing backwards. The rot would infect me before long. A cruel dissolution.

I wondered if I would reach my destination. It seemed too difficult, too far. Each step was a trudge through the sludge of congealing despair. The sailor who was a ghost who was a puppet had given me strength to endure, to press myself into the future, to strain myself through the sieve of reality, my desires dividing and extruding themselves into worms of glutinous determination. I was furious, truculent, muculent, and desperate.

A grisly hybrid of tenacious death and feeble life, I reached the river path and shambled rather than ambled along the uneven surface. I passed one of the sleeping tramps, and his soul rose from his slumped form as I did so, whisking itself away over the treetops. The sadness of this city, the casual deaths, always a new tragedy in some neglected corner. I hoped his soul would enjoy the space of the empty vessel it had chosen.

Back through the abandoned suburb, always upwards, into the wasteland, no less menacing as the sun rose in the east and illuminated the ruins, twisted metal and splintered wood, the brambles and weeds, the loops of barbed wire, powdered bricks. I had to rest, despite my reluctance, drawing in great racking sobs of tainted air, and leaning against a girder that speared from the shattered concrete at a low angle. The Urban Turban, that fairground phantom, boomed his metallic tube voice in my mind:

"Most ghosts rise up and keep rising."

But not Ronald. He had brushed my cheek and was hurtling sideways. He was being pulled by a force, I had no doubt. Just as the sailor had been dragged into the glass cage, into the puppet.

My brother was a kind individual but kindness is no protection against the plots and schemes of manipulators.

I recalled his words. "I did nothing wrong, offended nobody," he had said, but I wondered if I had misheard, if he had actually said, "offended a nobody," and now I remembered an incident.

Just a casual laugh he had once uttered, something trivial beyond measure but significant enough to a malevolent personality, to a maladjusted mind. Our trivialities frequently condemn us.

I forced myself to stand straight, to continue my journey over that hideous patch of forgotten terrain, towards the broken wall, through the chasm of sharp bricks, into the alley. My breathing was erratic, my vision flecked with flashes of black light. I was in the alley now. I reached the steel door on the wall of the institute and rattled the handle.

The door was still firmly locked, as I had suspected it would be. I swayed to the mouth of the alley, turned, approached the steps to the main doors of the building, mounted them slowly.

It was early in the morning but the institute was already at work. I passed through the entrance into the corridor beyond and kept going. I headed for the back room, the most obscure lab in the establishment. I had never been inside it, but I guessed where it was located. Hopkins worked with protoplasm and now I knew what Gruber worked with.

The word was dredged up from the slimy seabed of my subconscious. He worked with *ectoplasm*. He was a researcher into death and souls. A mediocre scientist who had stumbled on a discovery that would give him the renown he craved. I faltered, righted myself.

Wallace came out of a room, alerted by the commotion I was making with my heavy gait. He said, "Arnold, so you came back? For the operation. I knew you would see sense. I knew—"

Then he fell silent as I barged past him. The look of distaste on his face as my brother smeared him with putrefying flesh was extraordinary. Another door opened further along and Hopkins came out, a Petri dish in one hand, eyebrows knitted like duelling swords. Perhaps he was going to block my way but took a closer look at me, changed his mind, retreated into his room, slamming the door tight, bolting it from the inside.

I had reached the end of the corridor. The door that confronted me was low and grubby. The lighting in this part of the institute was weaker. This was where the low funded experiments were conducted. I assumed it would be locked but I guess Gruber had been distracted that morning. He wasn't a professional hitman but just a grasper, a parasite. The handle turned, I entered, shut the door behind me, gazed at him in his lab coat.

He stammered as he spoke, his cool words ruined by the erratic rhythm. He wanted me to know that he wasn't disconcerted by my arrival. He had rehearsed every eventuality. I was doomed.

He cleared his throat, tried again, and this time his voice was steady. "The poison is spreading from your brother to you. It's a chemical I use in my work. That's why I didn't care which of you I hit. To get one would be to get you both. It's for the sake of knowledge."

He paused, took a deep breath, continued, "All I had to do was wait for you to emerge from the entrance, take my shot, hurry down the alley and re-enter the institute through the steel door. That's an emergency exit that's hardly ever used. It suited my purpose admirably."

I took one step forward. He backed off, grinning unconvincingly, and stood behind a table on which a flask glowed faintly. It was connected to electrodes. I saw a fluttering deep behind the glass. I knew my brother's ghost was inside this prison. I knew it was the empty vessel that had diverted his soul from the liberty of infinity, from the intergalactic gardens of death. I spoke to Gruber, in a voice that filled the room to bursting.

"But why? What was the purpose?"

He scratched his head almost manically and said, "I needed results. Look at you! I didn't know what kind of ghost or ghosts you had inside. One or two? It was even possible you shared a mutated soul. I had to find out, you had to die. I had to collect whatever came out. It was one ghost, unsullied, pure. This in itself is useful research! I won't be stopped by your petty considerations, your paltry self-regard. Time to liberate your ghost too! You can join him in the jar, brothers reunited in an electric afterlife!"

I was dying anyway, but he didn't mean that. There was a gun in his grasp, absurdly small in his big hand, a Colt Model 1903 Pocket Hammerless, lethal at this range but almost comical in appearance. His aim wavered but my stomach, chest and head were always covered. I took another step closer and he licked his lips, flared his nostrils, growled.

He said, "I have discovered that the electrification of an empty vessel gives it a psychic allure that attracts loose souls. But it's the allure that matters, not the voltage itself. That will be the subject of my next paper. It will make me famous and I will be respected at last."

"The allure," I said, and then I added, "At last," and I took another step in his direction, another step closer to the flask. He stretched his arm even further with the pistol at the end of it.

"He laughed at me once, he mocked me."

"Deservedly," I said.

"Time to get it over with, to do the deed."

He squeezed the trigger.

The sound echoed from the walls. By chance the bullet tore into one side of my heart. My blood pressure dropped instantly, my vision blurred, I felt my soul tugging at the nerves and sinews that bound it tight. These cords loosened and the prisoner was set free.

Gruber shrieked with unholy glee.

Then his laughter underwent a transformation, performing a glissando slide down the scale of human emotions, turning from mirth into terror. My ghost had left my own body, it was seeking an empty vessel. The universe itself dragged it one way, the electrified flask another, but there was a third force, a vessel empty and more alluring than either.

My soul entered the body of my dead brother. Arnold became Ronald. The corpse jerked, its lips falling from its mouth with the sudden movement. Glassy eyes perceived Gruber dimly. I was on the other side now, in both senses. Could I adjust to my new situation?

My brother was the empty vessel.

I staggered forwards, shedding chunks of flesh, leaning to my left in order to remain upright, to counteract Arnold's dead weight. I steadied myself on the table and the flask trembled.

Gruber was fumbling with his gun.

I reached him before he could find his courage again. I pressed him into a corner with my double weight.

I lifted my rotting arm, green slime pouring from the elbow, and forced my fist into his mouth. He gurgled. My fist expanded, turning into a viscous fluid, a wedge of thick ooze. This fluid poured down his throat, saturated his nostrils. I kept pushing my arm and it vanished into him, melting, deliquescing, steaming as it did so, filling the room with sickly green vapour. His eyes were wider than eyes should ever be. They bulged but I was merciless. The light in them faded, then I felt his soul leave him.

It rose into the air, almost touched the ceiling, but the pull of the flask was too great as the cables hummed. His ghost veered, accelerated towards the glass and passed through into the jar.

He was alone in there with my brother's ghost.

I nodded once, collapsed.

Sprawled over Gruber's body, my soul left my brother's body, which had dissolved too much to be a vessel for anything. There was no indecision at all. I flung myself at the flask, found myself inside it, comforted by the electricity, a confined paradise for brothers.

Wallace and Hopkins didn't enter the room for another hour. They weren't able to summon up the courage until then. They found a flask with three flickers of pale light inside it, but the bodies on the floor were their main concern. They summoned the police. The flask was forgotten, eventually removed and put into storage. And no one ever asked what two of the flickers were doing to the third that struggled between them.

Rhys Hughes has lived in many different countries and currently lives in India. He began writing at an early age and his first book, Worming the Harpy, *was published in 1995 by Tartarus Press. Since that time, he has published more than fifty other books and his work has been translated into ten languages. He recently completed an ambitious project that involved writing exactly 1000 linked narratives.*

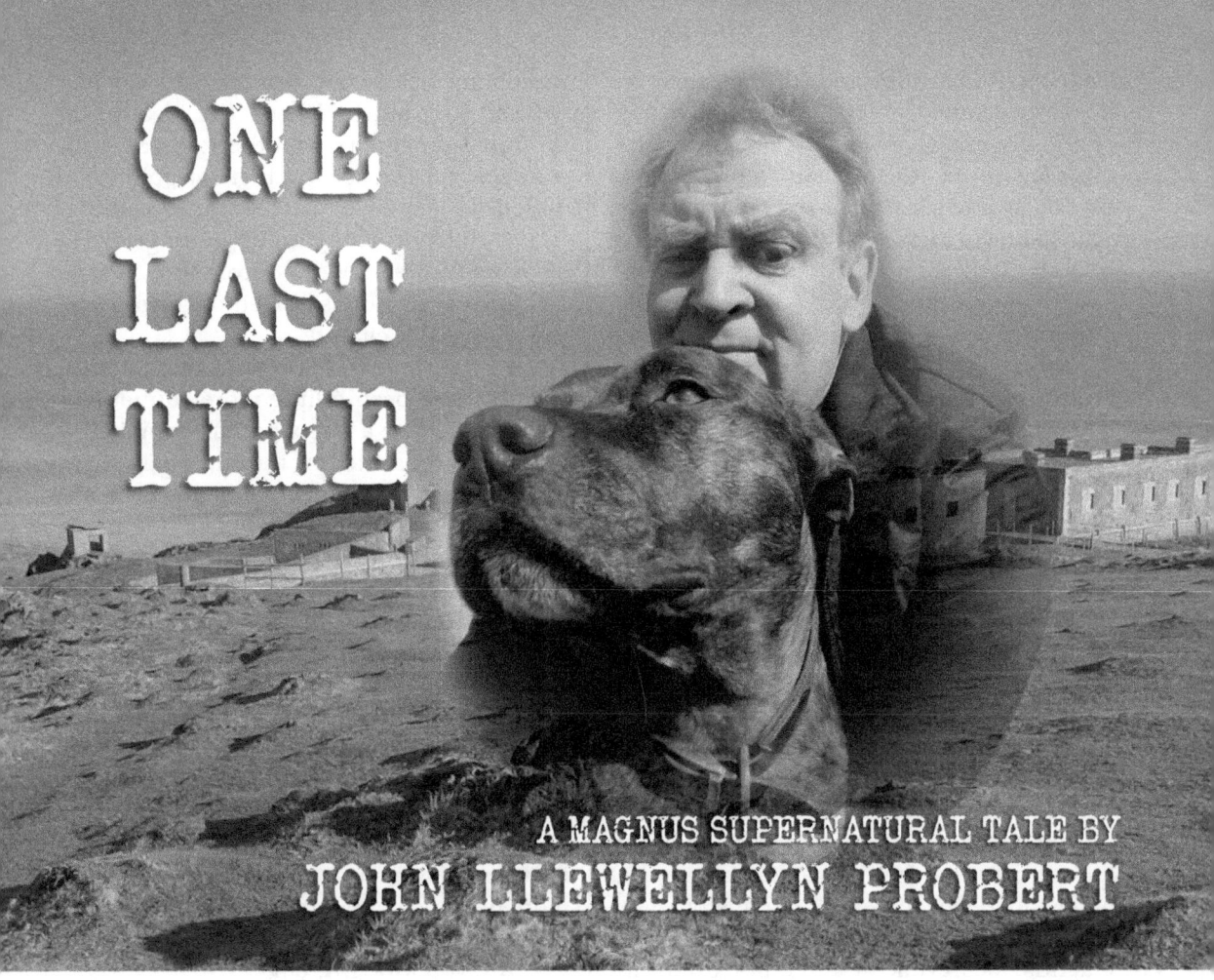

ONE LAST TIME

A MAGNUS SUPERNATURAL TALE BY
JOHN LLEWELLYN PROBERT

THIS IS NOT MY TALE TO TELL, BECAUSE I WAS ONLY WITNESS TO A SMALL PART OF IT. THE ONLY INDIVIDUAL WHO REALLY KNOWS WHAT HAPPENED IS MAGNUS, MY FAITHFUL STAFFORDSHIRE BULL TERRIER, and while I will admit he possesses quite an extensive, often to the point of bewildering, understanding of human vocabulary, that understanding is still very much limited to words for "food," "walk," and "adventure," a word the utterance of which sends him into paroxysms of joy followed by a mad stampede to the car. But as any dog owner will know, his eyes, his face, and his body language all provide their own way of helping him communicate, and it is partly through those that I have been able to piece together my own understanding of what happened to us one midweek morning in early June.

The heatwave that forecasters had promised was finally here, and we were out early to avoid the most extreme temperatures the day might have to offer. It was comfortably warm as we trudged our way up the incline leading to the top of Brean Down, a 310-foot-high promontory in Somerset that extends into the Bristol Channel between Weston super-Mare on one side and Burnham-On-Sea on the other.

For those who enjoy a challenge, a steep staircase cut into the rock can take you straight from the car park (and the tea rooms, should you be so inclined) to the top. Today, however, my brindle friend and I had decided to climb the slightly easier but nevertheless still steeply sloping route to the right that takes you to the summit of the promontory at the point where it arises from the mainland.

Magnus was maintaining his usual pace, seemingly unaffected by the gradient. He was wearing his harness and lead, as the area possesses many steep drops that a dog, especially one as low to the ground as he, may fall prone to in their rambunctious enthusiasm to see what is over the next rise. This did mean, however, that I required him to halt halfway up so I could catch my breath. Magnus stopped good-naturedly, sniffing items of doggy interest at the side of the path until I was all right to resume. Overhead, wisps of cloud formed crushed cobweb patterns in an otherwise faultless blue sky. I was soon ready to move on with Magnus trotting ahead of me, something he is only comfortable to do when he is on his lead. Otherwise he prefers to follow behind. I have come to believe the tension exerted by my holding his lead offers him reassurance that I'm on the other end, and with this he can forge ahead safe in the knowledge that I am still close to him.

We reached the top to enjoy the quite spectacular view offered on summer's days such as this. The sea was the kind of blue one hardly ever gets to experience in England: a deep, inviting, Mediterranean azure that almost made me forget the usual stony grey of its appearance during most of the year. Magnus, meanwhile, was unimpressed with what he saw. He gave it a single glance and then pulled on his lead to signify there were far more important items of concern to him on the worn gravel path ahead, and so we set off on the clifftop walk that would take us to the promontory's very tip.

Just before that, of course, would be the fort.

Brean Down Fort is going to be important a little later in our, or rather Magnus's, story. The extensive stone buildings that can be found there now were originally a Victorian naval fortification, built in 1870 to prevent invasion by the French and provide protection to Bristol Channel's ports. It was used for experimental weapons testing in World War II but is now an empty ruin, with most parts other than the most treacherous open to the public. What many amateur local historians, enthused with the opportunity to discuss all things pertaining to those periods, may neglect to tell you, however, is that settlements have existed all over the promontory since the Bronze Age. The site we had just left had been the location of an Iron Age hill fort, and the Romans built a temple on the second highest point, one which we would shortly be approaching. In fact, bits of pottery and Roman gold and silver coins are still found from time to time as more of the land is eroded by the sea and the changes in climate.

If I had known all of that beforehand, I might have been a little more cautious in taking Magnus, a dog who has exhibited a propensity for attracting the supernatural, to such a place. That said, we had been there before on a number of occasions and never experienced so much as a hint of the ghost of a gunner, or spectre of a centurion.

Magnus was forging ahead. We had quickly moved off the main path, which is the old military road that winds around the lower half of the north side of the promontory and does not offer such arresting views, and were tramping across turf. Suddenly Magnus came to such an abrupt halt that I nearly fell over him. This used to happen a lot when he was first adopted and was a far more nervous chap, but it's now such a rare occurrence that I was ill-prepared for it.

"Are you all right, boy?"

Magnus was staring back the way we had come, his eyes narrowed, almost as if he were squinting to better see something the actual existence of which even he was unsure. When I looked, there was nothing of note, probably because the squirrel or other wildlife that his exquisitely sensitive hearing must have picked up had made a swift getaway as soon as it had realised it had been spotted.

I gave the lead a gentle tug and Magnus resumed our walk, although he still kept turning back at intervals as if convinced there was something behind us. He halted again, more gently this time, narrowed his eyes once more and then looked up at me. We have spent sufficient time together and been on enough adventures that I took him entirely seriously as he seemed to be asking me if I could see what was causing him concern. There was nothing, I said, hoping my tone of voice and my shrugged shoulders would make my response clear. When that didn't work, I offered him a treat which was duly gobbled, and served to provide adequate distraction, at least for that moment.

Now we were passing the stone staircase that led directly up from the car park 310 feet below. Again Magnus halted. He glanced behind him, then at the steps, then at me.

"I still can't see anything," I said.

No, but I could hear something, coming from the steps. A series of scrapings and mutterings, stumblings and giggling as the first members of what turned out to be a school party on a field day outing emerged into view. Realisation dawned.

"Oh is that it?" I well knew Magnus's penchant for what can most accurately be described as human adoration. He had obviously detected the approach of a number of potential strokers and petters, perhaps even with food to spare, and I guessed he had got a bit over excited at the prospect. Already he had adopted what I call his "adorable" stance, complete with Staffy smile and vigorously wagging tail. I reassured the group of five teenaged girls who approached us, unable to resist his charms that, yes, he was friendly and yes, he would love some attention, but that it was best to exercise caution when approaching a dog as overly excited to meet new humans as he was at that moment.

This interlude of Magnus appreciation was interrupted by a distant bark of the human kind. It came from an older woman I assumed was the girls' teacher, calling them back to join a group which now numbered around thirty huffing and puffing youngsters who had emerged from the steep climb and were now busy taking photographs of themselves.

The dark-haired girl who had led her friends to us asked if she could take a picture of my canine companion. Magnus sat proudly and patiently next to her while I kept out of shot. It all seemed to be a success until the girl checked the image and I saw a frown cross her face. She glanced behind Magnus and me, looked perplexed, and then inspected the image on her phone once more.

"Is everything all right?" I asked.

"Must have been a trick of the light," she said. "For a moment I thought I saw—"

"Charlotte! Will you and your friends please stop being distracted and return to the group!"

The teacher's voice was loud enough to make Magnus jump, and before I could ask Charlotte what she thought she might have seen, she and her friends were gone, running to catch up with the rest of the group, which was already negotiating the next hill with the vigour of young people able to quickly recover from the stress of a 300 foot climb.

"I think we'd better let them get ahead," I said to Magnus, momentarily glum now he was no longer the centre of attention. When I looked again the group had already disappeared, surprisingly quickly, I thought, although I didn't grasp the significance of this until later.

Despite the forecast for the day, and despite the sky staying the same shade of almost blinding blue, the next stage of our journey was accompanied by a chill breeze the onset of which had coincided with the disappearance of the school party. We were halfway up the hill the Roman temple had once stood on when Magnus froze again. He looked behind us with a wary expression.

"Now come on, Magnus." There were occasions when I just needed to be firm with him. "There's nothing there."

Or was there? Now that I looked, I could not help but feel that the bushes furthest away from us looked somehow…different. Thicker, almost as if they were harbouring something, or rather a number of things, low to the ground and blue-grey in colour.

When I blinked the peculiar aberration of the foliage had vanished, as had the breeze, to be replaced by the slowly building heat of the morning. We carried on, uninterrupted, for another mile or so, and soon the barrack buildings, searchlight batteries, gun turrets, and other now-abandoned structures that covered the four acres of the distal promontory occupied by the fortifications came into view.

For anyone coming across it by chance, the main complex of Brean Down Fort could easily be mistaken for a Victorian prison, or high security hospital. The buildings possess the same grey no-nonsense functional look of an institution, and what remains of the visible gun pivots and neighbouring pill boxes could once all have been there to prevent prisoners escaping as much as foreign powers invading. Even the morning sunshine, and the calm blue of the sea either side and the sky above, couldn't shake the place's confrontational atmosphere. As we made our way down to the fort's entrance, accessed via a narrow bridge that crossed a dry moat, with drops on either side sufficient to severely injure a dog should he fall, I tried to shake off the feeling that there should have been more people around than just the two of us.

Where was the school party?

Admittedly they could already be inside, or inspecting the other small crumbling buildings that peppered the nearby cliffs. But if that was the case, they were being terribly quiet about it. The chill breeze had arisen once more, and just as we reached the entrance Magnus once again came to a sudden halt. I was quicker to turn this time and fancied, just for a moment, that there was something odd about the steep grassy hill we had just descended. Again I experienced the feeling that there was something unseen out there, and perhaps even several somethings, and that somehow they were hiding in plain sight. Even more concerning was that while Magnus's gaze remained fixed on the path we had just come down, I chanced to glance to the left, along the military road that wound away from the complex. Just for a moment I fancied I saw a figure dressed in grey. It wasn't wearing the combat fatigues of a soldier, however, but something much looser, more flowing, almost Druidic. Now where had that word come from? Never mind. The figure was gone and likely was never there in the first place.

Magnus still seemed convinced something was watching us. In an effort to rid him of his concerns I suggested we go in. The steel gate screeched as I opened it, making Magnus jump once more, and after passing over the bridge we found ourselves in the irregularly-shaped courtyard, barrack buildings to our left, the six major gun pivots on a raised concrete platform ahead of us, and the officers' mess, gunners' quarters, and stables flanking us to the right.

But no school party.

Or anyone else for that matter.

Sometimes the interior of places like this are cold even if they are open to the elements on a lovely day such as this was promising to be, and initially I assumed that was why it was so chilly. Once again, however, Magnus was far more clued up as to what was actually happening than I, and when he pulled at his lead to turn us round so we could see back across the bridge to the outside world, I beheld what would turn out to be my best and only glimpse of what I did not doubt my faithful companion could see in considerably stronger detail.

I counted four of them, grey-blue blobs bigger than sheep, evenly spaced across the grassy descent that led to the fort. Each was so insubstantial that I could see the rocks and bushes that lay immediately behind them. The outline of each was just as nondescript, such that the overall appearance of each could be likened to a nebulous mass of dirty, teased-out cotton wool. As they came nearer I noticed each moved with a kind of lolloping gait. Up and down, up and down, and all the while moving closer to the entrance of the fort.

Right to where Magnus was currently standing.

I pulled him back inside. When I looked again to see how close they were, all four had vanished.

"Perhaps we're safe in here," I said, as much to reassure myself as my faithful friend. Even as I spoke I suspected I was wrong, in part because, aside from the absence of anyone else in the hill fort, the sky had changed colour from blue to a strange washed-out indigo. The sun still shone but now, as its rays touched the barracks to our left, the walls began to change, the stone shimmering, with what lay beneath suggestive of an entirely different structure to that of simple Victorian sleeping quarters. Even so, Magnus wanted to venture inside. I wasn't happy about it, but he was determined and, with a great wrench of Staffy strength, he pulled us both into the building.

The barracks consisted of little but an oblong shell with a flagstone floor. Its small square windows were bereft of glass, while the roof open to that disturbing, unnatural sky allowed in plenty of light. Magnus led me to the centre of the room and then sat so he could see the entrance through which we had come, almost as if he was waiting for something.

When they arrived, the shimmering cloudy apparitions I had seen outside were now invisible, to my eyes at least.

But not to Magnus.

He got to his feet, first sniffing the air, and then directing that sensitive nose of his towards whatever was now standing right in front of him. And then an interesting thing happened. As he sniffed each in greeting (I counted him doing this four times) his behaviour began to change, and far from being scared or nervous, his reaction was one of joy. Before I knew it, he gave a low play bow to the invisible arrivals—front legs stretched out and leaning down heavily on his elbows. The response to this was presumably favourable as he then began to leap and tussle, cavort and play-snarl, looking for all the world as if he was playing by himself when in fact he was actually playing with four invisible beings.

Four invisible ghost dogs?

We had certainly encountered stranger things on our travels. From the direction I had seen them come and the way Magnus had been acting during our walk, I guessed they must have followed us from the site of the Iron Age fort at the other end of the promontory. Also, from how high Magnus was leaping and the angle of his eye line I assumed their breed must have been akin to Irish wolfhounds. I also began to wonder if the human figure I thought I glimpsed had been trying to call them back.

As regards Magnus leaping, I still had a tight hold on his lead, with the main length of the cord wrapped tightly around my forearm to better keep him under control. The practice has resulted in a couple of bruises in the past, and not a little muscle strain either, but despite his remarkable strength my brindle friend has yet to dislocate my elbow or shoulder. I was keeping the fingers

of my other hand crossed for that not to happen today, either.

A tight grip on his lead notwithstanding, I allowed Magnus as much free rein as I could, as he seemed to be greatly enjoying himself. He spent the best part of the next ten minutes playing with his new friends with such energy and verve that, even after that short time, I could see he was starting to tire. But it seemed the games were not over, and now he was being led outside.

Outside.

Where numerous National Trust signs warned of perilous and frequently fatal drops that required dogs to be kept on leads at all times.

I gripped the lead even more tightly.

Despite how tired he was becoming, Magnus was still whipped up into a frenzy, and I followed closely as he all but danced across the courtyard and headed south out of the compound. We found ourselves climbing onto a precipice where, twenty feet below, waves the same unnatural colour as the sky could be seen crashing with increasing violence against jagged rocks.

Magnus cavorted closer and closer to the cliff's edge until I decided he should go no further. It helped that Magnus's energy was somewhat depleted, but it still took all my strength to pull him back.

"Enough now, son!"

It is very rare that I speak to him with the firm severity of what I term my schoolmaster's voice. The benefit of this is that Magnus never fails to take notice, and now was no exception. Interrupted from his joyful reverie, he turned to look at me with an expression that convinced me he was under some form of supernatural glamour.

"Magnus!"

For a moment my voice calling his name caused whatever spell he was under to be lifted, but even so I could tell that, more than anything, all he wanted to do was continue playing. If he could speak, I do not doubt that his pleas would have been along the lines of "Can I go with them? Can I? My new friends? Can I go with them? Please?"

He was straining hard at his lead. I knew if I let go he would cannon straight off the cliff, plunge into the current below, and join those new supernatural friends of his for-ever. Despite the fact that, for all I knew, he might be eternally happy doing so, I could not bring myself to let him.

"If it's all the same to you," I said in tones now nowhere near as firm as I would have liked them to be, "I'd quite rather you stayed with me."

It was a little difficult to see exactly how he responded, as my vision was getting a little blurry at that point, but I was aware of the wind growing stronger, of the waves crashing more loudly and, above all of that, a faint sound of happy barking which, as it grew faint, seemed to be moving further out to sea. The next thing I knew, the tension in Magnus's lead had subsided. I looked down to see my friend bearing a very soulful expression as he stared out at a horizon whose sky was now rapidly returning to its normal blue. As the chatter of the school party began to slowly rise in volume behind us, Magnus sat down on the clifftop and I took up a position beside him, the sea churning and crashing below us, the fading of Magnus's invisible playmates an increasingly distant memory.

We stayed there for a long time on those windswept cliffs, the two of us gazing out across the water. I wondered what the intentions of his newfound friends actually might have been. Perhaps they weren't malignant at all. Perhaps their spirits had been trapped in the long-buried foundations of the Iron Age fort, and some combination of factors including the date, the weather (we were having the hottest summer on record), and Magnus, especially Magnus, had given them the chance to be free.

Magnus is a rescue dog. I could not begin to guess what was going through his mind right then, but I like to think he had been delighted to be given the chance to do some rescuing of his own. Perhaps all those ghost dogs wanted, maybe even needed, was the chance to play, one last time.

Eventually I put my arm round him. At that, Magnus turned and gave me the biggest and most heartfelt lick the side of my face has ever been lucky enough to experience.

I took that to mean he was happy he had decided to stay.

John Llewellyn Probert's latest books are the short story collection Chasing Spirits *(Black Shuck Books), the portmanteau novel* How Grim Was My Valley *(NewCon Press) and on the non-fiction front,* The Frightfest Guide to Mad Doctor Movies *(FAB Press). Coming up next will be a couple of novels, another short story collection and more film books, as well as articles for both US and UK film and literary magazines. He tries to fit in some sleep where he can.*

Magnus is a seven-year-old Brindle Staffordshire Bull Terrier rescue who has been part of the Probert household for just over two years. He is walked at least twice a day, and his favourite routes include the local beach where he loves to chase any crumpled linen that may flap across his path, the golf course after he was shown the 1945 Ealing classic Dead of Night, *and of course Brent Knoll, the subject of his first story, in* Nightmare Abbey 6. *After all that exercise his favourite way to relax is on the sofa where he loves to fall asleep in front of 1970s European horror films. He is very happy that his humans did not name him Zoltan.*

MUSIC, MADNESS, AND MURDER:
REVISITING HANGOVER SQUARE

MENTION THE "GOLDEN AGE" OF HOLLYWOOD HORROR AND THE FIRST STUDIO TO COME TO EVERYONE'S MIND WILL BE UNIVERSAL, with perhaps Val Lewton's 'B' unit at RKO a close second. Twentieth Century-Fox would be a bit further down anyone's list of producers of classic scares during this period, but in the mid-1940s that studio was responsible for a pair of classics made one after the other.

In 1944 Fox made *The Lodger*, the story of a landlady who realises her new tenant may well be Jack the Ripper. Realising they had a hit on their hands, plans were immediately made to reteam that film's star (Laird Cregar), screenwriter (Barré Lyndon), producer (Robert Bassler) and director (John Brahm). But what would serve as a suitable

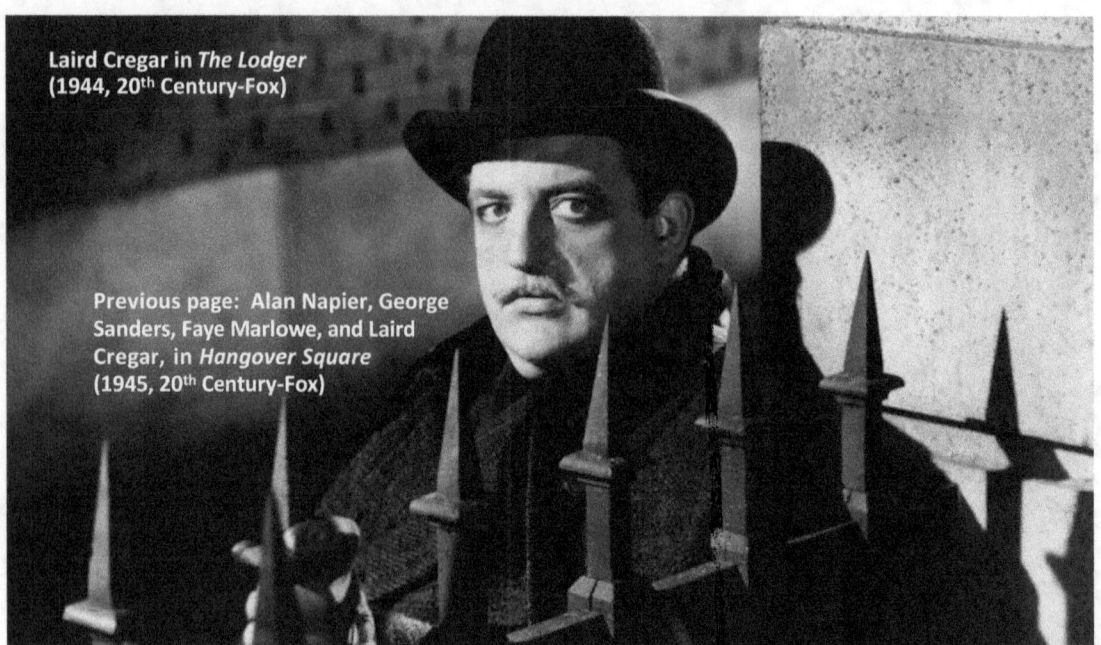

Laird Cregar in *The Lodger* (1944, 20th Century-Fox)

Previous page: Alan Napier, George Sanders, Faye Marlowe, and Laird Cregar, in *Hangover Square* (1945, 20th Century-Fox)

project? Attention focused on playwright and author Patrick Hamilton. The film version of his play *Gaslight* starring Charles Boyer and Ingrid Bergman had been a big hit in 1944 for MGM (it had previously been filmed in 1940 in the UK with Anton Walbrook, a film MGM had done their best to suppress). Hamilton and Lyndon knew each other and had, in fact, both had plays (*Gaslight* and *The Man in Half Moon Street* respectively) playing in London at the same time. In view of all this Laird Cregar was able to successfully persuade Fox to buy the rights to Hamilton's contemporary novel *Hangover Square*, a piece in which he was keen to play the lead.

The book tells the story of George Harvey Bone. A lonely, sensitive, unemployed man, George has a tendency to fall into what he terms "dark moods." He becomes obsessed

with a wholly nasty actress called Netta whom he regularly ends up humiliating himself before and whom he eventually drowns in her bath. He then kills himself, leaving a note asking that his cat be looked after. When Fox decided to film the property, Lyndon admitted he disliked the book, much more he couldn't bear to read it again, so instead he asked for the studio's three-page summary. And that was when everything changed. Reduced to its bare outline the screenwriter suddenly realised how to make Hamilton's novel work for a 1940s cinema audience.

George Harvey Bone was no longer a sad loser but instead a brilliant composer (a move Laird Cregar greatly approved of). Instead of just drifting into the dark moods that cause him to kill, now he was triggered by stress and a loud discordant sound such as scaffolding collapsing (the kind of narrative device that would also see use in Hammer's 1971 *Hands of the Ripper*). The murder of Netta was changed to her being dumped in a trench and covered in cement, but would be changed again, to a scene that turned out to be one of the film's highlights, at the insistence of Fox head Darryl F Zanuck. Also at Zanuck's insistence, the setting was changed from contemporary London to the Victorian era to allow re-use of Fox's (impressive) sets that had been built for *The Lodger*.

Barré Lyndon's final screenplay for *Hangover Square* ended up taking at least five separate drafts written over six months, with early versions having George's moods turning him into a suave criminologist. Cregar loved this idea and hated it when he later felt himself reduced to the status of a "mere murderer." Lyndon, meanwhile, disliked the music Bernard Herrmann would write to accompany the film (including George's concerto, which is the key to the whole picture) and had to be reassured by director John Brahm that it was "exactly what it needed to be." Watching the film many years later he relented and admitted he now appreciated its genius. But let's leave the production difficulties for now and concentrate on the film itself which, even though it had a difficult gestation, remains a standout in the careers of many involved.

After the opening credits we are informed that we are about to learn the story of George Harvey Bone of 12 Hangover Square (explaining the title succinctly) and that the "British Catalogue of Music" lists him as a Distinguished Composer.

The film proper opens on a hurdy gurdy. Both the tune it is playing and the flame burning at its side will come back to haunt both us and George as the film goes on. This is just the beginning of an impressive overhead shot showing us a busy Victorian street that then pans across to an upper

floor window where we see an elderly man stabbed, POV-style (and in fact similar to how Judith Myers' death is filmed in the opening of John Carpenter's 1978 *Halloween*). The residence is set alight (fire again) after which we see the killer's face. "Old Ogilvy's place" as we are informed, burns as the killer stumbles down the street in a daze. The killer is George Bone, and he's only now beginning to emerge from one of his "dark moods." As he reaches Hangover Square he hears piano music from his own

basement flat, where he finds his friend Barbara Chapman (Faye Marlowe, who only made eight films) and her father Sir Henry (Alan Napier, most famous as Alfred from the Adam West TV *Batman* but with a lengthy career that also included Universal's 1946 *House of Horrors* and work in Val Lewton's classic RKO movies). Barbara has been playing George's as-yet unfinished concerto, "the best work you've ever done" says Sir Henry who, it would seem, knows a thing or two about such stuff. He offers George a chance for it to be performed, with George as soloist, at his next "musical soirée," "provided it's finished in time."

"I'm enormously complimented," says George, in a line that apparently took many takes for Laird Cregar to get right. (More on that later.) George confesses to Barbara that he's just had another of his blackouts (the "another" being, of course, significant) with no memory of what he has done during it. Meanwhile in the street outside, a news vendor cries of horrible murder.

Concerned, George goes with Barbara to see Scotland Yard psychiatrist Dr. Middleton (George Sanders during what Alan Napier kindly termed his "uncooperative" period—more on that later, too). George wants to know if he could be capable of criminal acts, especially as

after this most recent episode he has found a knife in his pocket and blood on his coat. Middleton asks George about triggers to his condition, and we learn George has to be very worked up and stressed, after which any loud discordant sound will set him off. Middleton performs a blood test. There is a lit Bunsen burner (fire again) on his laboratory bench. After George and Barbara have left, Middleton tells a police superintendent that he thinks they should be followed.

Soon after, Middleton visits George at home to tell him (and Barbara) that the blood on George's coat has turned out to be his own from a head injury, and that his knife possesses no incriminating evidence. Middleton suggests that the best thing George can do is to take a break from his music and get away from it for a while, something we can already tell the artist is going to find virtually impossible. Middleton escorts Barbara to her home on the other side of Hangover Square,

denying George the opportunity to do so and thus gently driving a wedge between her and George that will have repercussions almost immediately. As they walk, Middleton engages in what, in future decades, would be considered typical giallo-style psychiatrist psychobabble designed entirely to warn the audience that things are likely going to get worse for George.

To take his mind off things, George attends a Saturday night "Smoking Concert." Smoking concerts were live performances attended by men only during the Victorian era and were very popular. The term is now obsolete although certain British universities like Oxford and Cambridge do still hold them, as does the University of Liverpool Medical School.

The smoking concert George attends at a local pub effectively seals his doom, because performing there is Netta Longdon (Linda Darnell, a beautiful actress from Texas who apparently arrived in Hollywood accompanied by her pet rooster). Netta is wearing a dress that was the result of careful discussions with the American ratings board. George is smitten and inspired to write a song which he plays for her. Cregar had been taking piano lessons and was at pains to do his own fingering for the pieces we see George performing. Netta immediately realises she might be on to a good thing, as does her lyricist / possible boyfriend / likely

ne'er-do-well Mickey (Michael Dyne). The three of them stagger home drunk to discover Netta's cat has been thrown out by her landlady. George offers to look after the animal (let's hope he does) and tells Netta she can come and visit it anytime. It's easy to read the cat as a symbol of Netta's insidious invasion of George's home life.

George's song earns Netta and Mickey a decent sum, and she admits relief that she now doesn't need to have any more to do with boring George. Oh but she does, says

Feline Netta (Linda Darnell) teases a male audience with her bawdy song and dance routine.

Cregar and Darnell with Michael Dyne.

Mickey, reminding her that the two of them might be sitting on a potential goldmine with George's songwriting ability, and he suggests she lead him on so they can obtain a few more.

Soon George is taking Netta out every night and neglecting Barbara, her father, and most important of all, his concerto.

During one such excursion the two of them "bump into" Mickey and theatrical producer Eddie Carstairs (Glenn Langan who, twelve years later, would be playing *The Amazing Colossal Man* for producer-director Bert I Gordon at AIP). George wants to take Netta to a symphony. She agrees but then immediately blows him off for a chance to sing at

the club Eddie and Mickey are off to, but not before she claims a headache and gets George to take her home. In an act of supreme villainy (Linda Darnell was initially reticent to play such an evil role, and it's easy to see why) she makes him finish her new song for her while she "rests up," then as soon as he goes round to her place to deliver it, she sends him on his way and sneaks back out. Back in 1945 you could probably hear the boos and hisses from the audience from outside the cinema.

But unbeknownst to Netta, George has paused outside her house to enjoy a coffee with a night watchman who is keeping an eye out for a delivery of gas pipes. When she leaves, George spots her. She brushes him off and her carriage leaves. All of this is witnessed by Barbara and her father. Barbara becomes the voice of the audience as she admonishes George before leaving him in the street. George is getting more and more stressed, and those gas pipes are arriving. Are they going to fall into the trench that

has been dug for them with a fearful dark mood-inducing clatter? They surely are.

George returns to his flat in a murderous mood, gives the cat some consideration but then leaves it alone. Instead, he knots a curtain tie-back, thuggee-style (as will be remarked upon shortly) before setting off into the night. We see the camera at a low angle as George strides through the wet streets, and we freeze frame once he has left the shot. We hear a girl scream.

By the time the police have arrived George is coming out of his daze and is back in Hangover Square. It turns out he has tried to strangle Barbara. The best place to see this scene is in house publicity stills, although there will be a flashback to it close to the end of the film. Barbara is still alive, and Middleton explains that her bruises fit with attempted strangulation by thuggee cord.

George, now entirely unaware of what he has done, comes to check on Barbara (who has no idea who her attacker was) and promises her that he will finish his concerto, which he ends up doing by candlelight. But oh dear, here comes Netta calling and using her womanly wiles to convince George to finish another song for her instead. She tries to steal a musical motif from George's concerto and succeeds! (Cue more booing from cinema audiences of the period, or perhaps sharp intakes of breath).

It's bonfire night, and some boys are on

the street asking, "Penny for the Guy," with some explanation for anyone (presumably US audiences) unfamiliar with this practice. This setup is going to be very important shortly. George goes to Netta's apartment and proposes to her when she quite obviously doesn't want him there, and guess what? The smooth Mr. Eddie Carstairs has got in first and plans to marry Netta next week. Enraged, George tries to strangle Eddie, but Netta intervenes and George leaves. More stressed than he has ever been so far, it just takes some violins falling over to send him into a mood. The curtain tie back gets knotted again and the cat has to make a dash for it. George returns to Netta's and witnesses her saying goodbye to Eddie.

Netta is not long for this world.

And quite right too, cinema audience members were no doubt thinking by this point. It looks as if the cat didn't escape, either, its body discovered as George carries Netta's body off. He joins a procession to the huge bonfire that has been built near the square and where everyone is being encouraged to dump their "Guys." George's Guy is, of course, dead Netta in a cheap mask, and soon her body is one of many being engulfed by the ensuing conflagration.

This scene is a standout, with George being encouraged to climb to the top of the as yet unlit bonfire and place Netta's body there because his "Guy" looks so fine. It's such a memorable, tense, and beautifully

composed scene that it's perhaps surprising to appreciate it wasn't in Barré Lyndon's original screenplay, where Netta's body was dumped in building foundations and covered with cement. Studio head (and co-founder of 20th Century-Fox) Darryl F Zanuck didn't like that, and insisted Lyndon come up with something better. Lyndon found himself thinking of Guy Fawkes night, which is still a tradition in England. Nowadays bonfires are only constructed in specially appointed places because of health and safety concerns, but back then everyone who could build a bonfire would, and some companies (Lyndon specifically thought of breweries, which is what we see here) would encourage their workers to build a bonfire in the works yard. Lyndon skilfully primes the audience with the "Penny for the Guy" scene so it's not so jarring when George ends up carrying Netta's body through a busy city street. Darryl Zanuck was delighted with Lyndon's solution to the problem and was happy to spend the money on what turned out to be an understandably complex scene, one that required not just all the members of the

studio fire department standing by, but other fire services as well. The bonfire itself was forty feet tall, and 200 extras were employed as revellers for George to claw his way through as he retreats from the blaze.

George is still in his mood when he's told his cat is dead, so when he comes out of it shortly after, he pours milk for it and looks for it under the piano. Distracted by seeing his concerto, he sits down and begins to play it, for us the audience as much as for himself. Brahm films his performance in a single master shot, once again utilising the overhead camera that slowly closes in on George but remains hovering over him.

Netta's show has understandably been cancelled as a news vendor outside the theatre informs us that no one can find her body. The police call on George, and not for the first time, it seems. Eddie has told them George was over at Netta's quarrelling with her on the night of the disappearance, the inspector says, as he fingers the curtain tie-back. The police are also aware of George's periods of "forgetfulness." Might he have had one that evening? George says he didn't

and that he can account for his actions. Meanwhile Sir Henry is delighted with the concerto's manuscript which he has been perusing in the room next door, and is making plans for rehearsals. The police seem to be happy that George isn't a suspect and decide to turn their attention to Carstairs, but Dr. Middleton isn't so sure and sets off to try and find Netta's body.

It's the night of the concerto's inaugural performance and there's snow in Hangover Square, where George confesses to Barbara that Netta is still playing on his mind. He's worried he may actually have had something to do with her disappearance. Barbara does her best to reassure him and reminds him that he also thought he had something

to do with the Fulham antiques dealer murder but he didn't. Except, of course, that he actually did.

Back at George's flat, Middleton has let himself in and confronts George as he returns home. Brahm keeps the doctor entirely in silhouette except for the knife he shows to George, who explains he has it for the sound holes of his violins. Middleton stays in darkness, with George brightly lit right next to him and dressing for his concert, as the doctor shows him an article he has found in George's flat about the thuggee cord, written by Middleton himself (which surely should have cast police suspicion on the doctor?). Has George ever made such a cord? Does George the killer make cords for his "art" while George the composer makes chords? There's certainly the chance that Lyndon slipped in some none-too-subtle wordplay there. George's gaze strays to the curtain tie, which Middleton discovers has wrinkles in it as if it has recently been knotted. He has also noticed George's singed trousers. The doctor's questioning persists, and we can see George is getting stressed, especially when Middleton comes right out and accuses George of murder. He tries to stop George going to his concert, warning him that his mind might break and cause

him "to do some terrible uncontrolled thing." "I've worked all my life for this night," says George, and his words have a double meaning of their own. Middleton insists George go with him to Scotland Yard. George seems to agree.

However, the next time we see him, George is at his concert. He's a bit late but he's there. Once again Brahm has the camera move up on high (as in the opening and bonfire scenes) as George takes his seat at the piano, and finally we get to hear George's concerto (or rather Bernard Herrmann's) in all its macabre glory. Meanwhile the camerawork itself is just as majestic, sweeping over not just the orchestra but the audience as well. As the piece plays, a policeman discovers Middleton locked in George's flat and lets him out. The police close in on George, the music mirroring George's building stress but also his sense of hopelessness. It's a tour de force of a climax that sees the music becoming increasingly frenetic as George mentally revisits his crime, including a brief shot of the attempted strangling of Barbara that we didn't see earlier, as well as the murder and burning of Netta. George eventually

collapses and Barbara takes over. In an adjacent room George admits that he now knows everything he has done. The police are going to take George away. Assurances that he won't hang are not enough—George must hear the end of his concerto. He throws an oil lamp that bursts into flames, because of course, out of all the many films that end in a fiery finale, this one absolutely has to. The auditorium begins to fill with smoke. The audience panics and leaves despite George's insistence that they must hear the concerto to the end. Middleton drags Barbara away, and as the flames rage higher and fire

Robert Bassler came onto the set and gave Sanders a severe talking to. In response, Sanders punched him with such force he laid the producer out cold. In later reports co-star Alan Napier had referred to Sanders as "uncooperative," which was putting it mildly. The "better this way" line was the result of rewrites but, for all we know, may well have been the best dialogue for Middleton to utter.

But other actors were awkward too, most notably star Laird Cregar. Troubled by both his homosexuality and his weight problem he insisted on going on a crash diet that meant *Hangover Square* had to be shot in sequence because of his continued weight loss. This was in part due to his desire to be a romantic leading man, and one cannot help but think that Netta's show being called "Gay Love," which ultimately leads to her death, was a piece of subtext that at that time was there just for the Hollywood community. The effects of dieting and the stress of so desperately wanting to be seen as a romantic lead led to Cregar repeatedly

engines arrive, only George is left, playing his concerto to completion. "Why didn't he try to get out?" asks Sir Henry outside. Middleton's reply? "It's better this way, sir."

It's the last line in the film and, like much of *Hangover Square*'s filming, was not without its problems, not least of which was Sanders, who repeatedly refused to perform his dialogue, claiming it all to be awful. He was so resistant to performing the original final line of the film that several takes were filmed, fiery finale and all, and when the camera came to rest on Sanders he simply stood there and said nothing. Producer fluffing his lines ("I'm enormously comple-mented" kept coming out as "I'm enormously complicated," a Freudian slip if ever there was one) and requiring multiple takes. Linda Darnell, who played Netta, would meet a tragic and horribly ironic end at the age of 41 from burns sustained in a house fire, while Cregar himself underwent abdominal surgery (the actual procedure itself is un-clear) straight after filming of *Hangover Square* completed and died shortly after. He was only 31.

Director John Brahm would never again reach the creative heights he achieved with *Hangover Square*. Despite delivering such a superb (and highly successful—the film made a $12 million profit for Twentieth Century-Fox) piece of work, it's likely the on-set turmoil (Cregar loudly stated he never wanted to work with the director again) had its consequences. Brahm would eventually end up working in television, where he de-livered some of the best episodes of *Alfred Hitchcock Presents* and *The Twilight Zone*. For composer Bernard Herrmann, whose score is still available on CD, this was, of course, still close to the beginning of a fruit-ful career of memorable works, many of them written for Alfred Hitchcock. The music is by turns ominous and threatening, sinister and soulful. It makes you scared of George while at the same time worried for him, and its title, "Concerto Macabre," makes for a fitting alternate title for the classic that is *Hangover Square*.

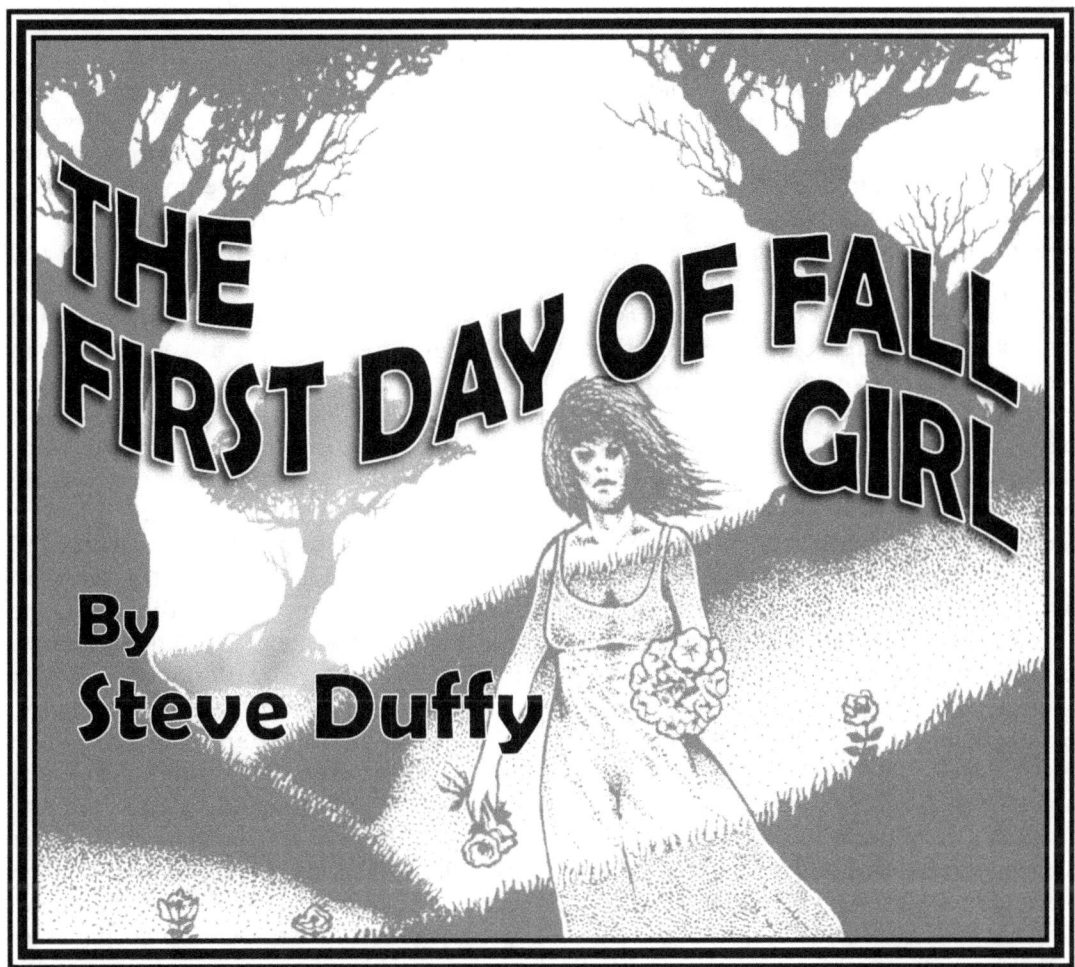

THE FIRST DAY OF FALL GIRL

By Steve Duffy

I **MOVED TO BERLIN IN THE SPRING OF 1990, EAGER TO DRAW A LINE UNDER LONDON.** My parents had died, and in dying left me financially secure for the foreseeable future, which back then seemed to stretch no further than the end of the 20th century. No one back then was looking beyond the grand climacteric of 1999: the new millennium seemed like an unconvincing trope from science fiction. England felt used up—too parochial, too clingy, too predictable—and I didn't want to spend a minute longer in its ruins. Berlin, I thought, was a place where the future might be breaking through. As you'll come to see, I was wrong on nearly every point that mattered.

I arrived in the interregnum between the fall of the Wall and Unity Day: people called it *die Wende*, reunification being dreamed up on the fly. The apartment I rented had formerly been the great dining room of a villa standing in its own grounds on the shores of the Graupnersee, out in the wooded southwestern suburbs. Back in London, a space of that size would have been subdivided into rabbit hutches with MDF partitions, all original features eradicated for the sake of tasteful blandness. Here, it was largely intact, and the bourgeois opulence made up

for any practical shortcomings. I fell in love with it at first sight: the floors of polished parqueting, the moulded plaster detailing on the walls, the tapestry of a hunt riding through a forest in diagonal lines like chessmen, the protagonists moving in and out of view between the trees.

The room was long and high-ceilinged, with large picture windows along one side and wide French doors that opened on to the gardens at its farther end. This combination of features made it practically impossible to heat: there was a large and ornate fireplace of black marble, but the chimney was blocked, and it was forbidden—*Hausregeln*, house rules—to light a fire in the grate. It being April, this detail escaped me at the time. Near the main doors to the communal reception was a knocked-through modern doorway that opened on to a tiny kitchenette, windowless and unventilated, that (I soon discovered) stank out the whole apartment if you tried to cook anything in there. A claustrophobic corridor at the farther end of the kitchen led to an even tinier bathroom, barely big enough to hold a shower cubicle. It was disturbingly expensive for what it was, not to mention what it lacked, but then I happened to be disturbingly well-off.

For the next few months everything was a release. I threw myself into the club circuit: Dschungel, already becoming passé by then, the exploding basement techno scene around Köpenicker Straße, UFO in Schöneberg, Prater at Prenzlauer Berg over in the newly liberated East. You learned about developments through word-of-mouth: "there's a new thing in the Todesstreifen," someone would say, and if you left it till next week to investigate, it might already be over. The music was primitive and obliterative, relentlessly forward-facing, owing nothing to the past; the party didn't stop till you crawled home wrecked at dawn, and the whole thing was endlessly conducive to prevarication, so far as my writing went.

You see, I'd come to Berlin to get on with my novel, or more accurately to start it. Like every other narcissist who mistakes his self-obsession for insight, I was planning to fictionalise a failed relationship from beginning to end—my own, of course. The idea, you'll be amazed to hear, was to parallel the end of one love affair (with Theresa, my ex) with the end of another (my disillusionment with England). Thank God, it never got written. I didn't even manage chapter one: my Amstrad sat gathering dust, a box of empty floppy disks alongside it, ready to store all the prose I wasn't producing. There was only one story that came to me during my stay in Germany, and that was a true one. I'm telling it here for the first time.

A LIFETIME OF WEAK-TEA English weather does nothing to prepare you for summers in the continental interior. That August the sun shone continually; I spent long enervated days in the shade, French windows thrown wide open, drinking cold Berliner Pilsners on a little raised dais at the end of the room— a stage, I guessed, where a palm court trio would have scraped through Viennese waltzes to aid the diners' digestion. I had the computer set up on a wrought-iron garden table on the dais, but I'm not sure I even plugged it in most days.

The heat lasted all through mid-September. On the night of the 21st, or more accurately the morning of the 22nd, I came home from a hot and sweaty club with a girl named Emmi. Like a lot of the German women I was seeing around that time, she had a directness about her, an intolerance for bullshit. There couldn't be a bigger contrast with that timid British diffidence, which is so often just an inability to state your requirements. Encounters with them, I found, were transactional but honest, friction-free, with no repercussions either way. It was very different from what I'd left behind in London, where every commitment, Theresa and the rest, seemed to come at an unsustainable cost.

"Take me home, why don't you," Emmi had commanded. This had sounded like a fine idea, so I'd bundled us into a taxi and told the driver *"Am Kleinen Graupnersee"* And so to bed, etc. She must have awoken before me, because when I came to, she was standing shower-fresh and naked at one of the windows, a slender silhouette against the morning sun.

"Get the coffee on, love," I said.

"Get it yourself, James Bond" she said amiably, not moving an inch. This was a nickname that amused her no end, and I'd decided to find it charming. "I'm watching your neighbour."

"What neighbour?"

"Your neighbour on the lawn."

"I really need a coffee," I said, reaching for my Marlboros on the bedside table.

"Does she always make this exhibitionist show?"

"She who? I don't know who you mean."

She grunted in impatience, crossed the

room to the bed and grabbed my hand, her skin still wet from the shower. *"Zack zack die Bohne,"* she commanded incomprehensibly. Ignoring my protestations, she dragged me across the room to the window. *"Naturistin?"* she asked, as if I'd know. She was gesturing towards the screen of trees that lay between the villa and the lake. *"Scharfe Titten, oder?"*

"Talk English," I grunted, and looked where she was pointing. Just the impression of movement, that was all, bare skin, a figure disappearing in the shade beneath the trees. By the time I'd blinked the sleep from my eyes it was already gone in a stray twinkle of sunlight off the lake. "She didn't have any clothes on, did she?" I'd never seen any of my neighbours going undressed around the place. There was probably a *Hausregel* against it.

"You also have no clothes, 007. Me neither. Are you going to make coffee, or do we all go run around playing the naked *Fangenspiel?"*

The woman, then; the enigmatic naturelover. That was the first time I saw her, though really that distinction belonged to Emmi, who'd got a proper look before rousing me. All I could swear to seeing was a blur of limbs, the swells and incurves of a body in motion between the trunks of the trees, like Duchamp's nude descending a staircase.

The male gaze is a swamp beast straight out of prehistory. Even though an actual naked woman was draped around my neck, hair wet and smelling of shampoo, it took only that glimpse of forbidden flesh outside to set off the little limping devil. "Look at you," said Emmi in amusement, giving me a brisk and playful tweak. "Take that junk to the kitchen and make coffee, Mr. Bond. And what about some music—there isn't a stereo in this place, or what?"

So, Emmi got her coffee, and I walked her to the U-bahn shortly after. She was meeting someone to see about a flatshare (she'd been squatting a condemned property in Kreuzberg for the last five months), and that was fine by me. I liked to award myself an interval of solitude after my first time with someone new: it helped me establish the parameters of my freedom. Back at the apartment, I collected the mail, brewed some more coffee and made myself comfortable out on the patio. There was a bank statement; a circular from the British Embassy with "Reunification—What You Should Expect" stamped next to the postmark; and a violet envelope with the address written in a childish rounded hand. I left them all unopened; I already knew what would be in them.

The woods around the lake were still charged with fierce green energy, and only a few of the beeches were turning gold. It would be October before the leaves had fallen from the old oaks and full autumn came to the Grunewald. Summer seemed languorously, deliciously extended: ideal weather for naturists, I supposed, thinking of that swift evasive figure we'd seen from the window. *Freikörperkultur* was popular in Berlin—it had been practised since before the first world war, or so its evangelists insisted on telling me. There were beaches set aside for nudists on several of the lakes, but I hadn't heard of one here on the Graupnersee.

Curious, in retrospect, how that glimpse of the naked woman kept coming back to me as the day wore on. There was, I suppose, nothing else to occupy me; my time was all my own. In quick succession, two women had crossed my path, twin pieces of a puzzle that needed to be placed in the right alignment to be solved. The concept fascinated me: wasn't this the type of synchrony writers fed upon, worked up in their heads until they found the framework for a narrative? I felt this observation augured well for my artistic development. This is the life, said the voice in my head, and you're living it: you're a free man in Berlin, now run with it.

All that afternoon I turned the idea around and around in my mind. Inside the apartment the phone rang several times; I ignored it, as I generally did. By way of research I strolled down to the lake. There was no one, clothed or unclothed, in the water or at its edge. Leave it for now, I decided; it'll work itself out. I was clubbed out for the weekend and the thought of going uptown seemed all too much, so I spared myself the stink of cooking in the apartment and walked to a nearby restaurant for dinner.

It was deep blue dusk as I was returning. Instead of following the main road I'd taken the short cut through the trees at the rear of the building. As usual, I had the quiet wood-chipped path to myself: the day was slowly ceding its heat to the evening, and all around me was the dense earthy smell of the forest. As I came around the corner of the villa, past my apartment, I happened to glance through one of the unlit windows. What I saw made me pull up short.

There was a shape moving deep inside the room, a quick and stealthy flitting from darkness into darkness. My first thought was that Emmi had come back unannounced; it would have been like her, I thought, but how had she got in? I knew I'd locked the door—had I left the windows open? Surely not. What struck me later was that I'd thought it was Emmi because the fast-moving silhouette had seemed to take the shape of a naked woman.

There was a lamp burning in the portico at the villa's main entrance, and there was the soft glow of candlelight up on the second floor, where the subdued sounds of dinner party conversation drifted through the half-open windows. That was all the light I had to see by. I crouched at the windowsill for a long time, trying to catch another glimpse of the intruder, but there was nothing. Only, you know how it is: the longer I looked, the more my imagination filled the shadows with the impression of movement.

I had to know, one way or the other. Letting myself in at the communal reception, I satisfied myself that the door to my apartment was locked. Bracing myself, I turned the key, barged through the door and switched on the lights, all in a panicky rush. There was nobody in there. Slightly nervous still, I checked first the kitchenette, then the bathroom; again, nothing. All the windows were fastened shut. Clearly, I'd been imagining things. Later that evening, in bed but not yet asleep, it struck me that I hadn't looked under the bed. I tried to see it as a sign of maturity that I didn't immediately switch on the lamp and check.

When I finally got to sleep, my dreams were intense and unrestful, though their content eluded me the instant I awoke, quite early the next morning. I was scrabbling round, eyes slitted, for the cigarettes, when again I had that tingle, the sense of furtive movement just outside the limits of vision. The morning sun was streaming in through the high windows, so I could hardly make out anything in the glare—not even which side of the glass the moving shape had been.

Wide awake now, I got up and made another sweep of the apartment: all clear. Outside, then? Apparently so, for when I glanced outside someone seemed to be running beyond the borders of the lawns, a glimpse lasting less than a second, just like yesterday. Really, just the sense of motion, that skipping figure inside the treeline, vanishing in the direction of the lake. My naturist neighbour, back again. And yet; and yet.

I went to get dressed—the day was appreciably cooler than yesterday, and I could feel my flesh creeping even in the warmth of the sun. The free-standing clothes rack was far enough away from both the bed and the window for me to be absolutely sure I hadn't touched it, but the shirts and trousers on their hangers were swinging softly to and fro, for all the world as if someone had brushed against them in passing, only moments ago.

Looking back, that was the point at which things began to crystallise. Overnight, the seclusion I'd prized so highly had become compromised: just a little at first, but palpably, and, it turned out, irrevocably. The final act was still days and weeks away, but now the idea was lodged in my head, and it never let go: the creeping awareness that I was no longer the sole inhabitant of the apartment.

"So THAT'S MY GHOST," I told Emmi. "Or whatever you want to call it."

She made a grimace. "You're sure."

"I'm not sure of anything," I said defensively. "That's the point, with ghosts. So little is knowable."

We were at a pavement table outside a café on Bülowstraße, a week or so after the two of us had first watched the woman through the window. Overhead there were dark clouds threatening rain.

"It's the *Naturistin*, you think? The woman in the garden?"

"I think so."

"But she was not a ghost." Emmi seemed certain.

"She's not a naturist," I countered. "I've searched all through the grounds, each time she's appeared, and there's never anybody. Where would a naked woman be running to, after all? Where would she leave her clothes? There's nothing—the place is quiet as the grave. And she's not just on the lawn, I think she's been inside the house. Remember I told you about the clothes rack?"

I ran through all the other things I'd seen: how the wall tapestry would sometimes ripple in the absence of a draught; sudden disruptions of light, shadows that came and went in an instant. I didn't tell her how it was wrecking my peace of mind, this intrusion of something that lay below the threshold of perception, something that barely registered on the senses except in the corner of the eye and the prickling of the scalp. I didn't know what it was, and I didn't know how to confront it. I knew what it was doing to me, though, and I didn't like it.

"So a ghost?"

"I didn't say that. I honestly don't know."

"Oh, but you think so. I can tell. Me? I'm not so sure."

I stubbed out my Marlboro with undue emphasis. "It's all just playing with words. You should come back with me. You'd feel it too. Then we could have this conversation for real."

"This is how you get girls back to your place." Openly amused now. "It's a threesome, already."

Thunder, and now the storm broke, fat round drops pinging off the tin tabletop. I jostled my way inside the café together with the rest of the fleeing customers. Emmi followed at her own pace, not caring about the rain. "So what will you do? Move away? Get a new place? You can join Paula and me in the new apartment, maybe, a boy with two girls, imagine. Another threesome, *oia*, it's what you like, no?"

I decided not to rise to the bait. "I don't know. I know what I'd do if I was in England."

"You'd call a, what is it, a medium? An exorcist?" Her laughter made people glance round at us.

"No, I'd hit the libraries." When she looked quizzically at me, I amplified: "I'd find out who'd lived in the place before me."

"You're taking this seriously. This *ghost*," deepening her voice in mock horror. "Are you really serious?"

"I have to take notice of it at the very least," I said, trying to keep my voice at a natural pitch. "I'm forced to. I think it's a woman; I suspect she's connected somehow to the house. It's in the history of the place, somehow, that's the only thing I can think of."

Emmi exhaled through pursed lips. "And you would find this out how?"

"There must be records," I said vaguely. "Newspaper archives. The electoral register, whatever it's called here. I'd want to know who'd lived in the house before, whether any significant event had happened there, a death, a disappearance, some sort of tragedy."

"I thought you were rationalist," Emmi said. She seemed perplexed; justifiably, perhaps.

"This is a rational approach." Even to myself I sounded defensive. I knew it was a prevarication.

"A rational approach to a fairytale."

"Aren't you even curious? I think I'd be curious."

"I'm curious why this matters so much to you." And to that I didn't have an answer. I'd already opened myself up beyond the point of comfort—after all, I'd known Emmi for so short a time. It would have been difficult to explain to anyone. Probably not to Theresa: she would absolutely have believed me, no matter how implausible it seemed. But Theresa was past-life now, unavailable. I had to deal with it the best I could. If only my German were better; if only I knew the places I should go.

"Come back with me now," I said again. "You'd see, honestly you would."

Instantly, Emmi stood up. "*Lass' gehen*,"

she said; *let's go*. I did mention her directness, didn't I?

On the U-bahn to Krumme Lanke we
kicked the thing around some more, to little
effect. Walking along the shortcut through
the woods, I found myself hanging back as
Emmi strode ahead. It wasn't that I was
nervous—well, a little, perhaps—more that
I wanted her first impression, unmediated,
uninfluenced, of what she'd find in the villa.
When I turned the last corner of the path,
she was already peering through the French
windows into the apartment.

"Hallo? Hallo?" She turned to me. "No
answer. Your ghost doesn't like me. So
jealous, this bitch."

Patiently, I walked her round to the
door, and again stood back to let her enter
the apartment first. I watched her as she
strutted up and down the length of the
room, and bit my tongue when she said,
"And so?"

"It's not a lapdog. It doesn't come to
order."

"Boring," she said, and flopped on to the
bed. "Does she come to you in the night?"
She humped up and down suggestively, setting the mattress springs to creaking.

I was about to issue a general denial
when all of a sudden she stopped bouncing,
held the duvet to her face with both hands
and sniffed deeply. "What are you doing?" I
asked her. Ignoring me, she got up from the
bed and went pacing around the room,
sniffing all the while like a dog on a scent.
"What is it?"

"You've had a woman here."

"No," I said, which was the truth. "There
hasn't been anyone here since you spent
the night."

Suspiciously: "So what is the perfume?"

"What perfume?" I didn't know what
she meant.

"Are you so used to it that you don't
smell it?" she demanded incredulously.
"You don't smell it. But it's everywhere.
It's unreal."

She must have been right; I must have
been used to it. I've wondered since whether
Emmi might have been tapping into the
same unease that I was feeling, just picking
it up through different sensory channels.

Still, at least something out of the
ordinary had happened, something that
Emmi couldn't laugh off quite so easily. It
took a while to make her believe that I hadn't
been sleeping with someone else—I suppose
I had that coming, given my demonstrable
lack of fidelity—but even after I managed to
convince her of that much, she still wasn't
buying into the rest of it, not entirely.

She did, though, end up agreeing with
me that the history of the villa would be
something worth researching. "Even if we
find nothing," she said, "you'll feel you have
done all you can." We were sitting out on the
lawn, away from the mystery fragrance—it
was eluding me still, but Emmi said it was
giving her a headache. The rain had come
and gone, bringing out all the richness of
autumn's sad scents.

"We?"

It turned out that Emmi's new flatmate
Paula was an archivist at the Landesarchiv
on Kalckreuthstraße. This was the reposi-
tory of all the documentation held by the
state on property in Berlin; there were gaps
in the data thanks to war and the upheaval
caused by the quadripartite division of the
city, but it was still the obvious place to
begin. Emmi said she'd get Paula to look
up the ownership of the villa, while she
herself would hit the Staatsbibliothek on
Potsdamerstraße to fill in the gaps, courtesy
of their newspaper archive on microfiche.
"I have the *Studentenausweis*," she said
archly, pulling the plastic cardholder from
her back pocket and waving the accredita-
tion at me. "I can also be the spy, Mr. Bond."

I suggested to Emmi she might stay the
night, stay as long as she liked, in fact, and
at first she agreed. Later, though, as we lay
together, she pushed herself up off the bed
and said apologetically *"Liebchen*, I can't."
Normally, I'd have taken it as a personal
rejection, but not this time. There was no
need for her to explain it; the reason was
there in her face as she wiped a hand across
her nose and mouth, in her haste to throw
open the windows. I still couldn't smell
anything, and I wondered whether a ghost
could be too insubstantial to occupy all of
the senses together at one time, whether
it might struggle to manifest itself as best

it could, sometimes one way, sometimes another, never fully able to reveal itself. I phoned for a taxi to take Emmi back to Schöneberg, and stayed out smoking on the front steps for a long time before returning to my compromised bed.

EMMI GOT BACK to me a week or so later, turning up at the apartment without warning, hammering on the windows and making me jump. Something was off in her manner that afternoon, a little more brittle than usual, perhaps a little more distracted. She dodged past my attempt to embrace her, and drew me instead to the table on the dais where she laid out the fruits of her and Paula's research, a little sheaf of photocopies and handwritten notes.

"Am Kleinen Graupnersee 15-17, a mansion built in 1908 by the chairman of Kowars AG, pharmaceuticals. Plutocrat, industrialist, big shot: this is Friedrich Kowars. But what good does it do him, Mister Big Shot? In 1916 his only son is fallen on the Western Front; three years after, Friedrich is gone in the Spanish influenza, and the house is sold to the family Gebel, bankers and moneylenders. The house is hard on its masters, for in 1923 Herr Gebel is also dead, and the family is now Frau Gebel and one daughter, Nera. Less than one year later, the widow has gone to join the husband—eia!—and the daughter inherits everything, at age 21. What a house, what a history!

"She is a spinster, this Nera, and remains so all her life. Do you suppose she is lonely, James? Can you picture her sitting at a window, here where we sit in this moment, looking at the leaves as they fall from the trees?" I could, only too easily. "Or in wintertime, watching the snow fall, and out on the water she hears the sound of the Seetaucher calling, one to another?"

"Go on," I said. I didn't want to think of lonely Nera listening to the loons call across the lake on a chill grey afternoon.

"So. We go forward now to year 1934, when the property passes into the hands of Nazi bureaucrat Dr. Franz Alberding. What has happened? Where is she, das traurige Nera? In the Berliner Tageblatt, nothing. In

the national press, nothing. I have to search deep, Mr. Bond; I have to look through the newspaper archives of the Jewish collection at the Berlin Museum on Lindenstraße. Here I find this." She smoothed out a photocopy on the table. "Tragischer Unfall einer jüdischen Erbin—can you translate, please?"

"Tragic accident of a Jewish..." The last word eluded me.

"Heiress," Emmi supplied. "Tragic accident of a Jewish heiress. It tells how she was found in the lake, James: drowned in the lake, one night in the autumn of 1934."

"An accident, then," I said. I was beginning to flesh out the shadows that had been evading me up till now.

"Certainly an accident—so says the Israelitisches Familienblatt, the polite newspaper of the Jewish community. I researched this deep, James, very deep. Well, so the conventions matter, you know, to the petit-bourgeois, you must not rock the boat. There are things of which no one wants to speak. But on the death certificate, we discover something else." She waited for me to say it.

"Suicide?"

"Genau so, Mr. Bond. Congratulations." She was affecting her usual flippancy, but there was a depth of emotion that I hadn't sensed in her before. "Poor Nera, whose name means the light of the candle, did you know that? The candle in the wind, yes, as in the song?" She puffed air through her pursed lips. "Und so. Easily blown out."

Neither of us spoke for a moment. She got up from the table, crossed the room to where the tapestry hung on the wall. "Have you ever really looked at this, James? Das, das Reh, the—"

"Doe," I supplied, joining her before the tapestry.

"The doe, yes, how she is running through the trees. And here der Jäger, the hunters, see how they chase her, how they come at her, so relentless. Always towards the lake, James; always towards the lake."

I wasn't following. "Then you don't think it was suicide?"

"Ah, you see a conspiracy now? You see Dr. Alberding and his stormtroopers chasing the poor little doe Nera, all the way into the lake?" She shook her head angrily. "You think we are all Nazis still, you British. So melodramatic. So...unnecessary."

"I don't know what you mean." The sarcasm was very like Emmi, but the underlying intensity was something I couldn't read.

"I mean that sadness hunts a person down, James. I mean that sadness, I don't know, depression, whatever word you use, let's say demons, why not—" her voice was getting louder, more strident—"I mean that those demons may drive a person all the way into the lake. I mean that when it is autumn and the leaves have fallen from the trees, and hope has gone, and she has been fighting for so-o-o long, and she is tired of fighting, sometimes that person, she will walk into the water and not struggle. And they will call it suicide, or else a tragic accident."

With that it was as if she was spent. She sat down wearily on the edge of the bed, running her fingers through her hair, then all at once pulling it forward to cover her face. "I try not to feel towards people an obligation, you know," she said through the veil of her hair, "and I don't like them to depend on me. I would just as soon leave them alone as carry them on my back. But when there is a dead girl, James, then I am on her side. Always on her side."

I didn't know what to say, or if she even expected me to say anything. After a little while she pushed her hair back again and said: "Yes, sometimes even crazy selfish Emmi will take a side. How about you, Mr. Bond? Do you take a side?" And again, I didn't know how to answer that.

"Emmi, why has this..." I was struggling to find a neutral way to put it, not wanting to set her off again. "Why has this affected you so much? You've gone a hundred and eighty degrees on this."

She exhaled. "I can't say. The first time I saw her, yes, I thought it was nothing, some stupid woman, why should I care? Then I smelled her in your bed, on your skin even, and I thought something else, I don't know what I thought, that you were sleeping around, fine, whatever, you

do what you do. But the third time was different."

"What third time?"

"I was trying to find the words," she said. "It's not easy."

"So just tell me." I waited while her mouth moved and she didn't speak.

"Today," she finally got it out, "just now, when I was walking through the woods to the house. I saw her again, your woman. She was looking in, here at these windows— she was watching you. She was wet—her hair was wet, the whole body, dripping, as one who has been in the water, yes?

"James, for a long time I stayed hiding in the trees, watched her watching you, and you so unaware. And when at last she turned away she saw me, it was no use, she saw me in the blink of an eye. *We saw each other*, James: I saw on her face this expression, and then I knew for real."

There was no lightness in her voice now, no guile, not even the stridency she'd shown before. "I felt like in this moment we understood each other, you understand? Like there was between us a connection? And when I tried to speak and she started to run away—towards the trees, always towards the trees and the lake with her— it was clear to me, everything was clear. She wasn't running just from me, she was running from everything. I think for her there's nowhere else to go."

I started to speak, but she stopped me. "And before she reached the trees, James, I don't know how to explain it, she had vanished. I watched her run, and then there was nothing."

EMMI STAYED THE NIGHT, but there was no real closeness between us beyond the forced proximity of two people sharing a bed. Neither of us felt like initiating contact, and you must remember that our whole connection up till then had been grounded in physical intimacy. She slept, or didn't sleep, turned away on her side, her knees hugged up against her chest, and after a while I got up and sat chain-smoking, the armchair turned towards the uncurtained French windows.

It was October, and the nights had a chill

in them. The moon was cold and infinitely remote through the bare-bone mesh of the tree branches, their dead leaves littering the lawn beneath. Now and again, I thought something moved in the shadows. Was she hiding from me? Twice now, Emmi had got a better look at her than I ever had. I didn't understand that at the time, but looking back, I wonder if it mightn't have betrayed a certain willed insensitivity, a deficit of empathy, perhaps.

At daybreak I made coffee, and brought it to the table where Emmi's haul of evidence was still spread out. Gathering the photocopies together, I filed them away in the roll-top bureau where I didn't have to look at them. Poking out of the pigeonholes like a standing reproach was my pile of unanswered mail, built up now over months. To distract me as much as anything, I took the letters back over to the table.

I opened the bank statements, and found nothing of interest (though in retrospect I ought to have—I was bleeding cash quite unsustainably at this point). I learned what reunification might bring from the embassy flyer (more accurately, I learned that no one was quite sure what was going to happen). I glanced through a letter from Alistair, a London acquaintance, keen to tell me what fun everyone was having (now that I was on the far side of the continent, seemed to be the subtext). After the third page of who he'd seen, what he'd been doing and did I know, I was ready to put it aside. When I read "Theresa's been on the phone a lot, asking after you," I went one further and tore it in two. The three violet envelopes with the loose loopy handwriting I left unopened.

Emmi rolled over when the autumn sunlight crept up to the bed. "I don't have coffee?" she said accusingly, and I fetched her a mug from the kitchen. When I came back she was at the window, staring at the mist as it rose off the surface of the lake like the vapour from the steaming coffee mug. Normally I'd have found her nakedness provocative. In the light of current events, I noticed only the gooseflesh, the lacelike mesh of tiny bluish veins beneath the skin where the summer's tan was already fading.

"Come away from there," I told her. She retreated to the bed, wrapping the duvet around her and sipping the hot coffee. "Did you dream about her?" she wanted to know. Truthfully, I said that I hadn't. I didn't ask her whether she had. From her initial position of skepticism and mockery, Emmi seemed to have adopted my ghost, perhaps even more completely than I had myself.

"Did I say," she said out of nowhere: "did I say that where she was watching, there by the window, there was a patch of wet, a little puddle? Where the little drops of water fell from her skin?" There seemed to be nothing I could usefully say to that, so I let it lie.

Emmi had a lecture to attend that afternoon, and I joined her on the ride into the city. Over by Prenzlauer Berg they were demolishing the Wall, and I watched the cranes levering away the graffitied breezeblock sections with half an eye while my mind wandered back in time, before partition, before the war, back to a time of stridency and fear. Back to the time of Nera Gebel, alone in her house by the Graupnersee.

Emmi's research had the villa commandeered by the Occupying Powers in 1945, closed up five years after, and uninhabited thereafter till the 1980s. It seemed a long time for a lonely ghost to be haunting an empty house. Viewed in this light, it seemed reasonable to ask why she hadn't begun to appear immediately after I moved in to the apartment. I wondered whether even here, out on the lawless fringes of the spirit world, there might still be rules, weird constraints based on unknowable edicts. Perhaps the souls of the dead were fated to wait out long stretches of the year in some sort of limbo, until the anniversary of their passing came around? Maybe they waxed and waned with the moon? But all this was pointless. Where would it get me, this train of thought? Round a table with the cranks and spiritualists, singing "Cherry Ripe" at seances?

I'd never believed in ghosts, had no place for them in my ontology, but now it seemed the proposition had been forced on me. Probably, though, there were no experts, not really. Wouldn't everybody's ghost be different from every other ghost? Surely no guidebooks or rituals could be expected to address such things exhaustively. I turned my back on all the kitschy apparatus of ouija boards and mediums, and tried to concentrate on practical matters: how I felt about what was happening, and what was to be done about it.

The first of these things was difficult to pin down. What I really wanted was to scale back the whole affair, make it manageable. How different it would be if I could sublimate everything, make it grist to the mill: a hook to hang a story on, something that I could shape into art and parlay into artistic validation. That was a non-starter, though. What was happening couldn't be downplayed. You couldn't live with that nagging sensation of being watched all the time, that much I did know. It manifested as a kind of clamminess, if you can understand that; a crawling of the skin that came and went and left its mark on you. I wondered how a fish in an aquarium might feel, its whole world open to the gaze of the observer through the transparent walls of its tank.

The second point of action came with even more difficulties. Was there anything I could actually do that might influence the working-out of this phenomenon? Its effect on me seemed to be far more obvious than any effect I could possibly have on it. I was very much the passive partner in this dance; I hadn't even seen the—call it the *apparition's*—face. That privilege belonged to Emmi, which felt ironic. In the beginning, she'd been laughing at me. A couple of nights at the apartment and one bit of snooping from behind a tree had turned her from militant rationalist into true believer.

Part of me, that part which shied away from commitment, wished she'd take the whole of the obligation on full-time. She was welcome to it, so far as I was concerned. In any case, I felt she was at least a part of it now, and so I took the U-bahn to Friedrichswerder, thinking to catch her coming out of the *Hochschule*. I had something in mind for the evening.

"NOT A SEANCE?" Emmi said, as dusk began to fall over the Graupnersee.

"No, of course not," I said, rather too hastily. "Just…"

"Just hold hands around a table." Something of Emmi's trademark acerbity was coming back. "With the candlelight."

"It's not—" I tried again. "Look. Can we agree that it wants to be seen?"

"It doesn't care, maybe. Whether or not."

"Then why is it hanging around me?"

"You're so egocentric. How can you even know?"

"I can't know," I said, trying to sound reasonable. "Neither of us can. But isn't it possible that, if we give it the opportunity…?"

"Possible, yes." She still seemed dissatisfied. "You know what I would do?" she said suddenly. "If I was James Bond, 007? I would move away. I would come to stay in Schöneberg with my sexy girlfriend Emmi and her sexy flatmate Paula. I would get a new apartment, whatever. A nice room in a nice new house, too new for ghosts."

It sounded appealing, the way she put it, but what if the phenomenon wasn't focussed on a place, but on a person? How could I be sure it wouldn't follow me there? "Let's see what happens tonight."

Emmi clicked her tongue impatiently. "Leave this shitty place to the dead."

"Or whoever."

"Oh, it's death." She sounded certain. "Can't you feel that? You're so self-centred, maybe you can't. But I can."

I denied it in general terms, but Emmi wasn't having it. "Yes you are, James. Part of you thinks it makes you important, this haunting, you think it puts you at the centre of things. No wonder your girlfriend left you."

"Actually, I left her," I said quickly. She made a face. "Whatever."

We were sitting at the table by the French windows. Between us, a candle left the farthest corners of the room in shadow. In the window-glass, our reflections were balanced perfectly against the sunset, a complicated mosaic of light and dark. I remember Emmi's pale thin features in the candlelight, how the shadows made her look haunted.

"Did she miss you, your girlfriend?" she asked, and I shrugged. "Yeah, whatever. Sometimes I don't think you are very nice, Mr. Bond."

"How can I know?" I said shortly.

"You think you can know a ghost from 1934. Or why are we here?"

I got up, fetched another bottle of wine from the kitchen; we'd drained the first one in no time at all. Emmi drank half a glass off at once. "This Pouilly-Fumé, oh la la, the rich man's drink." She sipped again, slower this time. "Actually it's good."

I tried to make it into a joke. "See, I may not be nice, but you can't complain about the drinks."

She laughed perfunctorily. Finishing the glass, she poured herself a fresh one, full almost to the rim. "But I should go more slowly. I want to be full aware for when the ghost shows herself, isn't that so?"

"I don't know. Perhaps it would help if we were drunk."

"We're writing our own rules, no?" She pushed the drink away, and a splash of wine dribbled down the side of the glass. "What will you do, when you have your proof?"

"Write it down, maybe," I said, indicating the Amstrad on the floor beside us. "In one form or another. Either as a true story, or as some sort of, I don't know—some sort of a fiction."

"Will it be her story you tell, or will it be yours?" And there was so much to unpack in that simple question that I couldn't immediately come up with an answer. When the silence had stretched out into minutes, Emmi spoke again, probably to herself: "Genau so."

"Maybe," I said, after a few minutes more, "maybe there's no other way to tell it. Maybe it's my story as much as it's hers. Yours too," I added, before she accused me of solipsism once more. "We're all involved in it, I think."

"I really didn't bargain for this, you know?" she said. "When I came home with you that first night, when we fell into that bed that smells of her now. I didn't expect luggage."

"Baggage," I corrected her. She waved it away.

"Whatever. James, you can be such an asshole, you know? I didn't expect *baggage*. There. Happy?"

"What happens between people, that isn't necessarily baggage..."

"Probably we are quite alike in that," she said, heedless of my interruption. "I like the simple thing, what feels good, no hang-ups, no complications, no bullshit. You too, only with you, doesn't it go something deeper? I look inside me, it's simple, it's fine, I'm not a bad person, I think. But inside you, it's also a little cold, right at the heart. Isn't that so?"

I didn't say anything. She nodded, as if my silence was assent.

"I saw in a film once, about spies, that they must have in their lives nothing they can't walk away from, like immediately, you know?" She clicked her fingers. "No *baggage*, no obligations. What do you say to that, Mr. Bond?"

And again I had no answer for her, even though the truth of the matter was staring us both in the face. When I'd met her, I thought we'd both bought into the same deal. If she turned out to be struggling with it in her way, then so was I in mine.

"Do you think Nera was like us?" Emmi was staring into the darkness outside. "Do you think she also had this fear of *baggage*? Or was she a romantic? Would she have given anything to share in the life of another? Isn't that much more likely, really? I ask myself this many times, James, in these last few days. It fascinates me, and I am afraid of it a little, of the answer, what it might be."

She tossed back some more of the wine, wiped her mouth with the back of her hand. "When I saw her, I felt... she runs towards the drowning only because she has nothing else to run to, you know? She would *like* to have that thing in her life—she wants it more than anything, I feel this somehow— but at the end there is only the lake. Everything else has turned away from her. Turned its back."

"She was lonely, yes, probably," I said. "Her circumstances, the times, the whole situation."

"And what it is, she didn't have the headset," Emmi said. "To deal with it, you need the headset, and she didn't have that. I feel her life as one big longing, you know? A minus, an empty space, a...a need that cannot be met."

I remembered something I'd read. "What is a ghost?" I quoted. "One who has faded into impalpability through death, through absence, through change of manners."

"Manners!" Emmi snorted. And under her breath: "*Gott schütze mich vor den Engländern und ihren beschissenen Manieren!*" When she wouldn't speak English, that was always a bad sign.

"Joyce was actually Irish," I said, wanting to score a point of my own.

She let out all the breath in her lungs in one giant sigh of exasperation, let her head fall to the wrought-iron tabletop like someone bludgeoned into submission. "Sorry," I said insincerely, then when she didn't immediately lift her head, "sorry" again. Through the opaque screen of her hair there came no answer.

She still wasn't moving. I was about to ask her what was wrong when she raised her head slowly, partway off the table. Now I could see where it had been resting: on the little pile of mail I'd left there that morning.

"What is this?" she said, picking up one of the letters—one of the unopened violet envelopes. Suddenly she held it to her nose, sniffed at it.

"Nothing," I said.

"No, it's something." She was glaring at me. "Smell it!"

I ignored her, twisted away when she thrust the envelope towards my face. But she wasn't having it. "Smell it now!"

To avoid an argument as much as anything, I sniffed the textured envelope. And it was like Proust's madeleine: that instant, comprehensive flash of memory that the olfactory sense is so good at unlocking. Beyond that recognition lay a train of thought I didn't want to follow.

"You get it?" she wanted to know. "Yes, you get it. So why didn't you tell me before?"

"I hadn't realised…" I began. But wasn't that bullshit, really? How could I not have known? How, when I'd woken up to the same scent for the best part of three years, on and off? How, when it was the last thing I smelled before I went to sleep?

"Who is this?" She'd sorted the three violet envelopes from the pile, was squinting in the candlelight at the return address.

"Theresa. Who is Theresa?"

"Give me those," I said, but I knew she knew. "It's none of your business."

"Oh, is that why I'm here? Because it's not my business? That's such bullshit, you know? You made it my business, James, when you took me to your bed and made me feel sorry for you. Now smell the damn things!" She made to open one of the envelopes, changed her mind and tossed them at me instead. "Why don't you open them?"

"I don't have to."

"It's your old girlfriend, yes? In London?"

I nodded. "I don't need to open them. I know what's in them." Which turned out to be correct only up to a point.

"I think it's because you're a liiiittle bit a bastard." Drawing the word out. "I think it's the easiest thing for you to just throw the people away if you have no more use for them."

"Fine!" I tore one of the envelopes open. "Let's see. Let's see what terrible sins I've committed." I could feel the evening, the whole future of our relationship, such as it was, coming apart, and in that moment all I wanted was for everything to be settled, one way or another. Over and done. A simple decisive action, an end to politeness and conventions. Picking a paragraph at random, I began to read aloud.

"I'm at the end of my tether, James. You won't answer my letters, you won't even answer the phone—I feel so alone, like the last four years were just a waste of time. Did I ever mean anything to you? I don't know what you want, I don't know where I stand—I don't know how much longer I can go on like this…"

I trailed off. It felt distasteful to be using Theresa's unhappiness as a stick to beat Emmi with. I kept on reading to myself, and left Emmi to simmer in silence.

Here were all the things we'd replayed night after night in those last weeks and months before my move to Berlin. How I'd betrayed her, how I wouldn't tell the truth, how I'd broken her heart, but still she'd take me back if only I'd love her the way she loved me… all the old accusations, the same capitulations, desperate concessions and frantic bargaining.

She didn't know what she was going to do, she really needed to hear from me. Why didn't I answer her? Well, we both knew why that was. I read on, and every sentence dragged me back to a past life I'd come hundreds of miles to escape. And she'd followed me after all. All that weight of responsibility was back; I'd only dodged it for a season.

Nauseous, I let the pages fall to the table. Immediately Emmi tossed another of the letters at me—the last of the three, as I saw from the postmark on the envelope.

More of the same, it seemed. First the condemnations, then the self-flagellation and protestations of forgiveness, ending as always with wretched, undignified pleading. But as page followed page, it began to run deeper. "You don't think I'll do it," I read; "you never thought I'd have the nerve. Well, maybe this time I will. I nearly did, that first time you said you were leaving, remember?" I remembered it only too well—the broken glass, the ambulance, the blood soaked deep into the mattress when I returned from the hospital. Her blood, and the smell of her perfume.

My face must have given me away, because Emmi was asking "What? What is it?" I didn't answer at first, and she made to grab the pages from my hand. Holding them out of her reach, I continued to read. "I shan't cut myself again. The blood frightened me that last time, and I don't want to spend my last moments being frightened, James, my soul's too much in pieces already. Just diving into nothing, that's what I want. Nothing, forever. I'm like you now, there's no heart left in me, it's broken. I just need it to be easy and quick I need it to be over, that's all. That's what you said to me, remember? For you it only ever meant a change of scenery, but for me—there's no use, you wouldn't understand. I want everything to be really, truly over. Draw a line under everything. Not cutting, but I'll find some other way—pills maybe, I've got enough pills, or I always felt at home in the water—" There was another page, but I couldn't stomach it.

"What does she say?" Emmi gave me hardly any time to answer, slammed her fist down on the metal table. Her wine glass fell to the floor, and the sound of broken glass reminded me unbearably of that night in Highgate, Theresa's half-hearted suicide attempt.

I was still weighing how to respond when Emmi snatched another of the envelopes from the table and ripped it open. "So I will see for myself," she was saying, voice slurring from the wine.

"Put that down," I told her, sounding ridiculously ineffectual even to myself, "that's not even from Theresa, that's from my mate Alistair, it's none of your business—"

Something fell from the opened envelope; a clipping from a newspaper. It descended in a drifting, sideways trajectory towards the mess of broken glass and spilled wine, and I grabbed it just as it began to settle in the puddle at my feet.

"*Body Found In Waltham Forest Reservoir*" was the headline.

Emmi dropped to her knees alongside me, tried to pull the clipping towards herself. I slapped her hand away; viciously, she slapped me back, but she made no more attempts to snatch the dampened, softened piece of newsprint. I laid it on the tabletop, tried to smooth it out without tearing it.

"Emergency services recovered the body of a woman, as yet unidentified, from Walthamstow's High Maynard Reservoir yesterday, Sunday 23 September. The body is thought to have been in the water for no longer than 48 hours, and police are investigating sightings of a woman behaving in an erratic manner on the footpath alongside the reservoir. Anyone in the vicinity of High Maynard on the night of Friday the 21st..."

I knew exactly where that reservoir was; I knew that footpath. Theresa and I had walked there so often in the cold clear spring of 1986, when we'd just started seeing each other. She'd talked about it many a time, called it one of her happy places, like Highgate ponds or the bend of the Thames beneath Richmond Hill.

Still on her haunches, Emmi had come around behind me and was reading over my shoulder. "It's her," she said. Since I was still fixated on the newspaper article, I had no way of knowing whether the blankness of her voice was mirrored in the expression on her face.

"It doesn't say," I said, and for answer she slapped down the letter that had accompanied the clipping. It was in Alistair's handwriting, and the first sentence read: "James, mate, I'm so very sorry."

"There were cormorants by the reservoir," I said, after what seemed like a long time. "They're quite ugly birds, I think, quite unkempt looking? They have a scolding sort of call..." I trailed off again. "They're not like the loons here. The sound they made always used to amuse her."

Ignoring me, Emmi was reading aloud from the clipping. "'The body is thought to have been in the water for no longer than 48 hours... sightings of a woman on a footpath on the night of Friday the 21st...' James, you don't *see* it?"

"See what?" All I could see was the reservoir, spring flowers along the banks, the two of us walking hand in hand, like people in love.

Her finger was jabbing at the words. "The night of Friday 21st! Can you really not see it?" Now I did. It was like a punch to the gut. Emmi pulled me round to face her.

"Friday, the night I come back here with you. That same night, Theresa is gone in the lake. And on Saturday morning for the first time we see the woman. Before, nothing. Afterwards, all the time. This woman, naked, wet, she leaves behind her a trail of water. And her perfume, we smell the perfume—god, James, how could you not have realised? How don't you *recognise* her?"

Because I hadn't been looking, I thought. Because I'd turned away on purpose, because it didn't suit me to face the truth. Because I'd willed it to be something else. Let it not be Theresa, let it be Nera. Let it be the past of this sad old house, and not mine. All lies, though, all deceptions. Smoke and mirrors.

I could hardly bear to look Emmi in the eyes. But she was looking away from me, staring wide-eyed at a place just over my shoulder. I twisted round to see what had caught her attention, and I wish I hadn't, now. Too late, too late.

For the first time, and as it turned out for the last time, I got to see her face. Distorted ever so slightly in the old dark panes of the French window, barely visible through the candlelight reflections in the glass, but of course I recognised her. How could I not? At first, I thought she was crying, but I think now it may have been the lake-water that ran out of her wet dark hair, ran in streams down her pale face, paler now than it had ever been in life. She was crouched low, squatting at the same level as Emmi on my side of the glass. They might have been reflections of each other, sisters from different fathers, one living, one dead.

I could feel Emmi clutching at me, hear her breathing at my ear, gasping something that I couldn't catch, but I had no time for her. All my attention was on the figure outside as she slowly moved back from the window, the pallor of her naked skin fading into shadow, all swallowed up in the autumn dusk. Her eyes seemed to disappear last of all, and their gaze, a reproach or an accusation, maybe nothing more or less than a testament, stayed fixed on me till the last. It's never really gone away.

Then Emmi was pushing past me, scrabbling at the latch of the French windows, throwing them wide open. She made to step outside, glanced down where she was about to set foot, pulled back. Staining the plain grey concrete a darker shade, a shallow puddle of water had collected. On the night air there was a stagnant smell, the faintest breath of scum and slime and a slow sucking bed of mud and weeds.

It took both of us to get past the threshold in the end. Holding hands for courage, we stepped around the puddle and followed her scent in the direction of the trees, where she'd always retreated. There seemed no need to run; it was clear where she'd be heading. We tracked that will o' the wisp as far as the shore of the lake.

It was very quiet. Even the constant grind of city traffic seemed muffled in the clustered woods. Overhead, the light pollution blocked out all but the brightest stars, just a handful of puckers in the spoiled, corroded glow of midnight. Out on the water, the nightbirds held their breath as a slow spreading ripple moved away from the shore, out towards the centre of the lake. So slight we might have imagined it, vanishing even as we watched, a perturbation of the moonlight leaving the depths beneath untouched, as soft and as silent as the belly of the night. Gone all too soon; gone for good, never to return except as memories and condemnations, each time autumn comes around.

Steve Duffy lives and works in North Wales. His most recent collection of weird stories, These And Other Mysteries, *was published by Sarob Press in 2024; he's currently in the process of putting together his next. Steve was the winner of the International Horror Guild's award for Best Short Story 2000, and in 2015 he received the Shirley Jackson Award for Best Novelette.*

Duffy writes that the house depicted in his story "is based on his memory of the house at Am Großen Wannsee 56-58, 14109 Berlin, [as shown below], which became infamous as the location of the Wannsee Conference in January 1942. The photo of the conference room gives the reader some idea of James's room."

GABRIEL'S HORN

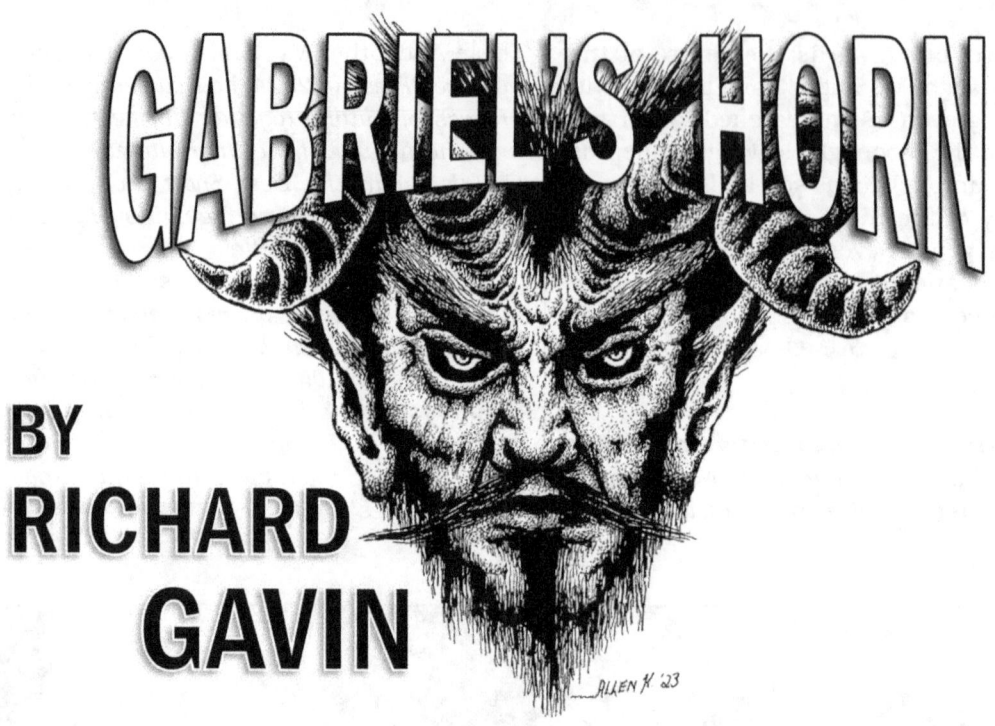

ALLEN K '23

BY RICHARD GAVIN

EVERYTHING ABOUT THE CEMETERY WAS IMPROPER, FROM THE CALLOUS WAY THE GRAVES HAD BEEN HEAPED AT THE BOTTOM OF THE GULLEY, to the brackish water that had been permitted to pool around the plots, to the felled trees that had smashed some of the markers to rubble.

Heloise inadvertently spotted the ugly place while cycling along one of the ravine's overhead trails. An overwhelming sense of indignity overcame her once she spied the anonymous headstones all facing different directions, and the plots that had no respectful space between them. She imagined the coffins piled messily upon one another beneath the soil, like logs in a firepit, and the thought saddened and sickened her.

No fencing distinguished the dead from the wilderness surrounding them. Many trees had cast their gnarly roots deep into the grave dirt, like wooden serpents boring to possess the old bones. The spurning of old graves was, Heloise knew, commonplace, perhaps even inevitable, for after all, given enough time, every bloodline must end. We all become faded strangers to this world, forgotten and forsaken.

And yet, the atmosphere of this place was one not so much of neglect as of disdain. It was this air of loathing that Heloise found frightening and compelling in equal measure. The fear percolated inside her as delicious titillation. Indeed, the allure of the secret charnel ground was magnetic.

Leaning her mountain bike against a walnut tree, she began a careful plunge down the earthen wall of the ravine to better explore her find. Her soles cut through years' worth of foliage, which covered the ground like dingy carpeting. The soil beneath it was wet and cold.

She hadn't yet reached the floor of the pit when the septic stench crowded her nostrils, nearly causing her to choke. She assumed the scent might be rising from the newly disturbed earth in her tracks, but the lower she went, the more cloying it became. Clearly, it radiated from the burial ground itself. Heloise shielded her nose with the neck of her sweater and pressed on.

When her soles touched the sludgy rim of the graveyard, she realized that no birds were anywhere in sight. She struggled to recall the last ones she had seen winging through the forest but could not. The tree limbs here were barren of all life.

The foul water seeped through her running shoes almost instantly. Reasoning that she could not get any more uncomfortable than she was now, she decided to explore the graves as thoroughly as she could. Many were submerged in the marsh, others had long ago lost their markers. Heloise hopped from semi-dry mounds to dryish rocks and finally onto one of the fallen logs. This last vantage allowed her to absorb the full scope of the graveyard's aberrations.

The symbolic grammar of the markers was unrecognizable. Absent were the customary crosses, Magen David, myrtle leaves. In their stead, crude scratches had been gouged on the shapeless lumps of yellowish stone. One of the markers had a partial animal skeleton bound to it. Heloise's best guess was that it was a bat, though the pin-like bones of only one of its wings remained intact. Above the area where the poor creature had been tied, a simple "X" had been savagely engraved.

Just beyond this grisly sight, a fluted shaft of dark, marbled material jutted from the highest mound in the graveyard. It seemed to command her to look. At first, she thought this object had been forged in the image of a torch, but once she had skulked near enough to touch it (though touch it she did not) she realized the object was a herald trumpet, the kind one sees in royal coronations. It appeared to have been forged from horn.

Her eyes followed the tapering pipe of the sculpture down to the mound of foliage around its base. A lone yellow eye glared up at her from the littered earth. Heloise flinched, recoiled, and nearly fell from the log in the process. The eye studied her unblinkingly.

Using the toe of her dripping runner, she gently kicked away the leaves and debris to uncover more of the face. The more she revealed, the faster her curiosity became obsession. She was soon down on all fours in the mud, clawing the entire tomb-like statue clean. The stench here was so intense it made her dizzy. Still, she persevered, compelled by some manic power of devotion.

When the spell finally passed, her hands were cold and raw and gloved in earth, and her skin and clothes were soaked with perspiration. But the task was accomplished. The funerary statue had been freed from its nest.

The monument was easily five times the size of the others in the burial ground, and far more ornate. The herald trumpet was but one detail of a sprawling tomb, wrought primarily from the same yellow stained stone as the rest of the markers. The base of the tomb was an angular slab upon which reposed a giant. Its face was a mask of negativity. Rage, terror, and madness were all conveyed in equal measure by the sculptor. This face was framed by a flowing mane and a long, unkempt beard. Upon the furrowed brow, a large pair of animal horns had been set. Their coiling shape led Heloise to conclude that they were ram's horns. Their rich colouring was like that of the trumpet. They too were likely forged from real horn.

Great but battered wings enveloped the torso like a ragged shroud, though these carven wings resembled snakeskin and not feathers. This serpentine aspect was also conveyed by the creature's phallus, which stretched out from a thicket of pubic hair and curved its way along the stomach with pornographic clarity. The image, despite being nothing more than a lump of shaped stone, made Heloise's blood rush to warm her face and her cleft at once.

The effigy's arms were bound taut to either side of the body by a long cord of thorns, akin to barbed wire, that was wound in a sadistic mummification. Teardrop shapes seeped from the countless wounds in bas relief, but because they were carved in the same whitish-yellow stone, they resembled leprous pustules more than droplets of blood.

Heloise squinted at the messy seam where the newly cleaned seraph sank into the soil. There, all around the heavy base, she could just make out the impression of hands, hundreds of them, each one frozen in a particular gesture. This fringe of appendages ran the circumference of the grave. A few of the hands clung to the thorny cords, but whether they were dragging the horrid angel to the depths or pulling him above-ground, Heloise could not tell.

Most of the gesturing hands seemed, to her educated eye, to be running in a kind of sequence, as if they were signing. But even with her lifelong working knowledge of various signing systems, only one was even vaguely like a word she knew, that of an open hand leaning toward what may have been a head. She had always known this sign for "listen."

Something deep inside her soul, some aspect of herself that seemed to have grown furious with frustration, decided to run with this thin lead, to interpret it as instruction. Unconcerned with whatever the result might be, Heloise rose to her feet, and she strained to listen. But the world could not reach her in that way. It remained enveloped in the same woolly insulation of silence that it had been since her birth. But somehow, here, today, this verity devastated her.

Dropping back down into the mud, her frame hitched with anguished sobs. Heloise did not truly know whether she was experiencing frustration or self-pity or rage. But no matter the precise nature of the feelings, they were deep and true, and they commanded expression.

She wept for a long time yet felt no true relief. Her truest sense was one of betrayal. Whatever power had called her to this ugly garden had deceived her. She rose and mentally prepared herself for the long climb back.

But before she started up the ravine, the power of the place once more pulled at her. This time it was more focused, clearer in its wordless instruction.

Heloise looked to the long heralding horn, at its funnel-like mouth. She went to it. With care, she climbed onto the bound giant, balancing herself by resting a hand on its phallus, the other on its taut throat. She leaned in, placed her head against the open bell, and she listened.

And for the first time in her twenty-two years on Earth, Heloise heard.

The horn affected her in ways far more potent and varied than it would have impacted a hearing person. The sound translated into visions of cascading fire, into horripilation of her flesh, into a smoky honey on her tongue. Though her body remained prostrate upon the statue on the slab, her spirit was swept elsewhere, to realms beyond her ken, and thus they would become secrets for her to guard within the chambers of her heart.

Heloise remained in this flung state for a very long time. She did not realize how many worldly hours had passed until she felt her body shivering and peered up to see the stars dazzling between the boughs.

The sound of the trumpet still vibrated through her, though she did not realize how badly the experience had depleted her until she began the arduous climb back to her mountain bike. The cabin was easily a mile from the ravine; a thought that almost caused Heloise to weep, for she scarcely had the strength to pedal.

Her mountain bike no longer had a working light, which made negotiating the trails as frightening as it was exhausting. She almost wished she had never come out here today. Almost. The gift of celestial sound was too radiant and precious, worth any suffering, any price.

By the time she reached Widget Road, whose ancient pavement had assumed the colouring of cheap unburnished tin in the moonlight, Heloise could no longer ride. She walked alongside her bike, leaning on it with such dependence that more than once she fell and sent its carbon fibre frame smashing against her own. She was no longer sure this was the right direction.

Inching her way along the Widget's shoulder of gravel and weeds, Heloise discerned a wisp of light crawling toward her in the distance. It grew brighter and more defined, bifurcating into a pair of headlights that held her in their glare.

The vehicle crept nearer and nearer, seeming to speed up once its driver spotted her. Cold panic shot through Heloise as she suddenly became aware of the easy prey she had become on this all-but-abandoned country road, weak and lonely in the dead of night.

The truck came to an abrupt stop,

and a shadowy figure hopped from the cab. Not until he stepped into the high beams did Heloise recognize Julius. He asked her where the hell she had been. Heloise began to cry...though she did not know whether it was from relief, fatigue, or a profound disappointment that her old life had intruded upon her current state and was threatening to pull her back, like the hands 'round the base of the giant's grave.

Julius knelt beside her, his face a mask of horror and concern. He signed to ask if she was hurt and she returned a simple no. He gently escorted her to the passenger door of the truck and belted her in before retrieving her mountain bike and laying it in the cargo bed.

The drive back to the cabin seemed protracted, despite the speed at which Julius drove. He rolled down the windows as far as they would go, transforming the cab into a wind tunnel. When Heloise tried to close the passenger window, he asked her not too, telling her that she reeked of sulphur. Heloise glanced down at her palms, still stained with the whitish-yellow dust of the gravestones.

Once inside the cabin, he draped an afghan around her shoulders and pulled the lasagna from the oven. Now several hours old, it was all but inedible. He made Heloise some tea, and after a few moments had passed, Julius could no longer contain his emotions, which were a stew of anger, fear, and relief. He signed with ferocity, his hands slapping together on certain words. He detailed how he'd spent hours walking trails, driving up and down the winding back-country roads, all the while dreading that one of the many worst-case scenarios running through his mind would soon become his new reality.

She circled one hand before her chest several times to tell Julius how sorry she was, then announced that she was going to bed. He did not join her for two more hours. Heloise knew this because she had neither the ability nor the desire to sleep. She merely played possum for Julius until she finally saw his chest rising and falling in the darkened room.

She slipped out of the bed, the bedroom, the cabin. She stood shivering on the covered porch, looking for the moon but not seeing it. Tonight's sky, ordinarily dazzling due to the area's lack of light pollution, was hazy and dull.

She had stepped into the night because, to her utter dismay, Heloise had found that her memory of today was already beginning to dissolve. What had only a few hours earlier been a tapestry of rich memory, intricate and vivid and seemingly eternal, had begun to unravel. Its threads of many colours were now being tugged by unseen forces, ones clearly determined to take this gift away from her.

Simply remembering what the giant's grave looked like was becoming a chore. She stretched her imagination to conjure his grim and graven face. Had the statue been cast in the image of one of the fallen angels of Biblical lore, she wondered? Having been raised in a house where science and skepticism were prized over scripture, Heloise had only a shallow pool of mythical knowledge from which to draw, but she was quite sure that the archangel Gabriel had been the one whose trumpet announced...what? The second coming? The end times?

Perhaps Biblical context was far less important than her personal encounter. Heloise closed her eyes and thrilled to the visions that filled the dark cavern of her mind. Shimmering light cascaded within the great dark cave inside her skull. Heloise could feel herself beginning to shake with delighted laughter and soon tears forged from being witness to something overwhelmingly beautiful began to drip from her chin. Such were the images that her soul had given her in place of sound. She was seeing the archangel's music. This was his gift to her.

Her legs then began to carry her off the cabin grounds and toward the woods. Heloise had no intention of walking, but allowed the journey, nonetheless. Her few brief pangs of confusion and uncertainty were quickly eased once she opened her eyes and discovered that the coruscating blaze that had fired her imagination had migrated to the tangible world around her.

• • •

THE FIRST THOUGHT to cross Julius's mind

upon waking was that Heloise must have forgotten to open the flue after starting the morning fire in the hearth, but he found only old ashes in the fireplace and no one else inside the cabin.

Flashes of Heloise's protracted journey angered him, and he flung open the cabin in the hope of finding her somewhere on the grounds. His eyes immediately began to sting from the hazy air. The thick fireplace smell was markedly stronger out here, far more so than it had been inside the cabin. Julius's heart sank at the implications of these elements.

Then he saw the sky's infernal colouring over the distant woods. Frantically, he raced to and fro, moving to the road, then back. He ran around the cabin and into the trees behind it. He tried in vain to discover tracks in the mud. Heloise was nowhere to be found. Julius feared the worst.

He hastily packed a knapsack with water, power bars, a flashlight. He had no idea how long or far he would have to hike to find her. Her mountain bike was still lying in the back of the pickup. She could not have gotten far on foot, or so he prayed.

Smoke billowed up from somewhere in the ravines, churning from the treetops, many of which had become towering torches. Visibility was atrocious. Not even the truck's high beams were able to slice through the dense haze. The poor air seeped in through the vents, and soon Julius was hacking. He caught a glimpse of his eyes in the rear-view mirror. They were bloodshot and teary. Why of all days had Heloise chosen today for another reckless exploration, he wondered? The gravity of the situation was becoming terribly apparent.

The hairpin turn at the end of Widget Road was one Julius always approached with over-caution, but today's toxic conspiracy of the forest fire and his fear blinded him to it. The truck went into the ditch at a bad angle. The axle snapped and Julius took a bad bump against the steering wheel.

IT MUST HAVE BEEN midday, he assumed, when the motorcade began to creep past him. Giddy from his concussion, Julius waved at the vehicles. A few moments later, emergency crew members were pulling him from the cab.

A police officer bridged their communication gap by scribbling a note for Julius, explaining that the area was being evacuated due to the wildfire. Julius tried to write Heloise's name, to urge the emergency crew to finish the search he had barely begun, but a terrible wooziness made the task all but impossible. Julius was piled into an ambulance while the rest of the villagers made their way to a nearby school that was serving as the evacuation centre.

THE FLEET OF FIREFIGHTERS managed to get the blaze under control in two days. Six days later it was out. The Bureau of Land Management acted quickly in the hope of getting residents back into their homes and to normal as swiftly as possible.

Investigators offered their best estimate based on burn patterns that the wildfire had started in a patch of lowland, though its actual cause remained undetermined.

Not long after the crisis had passed, stories from three of the Bureau members began to be shared around tavern tables or in the marriage bed. It was a tale of things inexplicable, and thus, things secret.

When the ravine that was to become central to the investigation was first passed through by the agents, one party of three had discovered a most remarkable formation. There, among the blackened trees and the smoking ground, was what looked to be a statue forged from ash. It was the image of two figures, one towering and inhuman looking, the other a nude female form. The woman was pressed against the winged beast, who appeared to be lifting them from the earth. A great trumpet was pressed to his mouth. One of the agents swore they saw a gap of empty space between the statue's feet and the ground. They appeared to float between the trees in a frozen instant, before a breeze pressed through the valley, crumbling them to a shapeless mass within the ruined forest.

Richard Gavin writes Gothic fiction and non-fiction that explores the bond between fear and the numinous. His stories have been

collected in six volumes, appeared in many annual "Best of" anthologies, and been translated into ten languages. His books of esotericism have been published by distinguished houses such as Theion Publishing and Three Hands Press. Richard resides in Ontario, Canada.

THE OTHER SHORE

BY KELLY WHITE

THE CHANGE IN THE AIR CAME SOON AFTER THEY LEFT THE MOTORWAY, THE UNDULATING ROAR OF PASSING CARS GIVING WAY TO THE SIBILANCE OF WINDING HEDGEROWS. The spring light glinted in the spaces between budding branches and fields unfolded on either side of them: swathes of pale-yellow stalks warming in the sun. The sound of the road rushed in through the open window and Fiona imagined she could smell salt on the breeze, even though they were still miles from the coast. Ahead of them, the horizon was a crisp line, the sea a hidden seam pressed against a clear sky.

She sensed a change in Sarah too, who sat forward in her booster seat, peering out of the window with all the curiosity of her four and a half years, as they meandered past charming redbrick cottages and old English pubs; watching as villages became hamlets, with only narrow lanes and unbroken countryside between them.

As Fiona turned the car onto a final steep hillside, the road dusty and crumbling at the edges, she glanced again at her daughter in the rearview mirror. Sarah's grip on her comfort blanket had finally loosened and it lay in her lap, almost forgotten. Fiona smiled to herself and realised the knot in her chest had eased too, just a little.

They reached the brow of the hill, and the sea was below them; an expanse of brilliant blue waves shimmering like the mirage of a heat haze. Fiona heard Sarah gasp.

The entrance to the park was marked by a wooden billboard. Its weathered image of a lighthouse against blue sky and golden sands was instantly nostalgic, even as Fiona noticed the slightly mismatched shades of its repainted lettering, the lower edge of the sign split and coming apart. Fiona couldn't help wondering about the state of their caravan, but quickly pushed the thought away. Summer holidays with her parents, in places as picturesque and uncomplicated as this, had given her some of her most cherished memories. This was the first time Sarah had been to the seaside and Fiona was desperate to give her daughter some happy memories of her own. She took a deep breath. Now that they were here, away from everything, she was sure Sarah would have fun. They both would.

Fiona pulled up in front of the modest

reception building and turned in her seat. "What do you think, sweetheart? Do you want to come with me to collect the key?"

Sarah hesitated, wringing her comfort blanket through her hands and tilting her head as she considered what to do. There was a distant look in her eyes that made Fiona want to scoop her up and hold her close. Then, with exaggerated care, Sarah placed the blanket on the seat beside her and reached for the belt buckle.

A MAN WITH A KIND, wrinkled face stood hurriedly as they walked in, leaning over the counter to shake Fiona's hand in both of his. He introduced himself as the owner.

"Phillip Jones. Welcome, welcome." He paused, waiting for her to speak.

"Fiona Clarke." She glanced down at Sarah, instinctively checking her daughter was still close. "We have a booking."

"Clarke. Yes, of course." Phillip nodded, casting about for something beneath the papers on his desk. "Here we are." He held the diary aloft, as if surprised to find it there. Leaning forward, he peered over the counter at Sarah. His broad smile faltered, a flicker of emotion passing over his face before the warmth returned.

"Is this your first time at the seaside, young miss?" His wiry eyebrows wiggled as he spoke.

Sarah retreated behind Fiona, hiding her face behind her long hair.

"She's just shy, aren't you, Sarah?"

Phillip chuckled, "Not to worry." He flicked through the diary and found their details, tapped at the card reader that sat on the countertop, then turned it towards Fiona.

She tried not to look too closely at the screen as she paid the remaining balance for their weekend break. The machine whirred, spewing receipt paper as Phillip turned with a flourish, waggling one finger in the air.

"Won't be a moment." He disappeared into a dim back office and started to hum, as if reassuring her he was still there, just out of sight.

Fiona glanced around the room. Early afternoon sun shone through windows on either side of them, dust motes trailing through the air, clinging to almost every surface. Three chairs stood against one wall, their bright blue seat fabric bleached by years in the ebb and flow of sunlight. Fiona wondered how long it had been since anyone sat there.

The counter was bare, except for a bell and the card reader, but the desk behind it was a confusion of papers; opened brown envelopes, their contents crammed back inside, old newspapers folded at the puzzle pages, and scrawled notes on torn out pages, crossed through until pen buckled paper.

A photo of a young girl was taped carefully to one raised edge of the desk. She was a few years older than Sarah, but the shape of her face, and her eyes, were uncannily similar. The girl's hair fell in unruly blonde waves; the reverse of Sarah's, which was dark and naturally straight. Was this who the owner had seen when he caught sight of Sarah? A daughter, or granddaughter, maybe? The girl stood awkwardly in front of a caravan, smiling for the camera. There was something odd about the image, but before Fiona could place it, she felt a pull on her t-shirt as Sarah twisted the fabric around her hand. She turned towards her daughter, who gazed up at her inquisitively, and gently pulled her close.

"Here we go." Phillip emerged from the office doorway, brandishing the key to their caravan. He handed it to Fiona and from somewhere amongst the papers on the desk he pulled a printed map of the park. He spun it around on the countertop and pointed to a caravan icon on the edge of the page. "Number thirty-five, right next to the beach."

Fiona smiled down at Sarah. "Did you hear that, sweetheart? We'll be right by the sea." Sarah's eyes grew wide before they disappeared behind her hair again.

Phillip produced a biro and circled their caravan on the map, then traced a road with the nib. "Just follow this down through the park. They're all numbered. Anything you need, I'm here until six, and this," he paused to cross out a landline number at the foot of the map and replace it with a mobile number, "is for out of hours emergencies."

He lifted the map and leaned over the counter. Giving Fiona a conspiratorial wink, he held the map out to Sarah. "Do you think you could look after this for your Mummy, young miss?"

Fiona was surprised when Sarah let go of her t-shirt and tentatively reached out to take it.

PEBBLED SAND ROSE in an embankment behind their caravan, the tall scrub grass at its peak rippling like curtains in the breeze. Sarah, excited now, pulled Fiona along by the hand towards the thunderous swell of the waves, only letting go to scrabble impatiently upwards. At the top she stopped short, her small body a silhouette against the sky. Fiona reached her as another wave thrashed against the beach, ribbons of foam stretching across the sand. She rested a hand on Sarah's shoulder, a familiar flutter of worry passing through her. The water was closer than Fiona had expected, the beach narrower, their caravan less than a stone's throw away. Sarah reached up and squeezed her mother's hand, interrupting her thoughts. The wind picked up, whipping their hair across their faces, and Sarah turned to Fiona, her eyes full of wonder.

"How far does it go, Mummy?" She asked.

Fiona knelt beside her. "Hmmm. I suppose it goes all around the world." She stretched out her arms, watching Sarah's eyes widen, then swept her up. "Like an enormous hug."

The embankment gave way steeply towards the beach, and they edged their way down towards the bulwarks of great black rocks which lay below them. To the north, the remains of wrecked sea defences stuck out of the sand at odd angles, as useful as scarecrows against the relentless tide. To the south, the distant tower of a lighthouse, bright white and crimson in the sunlight.

They ran towards the sea, Fiona pulling off her trainers and socks as she went, pausing only to help Sarah do the same. When the water hit her feet, she gasped at the cold. Sarah hesitated, retreating as the seawater rushed towards her, then chased it back out. As the next wave approached, Sarah held her nerve. She squealed with the cold, shocked but smiling. Fiona tensed as the wave hit her bare skin and laughed. The sting had already gone. If only life were that simple. She stretched her toes in the shifting wet sand, and watched as Sarah, emboldened now, ran at the next wave just as it hit the beach.

FIONA HELD OUT the shell in the palm of her hand. She hadn't realised they grew this large. It was flawless, with spiral striations and delicate pink markings.

"Go on," she said. Sarah carefully lifted the shell from her mother's palm. "Hold it up to your ear and listen. What do you hear?"

Sarah's face twisted in concentration, replaced a few seconds later with surprise. She pointed towards the waves. "I can hear the sea," her voice an exaggerated whisper.

Fiona couldn't help but smile. "Now you can always take the waves with you."

Sarah's tiny trouser pockets were already bursting with assorted shells and brightly coloured pebbles, so Fiona demonstrated how to hold up the edge of her t-shirt to carry things in it.

"Just remember to watch where you're going." She kissed the top of Sarah's head before her daughter could rush off in search of more seaside treasure.

Fiona watched Sarah move methodically along the beach, tiptoeing around clusters of pebbles on bare, sandy feet. She closed her eyes, took a deep breath, and reminded herself that her daughter was safe.

They were at the top of the beach now, out of reach of the waves, and black rocks loomed over them, shielding the eroding coastline. Patches of mud-brown lichen furred the rocks' lower edges, and water pooled in the shallow depressions between them. Fiona inspected a handful of these, hoping to find a sea anemone or a baby starfish to show Sarah. As she gazed past her blurred reflection into another rock pool, Fiona sensed Sarah close by, and a moment later, a second, smaller shadow settled beside her own.

"Look, Sarah," she said, bending quickly to scoop up a shell streaked with vein-purple threads. Fiona felt her daughter's hair brush against her arm as she plucked the shell from the pool. She looked over her shoulder. Sarah wasn't there.

Fiona stood, the skin on her arm turning a sharp cold. Sarah was further down the beach, still well within range of sight and hearing like Fiona had told her, but she couldn't possibly have been stood there, right beside her. Fiona felt a prickle against the back of her neck, the sensation creeping across her shoulders. She turned full circle, shivering. There was no one. She rubbed at her arms, encouraging the warmth to return to her skin. Someone had been close enough to touch her, she was certain of it. She shook her head. It must have been her imagination.

The chill lifted gradually, but her unease lingered, a splinter just below the surface. Fiona gazed after Sarah. She realised she was still clutching the shell tightly in one hand, its edges digging into the skin of her palm. Without looking at the water's surface, she dropped it back into the rock pool and walked along the beach towards her daughter.

IN THEIR RUSH to see the sea, neither of them had noticed the natural sandpit that lay behind their caravan. Sarah stopped mid-stride and Fiona almost toppled over her.

"What's the ma—?"

"Ssshhh, Mummy," Sarah pointed. Fiona noticed a small, furtive movement at the edge of the sandpit, a twitch of stone-grey fur, two black shining eyes peering at them.

Sarah raised her foot as if to creep forward. The rabbit jumped, its frantic little limbs kicking up sand as it made for the long grass and disappeared amongst the rippling stalks.

Sarah lowered her foot and sighed. "He must be shy, Mummy." She looked up at Fiona. "Like me." She said it so matter-of-factly that it made Fiona's heart ache.

Then Sarah's face brightened. "He just needs a friend, right, Mummy?"

Fiona couldn't help but smile. "That's right, sweetheart."

With the pebbles and shells carefully decanted into the sandpit, Sarah insisted that Fiona leave her to play. The anxiety that had occupied her these past months seemed, at least temporarily, to have lifted, and Fiona did not want to analyse it too closely in case she caused it to return.

Between hauling in their shared suitcase, food shopping, and Sarah's small rucksack of toys, Fiona peeked through the caravan's windows. Sarah was arranging shells in the sand, her lips moving as she chatted away to herself. With everything inside, Fiona paused to gently open a window behind the dining nook at the back of the caravan. She listened to the soft murmur of her daughter's voice, comforted that Sarah was so absorbed in whatever world she was creating.

Fiona unpacked their things quickly, folding their clothes onto the little shelf in the wardrobe, and filling the low, half empty bookcase in the main living space with Sarah's colouring books, pens, and pencils. Although the caravan was old, its fixtures carrying signs of make do and mend rather than renovation, Fiona was relieved to find that it was clean. The quick wipe down of the kitchen surfaces and bathroom were for her own peace of mind rather than because it needed doing, and as she worked, her own anxiety slowly started to ease.

JUST AS FIONA dropped a teabag into a mug, Sarah appeared in the doorway, hugging a bundle of fabric tightly against her chest. She looked up at her mother, then down at the thing in her arms and back again. She opened her mouth as if to speak and then stopped, caught between hesitancy and excitement.

Fiona knelt down in front of her daughter. "What have you found, sweetheart?"

Sarah considered the bundle in her arms for a few seconds before holding it out. It was a rag doll. A rabbit, with long, flat ears and thin limbs. It wore a dark, floral-patterned waistcoat that reminded Fiona of the fabric on her grandparents' sofa. Its eyes, nose, and mouth were stitched with black thread, and its white fabric body was stained and damp, half-caked in sand. It was a rather sad looking thing. Something in the angle of its features gave the impression it understood it had been abandoned.

Gently, Fiona took the rabbit and held it up. "Did you find it outside?"

Sarah hesitated again. Then, reluctantly meeting her mother's gaze, she nodded.

Fiona wondered if there was something her daughter wasn't telling her.

"Can I keep him?" Sarah's voice was quiet, uncertain.

A vague unease niggled at Fiona, unbidden. She dismissed it. She was tired of her negative thoughts interfering and she didn't have the heart to say no. "We would need to check that no one else is looking for him first."

A smile spread across Sarah's face and she rushed forward to hug Fiona. "Thank you, Mummy."

"I mean it. We'll need to ask at reception in the morning."

Sarah nodded and then looked at the rabbit seriously. "He needs a bath, Mummy."

Fiona laughed. "I think you both do."

WITH SARAH TUCKED up in bed, Fiona waited until her daughter's breathing was deep and steady before leaving her. She filled the kitchenette sink with warm soapy water and lowered in the rabbit doll, cradling its limbs almost like a baby. She worked soap into its ears with her thumbs until she felt the grit start to lift. The doll was handmade, and obviously made with love. Fiona could see this in every careful stitch, though the thread was starting to fray now from age and use. What a shame it had been left behind. She found herself half hoping that they would find the owner, even if it meant Sarah being disappointed. Maybe she could make Sarah a doll of her own? Fiona sighed. She doubted she would have the skill.

The rabbit's mouth and whiskers were slightly crooked, and Fiona tried to avoid rubbing at them too harshly, for fear of pulling those stitches loose. When she finished, Fiona emptied the sink and replaced the plug. She stretched her cramping fingers as the sink refilled, gazing down at the rabbit as it started to float. The material of its waistcoat ballooned slightly and in the fading light, the twist of its mouth became a knowing smile.

The bubbles swirling on the water's surface slowed, then stopped, and Fiona found herself leaning forward, unable to look away. The feeling of being watched settled over her. An intense cold gathered at her waist and Fiona tensed with the shock of it.

There was a sudden rush of water over her hands, and she realised she was clutching the edge of the countertop, the sink overflowing.

"Stupid," Fiona admonished herself, scrambling for the tap. She grabbed a towel and started mopping up the water, grateful that at least she had noticed straight away.

The rabbit was a forlorn looking thing, propped up against the dish rack. It seemed to gaze past her, its head tilted to one side. Fiona resisted the urge to glance over her shoulder and pulled her phone from her pocket.

"It's just a stuffed toy," she muttered to herself, then felt an inexplicable pang of guilt. She took a photo.

"Don't worry," she said to the rabbit. "If we can't find your little girl, I know another one who will take good care of you." Though even as she said this, she couldn't bring herself to look it in the eyes.

SHE WOKE SUDDENLY to a loud noise that dissipated with consciousness. Her heart racing, she listened, anticipating, but there was only the muted roar of the waves and the blood thumping in her ears. Finally realising where she was, Fiona rolled over to see Sarah curled up in the bed beside her. She forced herself to breathe in deeply, then out, all the way out, until there was nothing left.

Outside, at the top of the embankment, Fiona closed her eyes and listened to the waves. She allowed her thoughts to come and go with her breath, trying not to cling to them. She was aware of leaving Sarah alone in the caravan, if only a few metres behind her with the door locked. She knew her daughter was safe, but Fiona breathed this out too, until she could no longer hear her own breath over the sea below her.

When she opened her eyes again, Fiona's heart had slowed and the distorted memories that had woken her had lost their edges. Darkness lay over the beach, the depth of it waning as her eyes adjusted. The only light came from a sliver of the moon, glowing like a rim of light around a closed doorway. With this, the image of Sarah's huddled body, half-buried amongst Fiona's clothes at the bottom of her wardrobe. Sarah's face red, her eyes swollen from crying. Fiona pushed it away, frustrated tears stinging the corners of her eyes. She doubted there was enough breath in her body to let go of that memory.

FIONA WALKED INTO the caravan's living area to find Sarah already in the dining nook, kneeling on the seat so she could reach the table. She was engrossed in a drawing, her face obscured by her long hair as she leaned over the paper, seashells and colouring pencils scattered across the tabletop. The rag doll rabbit sat on the table in front of her, slumped slightly under the weight of its ears. From across the room, it looked as if it was leaning forward in fascination, watching Sarah draw. Fiona smiled at the thought. Her unease from the night before seemed suddenly foolish in the morning light.

Sarah's comfort blanket lay forgotten on the carpet and Fiona picked it up, unsure whether this was a good sign or not. She flicked the switch on the kettle and wandered over to Sarah, shuffling along the bench next to her daughter. She kissed the top of her head.

"Good morning, sweetheart."

Sarah beamed up at her, then held up her drawing. "This is for you, Mummy."

Fiona took it. It was a drawing of the pink shell she had found yesterday.

"Well, thank you." She marvelled at how her daughter, at only four years old, had mimicked the variations in colour on the shell's surface. When she looked up, Sarah had pulled the rabbit towards her so that it now sat on the edge of the table. "This is very good, Sarah."

Sarah smiled. "Thank you, Mummy." All of a sudden, she snatched up a shell from the table, excited. "Mummy, do you think Rabbit will be able to hear the waves too?"

Fiona laughed as she shuffled out from behind the table to make a cup of tea. "I'm sure he will."

When she crossed the room again with her mug and an orange juice for Sarah, her daughter was holding the shell to the rabbit's ear, gazing intently into its stitched features.

Fiona reached across the table and gave the rabbit's leg a squeeze. "He's still

a bit damp from his bath. Do you think he'd like to come to the beach with us and dry out?"

For a few seconds, Sarah didn't respond. Then, still gazing at the rabbit, she shook her head. "Ka—" She stopped.

Fiona reached for her daughter. "What is it, Sarah?"

Sarah flinched. She turned to Fiona, blinking as if just waking up. She shook her head again. "He wants to stay here."

THE SHARP PEAL of the bell filled the reception room. Sarah gasped, then immediately reached up and rang it again.

Phillip appeared in the doorway, the shadow of annoyance leaving his face as soon as he saw Sarah. "Well, hello there, young miss."

He crossed the space to the counter and gave her an exaggerated wave. Sarah shuffled closer to her mother, but waved back.

"I'm sorry to disturb you." Fiona repositioned the strap of the beach bag on her shoulder, fishing her phone from an inside pocket.

Phillip turned his attention to her and smiled. "No, not at all. What can I do for you?"

His manner instantly put Fiona at ease, and she realised she had been anxious about enlisting his help, though she couldn't say why. She certainly didn't want Sarah to be disappointed if she couldn't keep the rabbit, but all the same, that would be an important lesson for her daughter to learn. Now they were here, Fiona was sure it would be fine. Even if the rabbit had been reported missing, she doubted that its owner could be contacted after all this time. She pulled up the photo she had taken the night before and held her phone out to Phillip.

"Has anyone reported this missing? Do you recognise it?"

He took the phone from her, his eyebrows creasing as he squinted down at the screen.

His eyes widened and he opened his mouth as if he were about to speak, but then he looked up and started to shake his head. "No, I'm sorry." He held the phone out to her. "No one has reported the little guy missing as far as I know."

Fiona took the phone, unsure she believed him.

"Does that mean I can keep him?" Sarah's voice was tentative. She looked up at Phillip and Fiona in turn. The old man met Fiona's eyes, and for a split second, she saw them flash with something close to panic.

Phillip looked away, gazing down at Sarah as if trying to decide what to say. He forced a smile. "He must have been out there an awfully long time, young miss. He has to be more than a bit raggedy by now?"

"Mummy gave him a bath, didn't you Mummy?"

Phillip rubbed the back of his neck. "Surely, you don't want—"

"He was lonely." Sarah's voice wobbled as she spoke.

Fiona didn't understand. What could he possibly object to? If no one was looking for it, what harm could it do to let Sarah keep the rabbit? Not wanting to argue, she knelt beside her daughter.

"But he has you to look after him now, doesn't he, sweetheart? Of course you can keep him."

As Sarah squeezed her mother tight, Fiona glanced up at Phillip watching over them, only for the old man to look away at something on his desk.

THEY WAITED FOR the bus, sat on a low stone wall opposite the entrance to the caravan park. A laminated poster, tied to the bus stop with lengths of tattered ribbon, obscured Sarah's view, and she leaned forward to peer around it. Fiona noticed rain had found its way beneath the plastic, and all that was left now was a red smear of swollen letters and the indecipherable swirl of ink that had once been a photo. The layout was immediately familiar, and Fiona found herself wondering who had gone missing, and if they had ever been found. She reached for Sarah, but stopped herself, forcing her hands to grip the rough grain of the wall instead. She had nursed her anxieties for long enough. It must not happen here too. But the alarm in Phillip's eyes. His reluctance for Sarah to have the rabbit. She admonished herself for letting him get to her. For letting her own imagination get the better of her.

She thought about those summers with her parents. They were impressions now, rather than a distinct series of images in her mind; the glowing warmth of a hug. Fiona knew this holiday was the break she and Sarah needed to make a fresh start, if only she let it. The small seaside town a couple of miles along the coast, with its promenade, shops and arcade, had a little more to entertain Sarah and would give them a chance to explore, to fully relax into their new surroundings.

Fiona watched Sarah kicking her legs out as she swung round to look back and forth along the road, her little body a pendulum, somehow maintaining its balance. When the bus appeared around a curve in the road, Sarah jumped down from the wall, grinning, and instinctively reached for her mother's hand.

THE SEAFRONT WAS bustling. They walked past cheerful shop fronts, customers squeezing past one another through open doorways; cafes with groups of friends sat around bistro tables, parasols unfurled, if not already open. A peal of jingles spilled along the promenade from the arcade, though when they reached it, its fairy light colours were muted by the sunshine. It was a day for being outside, bright and warm for the time of year, and everyone was making the most of it, the beach already filling with young families and sunbathers dozing in the late morning sun.

Sarah bounced along at Fiona's side, pointing out things she recognised, and some she didn't, with an awed, "Look, Mummy!" She spotted a shop awning laden with plastic buckets and spades and picked out a vivid green set, jumping up and down as the shop owner reached to retrieve them.

Before Fiona could pull the old towel from her bag, Sarah was racing down the beach towards the sea, pausing suddenly to look back at Fiona for permission. Fiona gave her a nod of encouragement and mouthed, "Go on," and settled down on the towel to watch her.

As she sat there, with the light and the colour and the noise of everything going on around her, watching Sarah fill a plastic bucket with seawater, Fiona finally felt herself relax. This was what she had wanted for her daughter, and it was everything she imagined it would be.

Sarah walked up the beach with her bucket held out in front of her, its handle stretched under the weight of the water. Her tongue pressed between her lips in concentration, she lowered it to the sand, tipped it over, then rushed off for more.

Fiona watched as Sarah built sandcastles, patting the top of the bucket when asked, and hiding a smile at the increasingly elaborate series of towers, until Sarah stood back to admire her work.

She tilted her head to one side. "What do you think, Mummy?"

"They're beautiful."

Sarah beamed, then grabbed her bucket. She spun on the spot, looking down at the sand, then bent to pick up a shell, then another one. Between them, they filled the bucket, then knelt next to the castles, carefully pressing shells into their soft walls. Under Sarah's instruction, Fiona built battlements between each tower, drawing the sand up between her hands. When one of these walls crumbled, overloaded with shells like in a game of Buckaroo, Sarah gasped, and Fiona was afraid she would be upset. But Sarah started to giggle. Fiona laughed too then, relieved that her daughter still knew how to have fun after all. As Sarah continued to giggle to herself, Fiona managed to take a couple of photos with her phone.

When they were finished, the bucket finally empty of shells, Sarah beckoned her mother over to where she was standing. "Take a photo, Mummy."

Fiona knelt beside her and held her phone up. She showed Sarah where to press and the camera clicked as it took the photo.

"It really is beautiful, Sarah." She kissed the side of her head. "Did you have fun?"

Sarah nodded, pointing at the middle tower with her spade. "This is the Keep, Mummy. Where we live. And the rest of these—" She swung the spade through the air to indicate the remaining towers. "They're here to keep us safe."

"Where did you...?" Fiona stopped herself, her surprise disappearing in a flare of guilt as she realised she hadn't been able to protect her daughter. Of course, Sarah was aware of that responsibility, after all they had been through. She took a deep breath, resolving not to dwell, when Sarah gasped.

"What, sweetheart?"

"A moat." Sarah started to dig. "Katie said castles need a moat."

Fiona frowned. "Who's Katie?"

Sarah stopped digging but didn't look up. "She's..." She paused, searching for the right word. "My friend." She started digging again.

"From nursery?" Fiona tried to remember the names of the other girls, but Sarah was shaking her head. "From the caravan park?"

Sarah paused again, her face creasing with anxiety. Fiona realised she was interrogating her. "It's okay, sweetheart. I was only curious." She hesitated, then added. "Maybe you could introduce us?"

Sarah looked up at Fiona. "But you can't see her, Mummy."

THEY WALKED BACK to the bus stop slurping ice creams, licking the softening edges of the wafer cones before the melted ice cream could hit their fingers. The beach bag over Fiona's shoulder now held the comforting weight of a bottle of wine, which she had hesitated over, until she reminded herself that she was on holiday too. The unease that had receded from her at the beach now felt like silt, settling in the pit of her stomach, and Fiona found herself looking forward to putting Sarah down for a nap, so she could wash it away again.

Sarah giggled, trying to catch rivulets of strawberry sauce before they dripped to the floor, only to end up dipping her nose in it. Fiona laughed in spite of herself.

"What, Mummy?"

"You have a little something here." Fiona pointed to her own nose.

Sarah crossed her eyes and stuck out her tongue. "I can't reach." Then they were both giggling, Fiona struggling to keep her hand steady as she dabbed at Sarah's nose with a tissue.

Fiona hadn't pressed Sarah any further about Katie. She realised, somewhere between the aisles of the shop, that Sarah must have made up an imaginary friend. She had ruled out the other possibilities, another guest at the caravan park, or a local girl. She had seen no one else at the park, with Sarah or anywhere else, and that part of the coast was fairly isolated, the reason why their break had been so cheap. What she had seen was Sarah chatting away to herself. It was obvious. Sarah had created a rationale for finding the rabbit doll. An imaginary friend had given it to her. Sarah had a good imagination, that was all. Yet something about it unnerved her.

THE GLASS WAS COOL against her forehead. Fiona held it there with her eyes closed, listening to the waves in the distance. She was outside, sat on the caravan's narrow, metal steps. The sun glowed behind her eyelids. She took another deep breath, held it, then forced it from her lungs. She lowered the glass to her lips and took a sip; opened her eyes, blinking. The sun was still high, glinting against the siding of the caravans around her. Even in the bright sunlight, they seemed to slump under a pervasive emptiness, windows dark and devoid of movement.

She had been naïve to think that one short holiday would wash her anxieties away. Instead, they had found new shadows to steep in. She took another, longer drink. Naïve was the kindest word she could manage. It had been months.

She'd known as she walked through the door that he had left. It wasn't the empty spaces where his belongings had been, she only noticed these later, but the silence. She felt the easing of an oppressive weight and the crush of grief simultaneously, leaving her numb to both. All she felt then was blind panic. Where was Sarah?

Fiona raced through the house, calling Sarah's name, her ears ringing, her vision blurring with tears. She searched once, then again, forcing herself to slow down, to listen. She was shaking. She had dropped her phone somewhere and she couldn't remember when she last had it in her hand. The house felt disjointed, as if the rooms were in the wrong order. Then a small, familiar sound made her stop. The creaking hinge on her wardrobe door.

Fiona drained her glass and set it down beside her. The breeze had changed

direction, stealing some of the day's warmth, and she pulled at the sleeves of her sweater before reaching for her phone. Fiona found the photos of Sarah at the beach; big grin stretched across her face. Fiona was awed by Sarah's resilience, when she felt so fragile. She scrolled through the photos slowly. Sarah's smile was infectious, the twinkle back in her eye, and Fiona couldn't help but smile too. Maybe they would be okay, after all.

As she continued to scroll, Fiona reached the photo of the rabbit doll she had taken the night before. She paused, her thumb hovering above the screen. Seeing it again, propped against the dish rack, she supposed Phillip was right. It was old and worn, and there was something strange in its features that even now, Fiona couldn't articulate. But it was just a doll, and Sarah was so taken with it, it shouldn't matter what Phillip or Fiona thought. She felt her earlier annoyance at him subside. He had only been trying to help. She moved to press the lock button, already lowering the phone to replace it on the steps, when she noticed a shape in the corner of the photo.

She lifted the phone again, tilting the screen away from the sunlight. A coldness crept through her, tightening in her chest. It was a child's hand, pale and not altogether there.

Fiona stared at the small, outstretched fingers reaching for the rabbit's foot, the rational voice in her head suddenly distant, its withdrawal almost a relief. Somehow, she could see the girl's fingernails had lifted away, the skin beneath black with rot.

Tears welled in the corners of her eyes. Around her, the air changed. She felt heavy and sensed something shift behind her, in the doorway. She couldn't move, her body thick with dread.

Sarah screamed.

Fiona hurled herself through the doorway, the caravan a blur until she reached the bedroom door. The rabbit lay on the floor in front of her, the bedsheets thrown back, bed empty. Fiona felt a familiar flush of panic, until she realised Sarah had squeezed herself into the space between the bed and the wall. Fiona made herself cross the room. She scooped Sarah up, her daughter's hands clutching at her, her breath faltering between sobs.

"Oh no. No, no."

"Oh, sweetheart." Fiona held Sarah tight, every instinct screaming at her to get her daughter out. She glanced back, already out of the room. The rabbit lay prone on the carpet, a little dead thing, withered and mouldering. Fiona blinked and the impression was gone. Then she was outside, crossing the grass to the caravan opposite.

She slumped onto the steps, shifting Sarah's weight onto her lap and pulling her close, stroking her hair. "It's okay now, sweetheart. Mummy's here. I've got you."

Sarah's body heaved against her and Fiona felt her daughter grasping at her sweater, twisting the material in her fists as Fiona tried to calm her.

Sarah spoke between sobs, her face still pressed against Fiona's chest. "Oh, Mummy. It. It was HORRIBLE." She looked up and Fiona saw the terror in her eyes, before Sarah twisted away from her. "She can. Take. It. Back." Sarah shouted the words in the direction of their caravan before burying herself again in Fiona's arms.

They sat, holding tightly to one another, the tears running freely down Fiona's face. She clung to her daughter, hushing her, trying to reassure her, replaying the last twenty-four hours in her mind.

She avoided looking back at the caravan, afraid she would see the girl standing in the doorway, knowing that Sarah already had.

THE SOFT SHUFFLING footsteps were somewhere to her left. Fiona tensed, clutching Sarah tighter. She wanted to squeeze her eyes closed. Instead, she forced herself to look.

Phillip rounded the caravan and stopped when he saw her. Fiona let out a long, ragged breath, and felt her adrenaline draining along with it.

"Oh dear." Phillip closed the gap between them; his face creased with worry. He glanced at the doorway of their caravan and Fiona felt a flicker of anger. She grasped for it.

"Did you know?" She was surprised by the sharpness in her own voice. He knelt beside them, steadying himself against the side of the caravan, confusion in his eyes.

"Are you both okay? What happened?" Fiona felt tears fall against those already drying on her cheeks. Embarrassed by his concern, she wanted to turn away and bury her face in her daughter's hair.

Phillip placed a hand on her arm and she flinched. She searched his face. No, he didn't know. At least, not everything.

"Let me help you." He stood up and held out a hand.

Exhaustion thickening in her limbs, Fiona gripped his hand for balance and heaved herself to her feet, Sarah shifting against her, tightening her grip.

"Thank you." She didn't know what else to say.

Phillip ran a hand through his hair, shaking his head. "I came to apologise. About the rabbit. I owe you an explanation."

The rabbit. She would have to deal with it, with Phillip here, before she lost her nerve. She closed her eyes and took a deep breath, trying to supress the dread that threatened to overwhelm her, aware of Phillip beside her. She turned and gently lowered Sarah back onto the steps.

"Can you watch her?" she asked Phillip. "I'll be a few minutes."

He nodded. "Of course."

"No, Mummy." Sarah clung to her with a fierceness Fiona hadn't realised she was capable of.

"It's okay, sweetheart." Fiona brushed the hair from Sarah's eyes, holding her face in both hands. "Mummy will be right back. I promise."

She gazed at her daughter, waiting for Sarah's grip to loosen, then fall away, almost hoping that she wouldn't let go.

The caravan was empty, the rabbit doll undisturbed on the bedroom floor. Fiona scooped it up using Sarah's bucket and spade, not wanting to touch it again, and rushed back outside. Behind the caravan, Fiona worked quickly, shovelling until sand gave way to soil, then still further, until she had a hole deep enough and wide enough that she would be able to curl up into it herself. She tipped the rabbit in and filled the hole in after it.

FIONA DROPPED THE suitcase next to the door

and considered the bucket and spade in her other hand. In her mind, she could still feel the weight of the rabbit doll inside. She hesitated; it would be easy to leave them behind. Sarah started to giggle behind her and Fiona sighed, balancing the bucket on top of the suitcase before turning around.

Phillip was pulling at the sides of his mouth, crossing his eyes and sticking out his tongue. Sarah, wriggling with laughter, could barely stay upright on her seat. She saw Fiona and pointed at Phillip. "Look, Mummy."

Phillip turned, fingers still stretching his mouth. He spluttered and straightened up. "Sorry."

Fiona smiled. "Don't be. Thank you for watching her."

Sarah wandered over then, lifting both arms, waiting to be picked up. Fiona wanted desperately to bundle her daughter into the back seat of the car and leave, but reason stopped her. Sarah was a lead weight in her arms.

THEY SAT WITH the empty wine bottle between them, Phillip turning his glass slowly in one hand, nursing the last drop. Fiona sat against the wall, staring through the window as the sandpit grew indistinct in the failing light.

He had shown her, tapping at her phone screen and handing it back to her: *Six-Year-Old Girl Missing on Family Holiday; Search for Missing Girl Continues Along Norfolk Coast; Missing Girl's Parents Fear Drowning.* Each headline brought a rush of nausea, the memory of losing Sarah for mere minutes compared to this. She thought of Sarah, terrified, and started to shake.

"We never found her body." Phillip's voice was quiet, resigned. "I kept looking. Even after the police stopped. After her parents... My wife..." He trailed off and slumped onto the seat. "When I saw the rabbit..." He paused. "I didn't know what to think."

Fiona could sense him watching her as she scrolled. She recognised Katie's photo, carefully cut from a newspaper and taped to Phillip's desk, the rabbit propped up at her feet. Fiona looked up from the screen and their eyes met. Guilt had been a life raft for them both.

She hesitated over showing him the photo again, but she needed to be sure. "In the corner."

She watched his eyes go wide; a deep, dreadful keening welling in his throat. Fiona gently took the phone from him, placed it facedown on the table and fetched the bottle of wine.

They sat while the sun crept lower, the room cast in warm hues as Fiona told him of all the times she had searched her daughter's body for bruises that might match her own.

Hours passed. There was nothing beyond the window now but full darkness. Fiona imagined the waves breaking against the sand, receding, swelling, breaking, the water black, slick, dredging up something wretched.

She opened her eyes, gasping. Phillip's hand was on her shoulder, his face full of concern.

"Go and get some sleep. I'll stay. Keep watch."

"FIONA!" PHILLIP'S VOICE boomed inside her head and Fiona lurched awake, her heart hammering. The haze of early morning light exposed the empty space in the bed next to her.

"Sarah?" Fiona whispered.

Phillip hovered in the doorway. "Quick." His voice softer now he had woken her. He turned away and Fiona scrabbled out of bed to follow him, panic already flaring high in her chest.

The caravan door was open, and beyond it, the unfurling white drifts of a sea fret filled the morning air. The suitcase had been nudged aside and Sarah's bucket and spade were gone.

Phillip was at the kitchenette, pulling at drawers and cupboard doors as Fiona raced outside, bare feet on metal, grass, sand. "Fiona, wait!"

"Sarah!" Fear rose like bile in her throat; Phillip's voice lost beneath her own. She stopped, heaving air into her lungs and shouted again, and again.

A lurching beam of torchlight cast faint shadows through the mist and came to rest at her feet; disturbed sand around a frantically dug hole; the rabbit gone. Phillip pushed the torch into Fiona's hands, and she stumbled forward towards the embankment, grasping scrub grass, fingers digging into pebbled sand.

The fret lay thick against the beach. Fiona screamed Sarah's name until her voice grew thin and slipped out of her own hearing, lost beneath the white roar of the waves. She rushed forward, the jagged remains of wooden revetments rising out of the grey; silent figures watching her in the waning torchlight. She wanted to scream at them. She felt light-headed, directionless, the thin line between headland, horizon and sea lost to her.

The ice-cold sting against her ankles made her gasp. She felt the torch slip from her fingers; heard it slap the water; Phillip's voice reverberating in the distance, the sound of her daughter's name retreating like the waves at her feet, until all she could hear was her own breathing. In. Out. In. Out. Her whole body shaking with the effort.

Somewhere close, Sarah giggled.

The two girls knelt in the sand with the bright green bucket between them, Sarah shovelling sand while Katie held it steady.

Fiona lowered herself to her knees, watching as Sarah put down the spade and she and Katie lifted the bucket together, tipping it over. Katie patted the top of the bucket with one hand, her skin perfect and unblemished. The girls smiled at each other as they lifted it to reveal the sandcastle underneath.

The air rippled like shallow water over sand, black rot blooming across Katie's hands, up her bare arms. Her wild blonde hair suddenly lank and dripping. Fiona felt a sickening wrench in her stomach, then misery, fear, a loneliness so terrible it threatened to overwhelm her. She cried out, stumbling back as Katie and Sarah turned towards her.

"Mummy!" Sarah grinned. "We built them together." She started to point at the crumbling sandcastles that surrounded them, then stopped, her smile faltering as she saw her mother's fear.

Fiona struggled to her feet under the weight of Katie's attention. She couldn't bring herself to look her in the eyes, knowing now that was all the girl needed. Instead, she focussed on Sarah as she prepared to move. "They're beautiful, sweetheart."

Phillip grabbed her wrist, holding her back. Fiona hadn't sensed him behind her. She turned to him, about to pull away, but the look in his eyes stopped her. He held her gaze, until he saw she understood.

Fiona watched him crouch down in front of Katie, tears in his eyes. She saw the moment he felt it; her pain, all at once. Then he smiled, pulled at the sides of his mouth, crossed his eyes and stuck out his tongue.

Katie beamed, letting go of the bucket to copy him.

Fiona darted forward, lifting Sarah into her arms. She clung to her as she ran, not daring to look back, her own breathing loud in her ears, a roar of static—the sea—then Sarah's voice, almost a whisper. "It's okay, Mummy."

Fiona stopped, sobbing, squeezing her daughter against her. She could smell the salt in Sarah's hair, against her skin, as her daughter shifted in her arms to kiss her.

"It's okay, Mummy. I'm here." She struggled to brush the hair from her mother's eyes. "Look."

The beach lay pale before them, the sea fret thin enough now for Fiona to see the line of panicked footprints she had left trailing behind her. She traced their route back to the small cluster of sandcastles, barely shadows against the shore, and the two silhouettes still crouched in the sand. Fiona glimpsed movement, something tipping over, then a glint of sunlight, and they were gone.

Kelly White is a writer based in the UK. Her short fiction has been published in *Supernatural Tales* and in anthologies from Black Shuck Books and Knight Watch Press. She holds an MA in Creative Writing from the University of Birmingham. "The Other Shore" grew from a happy childhood memory of a typically British seaside holiday in the early '90s and a love of ghost stories. ■

FEAR IN FOUR COLORS

THE HIDEOUS HISTORY OF AMERICAN HORROR COMICS

BY JOHN M. NAVROTH

CRIME AND HORROR "COMIC" BOOKS

DELINQUENCY

PART VI: INDICTIMENTS & INDIGNITIES

FEAR IN FOUR COLORS:
THE HIDEOUS HISTORY OF AMERICAN HORROR COMICS

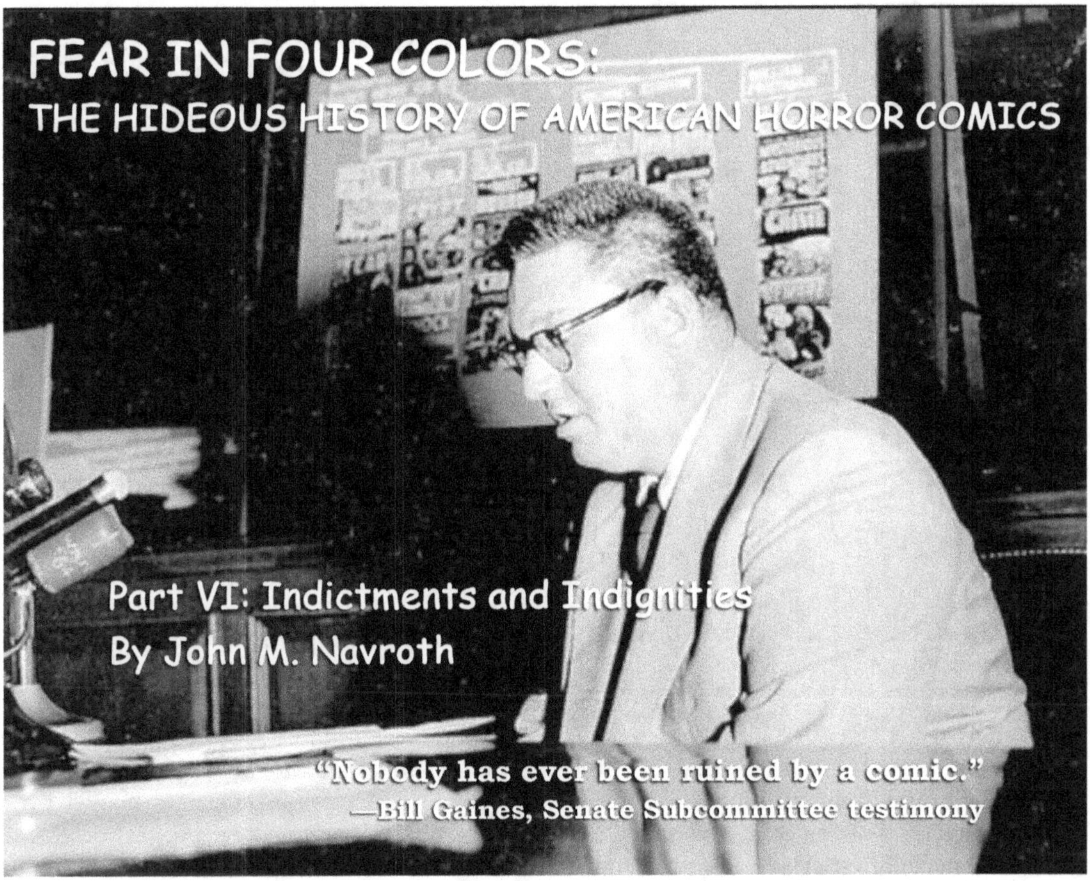

Part VI: Indictments and Indignities
By John M. Navroth

"Nobody has ever been ruined by a comic."
—Bill Gaines, Senate Subcommittee testimony

O N APRIL 19, 1954, THE FIRST EDITION OF PSYCHIATRIST DR. FREDRIC WERTHAM'S BOOK, *SEDUCTION OF THE INNOCENT* WAS PUBLISHED BY REINHART & COMPANY, INC., NEW YORK. Two days later the *Senate Subcommittee on Juvenile Delinquency* convened and in a few short months, the comic book industry was reduced to a near-barren landscape. As a result of the fallout, publishers had no choice but to self-regulate their product in order to stay in business. As we shall see, some did not survive and became the first casualties of the war on comics.

Wertham was born Friedrich Ignatz Wertheimer to Sigmund and Mathilde Wertheimer on March 20, 1895, in Nuremberg, Germany. In 1921, he graduated medical school from the University of Würzburg and continued his postgraduate studies at universities in France and Austria. The following year he immigrated to the United States and began working at the Phipps Psychiatric Clinic, Johns Hopkins University in Baltimore, Maryland. He published his

The author of THE SHOW OF VIOLENCE and DARK LEGEND

SEDUCTION OF THE INNOCENT

Fredric Wertham, M.D.

the influence of comic books on today's youth

first book, *Significance of the Physical Constitution in Mental Illness* in 1926 with Florence Hesketh. The following year he changed his name to Fredric Wertham and married Hesketh. In 1932, he was appointed senior psychiatrist at Bellevue Mental Hygiene Clinic (later re-named Bellevue Hospital), New York, N.Y., and in 1936 was appointed its director. In 1940, he accepted the directorship of psychiatric service at Queens Hospital Center, Jamaica, New York.

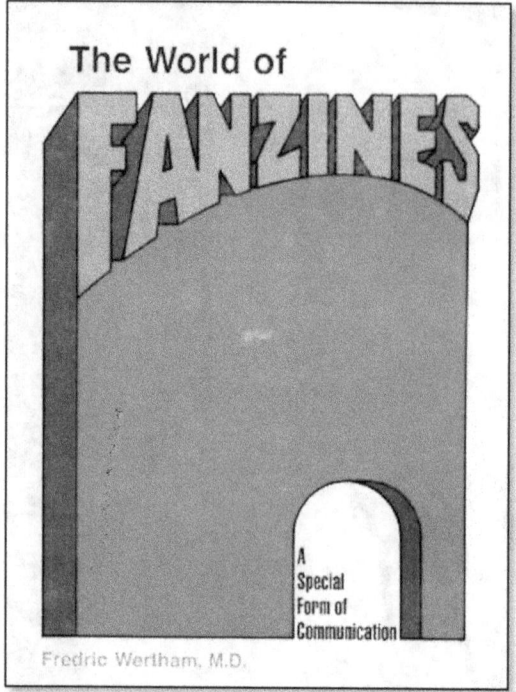

The World of **FANZINES**

A Special Form of Communication

Fredric Wertham, M.D.

APPROVED BY THE COMICS CODE AUTHORITY

Look for the COMIC BOOK with this SEAL

He opened the Lafargue Clinic in Harlem, New York, N.Y. in 1946, a psychiatric clinic specializing in the treatment for poor African Americans. The following year, he opened the Quaker Emergency Service Readjustment Center for sexually maladjusted individuals in New York, N.Y.

After the publication of *Seduction of the Innocent* and his testimony at the hearings, Wertham published three more books, the last being *The World of Fanzines: A Special*

Form of Communication (Carbondale and Edwardsville, Ill.: Southern Illinois University Press, 1973). By that time, his view on comics appears to have tempered (especially since the Comics Code Authority had been in effect for nearly thirty years), stating: "In my analysis, the editing of fanzines is a constructive and healthy exercise of creative drives." Wertham died on November 18, 1981, in Bluehills Farm, Kempton, Pennsylvania, at the age of 86.

On April 21, 1954, at 10:00 A.M., the *Hearings Before the Subcommittee to Investigate Juvenile Delinquency* began its two-day proceedings focusing on comic books, presided over by Senator Robert C. Hendrickson (New Jersey). The morning session was comprised of introductory statements from Richard Cledenon, Executive Director of the committee, Dr. Harris Peck, Director of the Bureau of Mental Health Services, Children's Court, N.Y. and Henry Edward Schulz, General Counsel, Association of Comic Magazine

The now-infamous Fredric Wertham.

Previous page, top: EC Comics publisher William Maxwell (Bill) Gaines testifies.

Thomas D. Hennings, Estes Kefauver, Robert C. Hendrickson, and Richard Clendenen.

Publishers, Inc. (ACMP), N.Y. The ACMP was formed in 1947 in an attempt at self-regulation in the face of increased criticism. A code was drafted in 1948, but was largely ignored by publishers, some who had already adopted their own advisory boards. At the time of the hearing, Schulz confirmed: "The association, I would say, is out of business and so is the code."

The afternoon session began with Wertham's testimony. He let fly with a fusillade of comments condemning comic books, from their violence and bloodletting to their obstruction of proper learning. "We have found all comic books have a very bad effect on teaching the youngest children the proper reading technique, to learn to read from left to right," he claimed. "This balloon print pattern prevents that. So many children, we say they read comic books, they don't read comic books at all. They look at pictures and every once in a while, as one boy expressed it to me, 'When they get the woman or kill the man then I try to read a few words.'"

At the time of his testimony, Wertham, a social liberal, was head of the Lafargue Clinic in Harlem, N.Y. (named after Cuban-French Marxist Paul Lafargue, Karl Marx's son-in-law) where underprivileged black children and youth were treated for mental health disorders, many of whom were also juvenile delinquents. One of his more quotable quotes of the day was: "I think Hitler was a beginner compared to the comic-book industry. They get the children much younger."

EC's Bill Gaines was the sole comic book publisher representing the industry on the first day and he did so voluntarily. Gaines had prepared for his appearance in the afternoon session (suspiciously scheduled after Wertham) and was allowed to first give a statement on his views on comics and attempt to dispel their negative influence on readers. While Gaines' testimony has been well-documented, a portion of it here will emphasize the veracity of the line of questioning:

HERBERT WILTON BEASER, ASSOCIATE CHIEF COUNSEL: There would be no limit actually to what you put in the magazines?
BILL GAINES: Only within the bounds of good taste.
BEASER: Your own good taste and salability?
GAINES: Yes.

SENATOR ESTES KEFAUVER, D-TENNESSEE:
Here is your May 22 issue [*Crime Suspen-Stories* #22]. This seems to be a man with a bloody ax holding a woman's head up which has been severed from her body. Do you think that is in good taste?

GAINES: Yes, sir; I do, for the cover of a horror comic. A cover in bad taste, for example, might be defined as holding the head a little higher so that the neck could be seen dripping blood from it and moving the body over a little further so that the neck of the body could be seen to be bloody.

KEFAUVER: You have blood coming out of her mouth.

GAINES: A little.

KEFAUVER: Here is blood on the ax. I think most adults are shocked by that.

HENDRICKSON: Here is another one I want to show him.

KEFAUVER: This is the July one [*Crime Suspen-Stories* #23]. It seems to be a man with a woman in a boat, and he is choking her to death here with a crowbar. Is that in good taste?

GAINES: I think so.

HERBERT J. HANNOCH, CHIEF COUNCIL:
How could it be worse?

In retrospect, many have questioned the wisdom of Gaines volunteering to testify and if the outcome of the hearings would have been different if he hadn't done so. Based on how the cards were already stacked against the entire industry, it seems unlikely.

Gaines himself later gave an explanation for his overall sub-par performance, admitting that he misjudged the timing of taking his prescribed diet pills (Dexedrine). The dose began to wear off during his testimony, he claimed, leaving him exhausted and on the ropes from a panel of relentless adversaries who would have not let up had they been allowed to continue.

On Thursday, April 22, 1954, the second session convened at 10 A.M. The first witness was Gunner Dybwad, Executive Director of the Child Study Association of America, followed by William K. Friedman, associate publisher and editor of *Mysterious Adventures* and *Fight Against Crime* (Story Comics), Dr. Lauretta Bender, Senior Psychiatrist,

Bellevue Hospital, N.Y., and advisor for DC Comics, Monroe Froehlich Jr., Business Manager of Magazine Management Co. (Marvel Comics), William Richter, News Dealers Association of Greater New York, Alex Segal, President, Stravon Publications (who advertised in comic books), Samuel Roth, a publisher who had been jailed several times for possessing or selling obscene materials, and Helen Meyer and Matthew Murphy, Vice President and Editor of Dell Publications.

After the conclusion of the hearings and with the looming fear of government regulation, the comics industry circled their wagons and formed the Comics Magazine Association of America (CMAA). Drafted by members, the Comics Code Authority was adopted on October 26, 1954. Included in the guidelines were prohibiting the use of the words *horror* or *terror* in the title of a comic book and forbidding subjects such as vampirism, zombies, ghouls and "werewolfism." These and other severe restrictions effectively eviscerated most of the EC line as well as dozens of other publishers' crime, horror and mystery titles.

There is another chapter in the infamous hearings: a third session was held on Friday, June 4, 1954. The main topic was "tie ins," a practice allegedly used by distributors to essentially coerce newsstand dealers into stocking titles they were reluctant to carry

(i.e., crime and horror comics). It was also claimed that distributors would not ship better-selling magazines unless they also accepted the comics. The argument continued back and forth throughout the day between distributors and dealers. In the meantime, the case against comics swelled to even larger proportions.

On March 15, 1955, Senator Kefauver issued an "Interim Report of the Committee on the Judiciary" as a part of the *Investigation of Juvenile Delinquency in the United States*. The following are selected introductory statements from the document. Opportunistically, the full text of the Comics Code Authority was included in the interim report.

- Members of the subcommittee have emphatically stated at public hearings that freedom of speech and freedom of the press are not at issue…they agree that these freedoms, as well as other freedoms in the Bill of Rights, must not be abrogated.

YOU STUPID OLD FOOL! I'VE STOOD FOR YOUR MISERLY, PENNY-PINCHING WAYS LONG ENOUGH! FROM NOW ON IT'LL BE MY MONEY... AND I'LL SPEND IT MY WAY! DIE, EZRA...DIE!

AGHRRRRRRRR!

Kids often shared their comics with friends. Left: "Stick in the Mud" (*Fight Against Crime* #19).

- The subcommittee has no proposal for censorship. It moved into the mass media phase of its investigations with no preconceived opinions in regard to the possible need for new legislation.
- In its investigations of mass media, as in its investigation of other phases of the total problem, the subcommittee has not been searching for "one cause" [of juvenile delinquency].
- Due in part to the comparatively recent introduction of comic books, there remains a considerable area which deserves careful and *scientific* exploration [emphasis added].
- The subcommittee was concerned only with those [comic books] dealing with crime and horror.
- The so-called crime and horror comic books of concern to the subcommittee offer short courses in murder, mayhem, robbery, rape, cannibalism, carnage, necrophilia, sex, sadism, masochism, and virtually every other form of crime, degeneracy, bestiality, and horror. These depraved acts are presented and explained in illustrated detail in an array of comic books being bought and read daily by thousands of children. These books evidence a common penchant for violent death in every form imaginable. Many of the books dwell in detail on various forms of insanity and stress sadistic degeneracy. Others are devoted to cannibalism with monsters in human form feasting on human bodies, usually the bodies of scantily clad women.

What followed bordered on the sanctimonious and was significantly more punitive in tone to the comparatively even-handed opening comments.

"It will be clearly seen that the major emphasis of the material then available [at the time of the hearings] on America's newsstands from this segment of the comic book industry dealt with depraved violence." The examples provided were:

- "Bottoms Up!" (*Mysterious Adventures* #18, Story Comics, February 1954).
- "Frisco Mary" (*Crime Must Pay the Penalty* #37, Ace Comics, March 1954)
- "With Knife in Hand" (Strange Tales #28, Atlas Comics, May 1954).

- "Head Room" (*Haunt of Fear* #24, EC Comics, March-April 1954).
- "The Orphan" (mistitled as "Orphan" in the report. *Shock Suspenstories* #14, EC Comics, April-May 1954).
- "Heartless!" (*Fight Against Crime* #17, Story Comics, January 1954).
- "Stick in the Mud" (Fight Against Crime #19, Story Comics, May 1954).

The remainder of the document continues in great detail, carefully enumerating the transgressions of crime and horror comics, all couched in political double-speak typical of bureaucratic decisions that obviously intend to influence the outcome of an argument, but still claim to remain neutral. However, it was emphasized that publishers were to have the primary responsibility for the content of their publications.

The report is an illuminating look at what clearly reads as the subcommittee's summation after they had nearly a year to percolate their views into a stronger brew, as well as fully assimilating Wertham's respected opinions into their findings

Since the government essentially washed their hands of the legal problem of comic books, it would have been interesting to see what might have happened if the rush to form the Comics Code Authority had been postponed.

Nevertheless, comic book publishers were reeling with concern for their collective future. In what was tantamount to a last gasp, Bill Gaines vented his frustration by running a satirical editorial, "Are You A Red Dupe?" on the inside front cover of *Haunt of Fear* #26 (July-August 1954). Co-written by EC's business manager Lyle Stuart and drawn by Jack Davis, it took a nasty swipe at Wertham by associating him with communism. Treating it as a joke, Gaines made the blunder of sending a copy to the subcommittee, which could not have possibly put him in good graces with them, especially when Joseph McCarthy was still busy rooting out communists from the country at the time. Gaines later tasked Al Feldstein to write a piece in *Shock SuspenStories* #18 (December 1954-January 1955) titled, "A Special Editorial: This Is An Appeal For

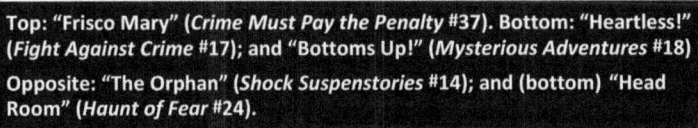

Action!" urging protests opposing the campaign against comics.

As far back as 1951, publishers had taken a stand against criticism. "The Case for Comic Books" appeared in *Mister Mystery* #3 (Stanley Morse, Dec. 1951-Jan. 1952). The editorial amounted to little more than a cry in the wilderness and was only printed once. In the meantime, humorous pokes at Wertham began to appear in comics such as *Mad* #34.

At the end of the day, is it fair to say that the Comics Code Authority was solely

Top: "Frisco Mary" (*Crime Must Pay the Penalty* #37). Bottom: "Heartless!" (*Fight Against Crime* #17); and "Bottoms Up!" (*Mysterious Adventures* #18)

Opposite: "The Orphan" (*Shock Suspenstories* #14); and (bottom) "Head Room" (*Haunt of Fear* #24).

ARE YOU A RED DUPE?

IN THE TOWN OF GAZOOSKY IN THE HEART OF SOVIET RUSSIA, YOUNG MELVIN BLIZUNKEN-SKOVITCHSKY PUBLISHED A *COMIC MAGAZINE*...

...SO THEY CAME AND *SMASHED* HIS FOUR-COLOR PRESS...

...AND *HUNG* POOR MELVIN THE NEXT MORNING!

- HERE IN AMERICA, WE CAN *STILL* PUBLISH COMIC MAGAZINES, NEWSPAPERS, SLICKS, BOOKS AND THE BIBLE. WE DON'T *HAVE* TO SEND THEM TO A CENSOR FIRST. NOT *YET*...
- FOR THERE ARE SOME PEOPLE IN AMERICA WHO WOULD *LIKE* TO CENSOR... WHO WOULD *LIKE* TO SUPPRESS COMICS. IT ISN'T THAT THEY DON'T LIKE COMICS FOR *THEM!* THEY DON'T LIKE THEM FOR *YOU!*
- THESE PEOPLE SAY THAT *COMIC BOOKS* AREN'T AS GOOD FOR CHILDREN AS *NO* COMIC BOOKS, OR SOMETHING LIKE THAT. SOME OF THESE PEOPLE ARE NO-GOODS. SOME ARE DO-GOODERS. SOME ARE WELL-MEANING. AND SOME ARE JUST PLAIN MEAN.
- BUT WE ARE CONCERNED WITH AN AMAZING REVELATION. AFTER MUCH SEARCHING OF NEWSPAPER FILES, WE'VE MADE AN ASTOUNDING DISCOVERY:

THE GROUP MOST ANXIOUS TO DESTROY COMICS ARE THE COMMUNISTS!

- WE'RE SERIOUS! NO KIDDIN'! HERE! READ THIS:

THE (COMMUNIST) "DAILY WORKER" OF JULY 13, 1953 SAID THAT COMICS PLAY THE CONSCIOUS ROLE OF:

"...BRUTALIZING AMERICAN YOUTH, THE BETTER TO PREPARE THEM FOR MILITARY SERVICE IN IMPLEMENTING OUR GOVERN-MENT'S AIMS OF WORLD DOMINATION, AND TO ACCEPT THE ATROCITIES NOW BEING PERPETRATED BY AMERICAN SOLDIERS AND AIRMEN IN KOREA UNDER THE FLAG OF THE UNITED NATIONS."

THIS ARTICLE ALSO QUOTES GERSHON LEGMAN (WHO CLAIMS TO BE A GHOST WRITER FOR DR. FREDERICK WERTHAM, THE AUTHOR OF A RECENT BLAST AGAINST COMICS PUBLISHED IN "THE LADIES HOME JOURNAL"). THIS SAME G. LEGMAN, IN ISSUE #3 OF "NEUROTICA," PUBLISHED IN AUTUMN 1948, SAID:

"THE CHILD'S NATURAL CHARACTER... MUST BE DISTORTED TO FIT CIVILIZATION... FANTASY VIOLENCE WILL PARALYZE HIS RESISTANCE, DIVERT HIS AGGRESSION TO UNREAL ENEMIES AND FRUSTRATIONS, AND IN THIS WAY PREVENT HIM FROM REBELLING AGAINST PARENTS AND TEACHERS... THIS WILL SIPHON OFF HIS RESISTANCE AGAINST SOCIETY, AND PREVENT REVOLUTION."

- SO THE *NEXT* TIME SOME JOKER GETS UP AT A P.T.A. MEETING, OR STARTS JABBERING ABOUT THE "NAUGHTY COMIC BOOKS" AT YOUR LOCAL CANDY STORE, GIVE HIM THE *ONCE-OVER*. WE'RE NOT SAYING HE *IS* A COMMUNIST! HE MAY BE INNOCENT OF THE WHOLE THING! HE MAY BE A *DUPE!* HE MAY NOT EVEN *READ* THE "DAILY WORKER"! IT'S JUST THAT HE'S *SWALLOWED* THE *RED* BAIT... HOOK, LINE, AND *SINKER!*

From Haunt of Horror #26

responsible for dismantling the comic book empire of 1950s as so many pundits claim? The answer is: not entirely. Other circumstances must be considered to determine a clearer picture of the cause of the industry's collapse.

Perhaps the greatest underlying factor rests on one critical event that occurred in 1955: the American News Company was dismantled in an anti-trust lawsuit. American News was the largest distributor of comic books in the United States, supplying well over 100,000 retail markets with over three hundred titles, more than half of those that were published. Coincidentally, Union News Company was a subsidiary of American News and happened to be the largest retailer of magazines, owning and operating

A SPECIAL EDITORIAL

THIS IS AN APPEAL FOR ACTION!

THE PROBLEM: Comics are under fire . . . horror and crime comics in particular. Due to the efforts of various "do-gooders" and "do-gooder" groups, a large segment of the public is being led to believe that certain comic magazines cause juvenile delinquency, warp the minds of America's youth, and affect the development of the personalities of those who read them! Among these "do-gooders" are: a psychiatrist who has made a lucrative career of attacking comic magazines, certain publishing companies who do not publish comics and who would benefit by their demise, many groups of adults who would like to blame their lack of ability as responsible parents on comic mags instead of on themselves, and various assorted headline hunters. These people are militant. They complain to local police officials, to local magazine retailers, to local wholesalers, and to their congressmen. They complain and complain and threaten and threaten. Eventually, everyone gets frightened. The newsdealer gets frightened. He removes the books from display. The wholesaler gets frightened. He refuses shipments. The congressmen get frightened . . . November is coming! They start an investigation. This wave of hysteria has seriously threatened the very existence of the whole comic magazine industry.

WE BELIEVE: Your editors sincerely believe that the claim of these crusaders . . . that comics are bad for children . . . is *nonsense.* If we, in the slightest way, thought that horror comics, crime comics, or any other kind of comics were harmful to our readers, we would cease publishing them and direct our efforts toward something else!

And we're not alone in our belief. For example: Dr. David Abrahamsen, eminent criminologist, in his book, "Who Are The Guilty?" says, "Comic books do not lead to crime, although they have been widely blamed for it . . . In my experience as a psychiatrist, I cannot remember having seen one boy or girl who has committed a crime, or who became neurotic or psychotic . . . because he or she read comic books." A group led by Dr. Freda Kehm, Mental Health Chairman of the Ill. Congress of the P. T. A., decided that living room violence has "a decided beneficial effect on young minds." Dr. Robert H. Felix, director of the National Institute of Mental Health, said that horror comic books do not originate criminal behavior in children . . . in a way, the horror comics may do some good . . . children may use fantasy, as stimulated by the "comics" as a means of working out natural feelings of aggressiveness.

We also believe that a large portion of our total readership of horror and crime comics is made up of adults. We believe that those who oppose comics are a small minority. Yet this minority is causing the hysteria. The voice of the *majority* . . . you who buy comics, read them, enjoy them, and are not harmed by them . . . has not been heard!

WHAT YOU MUST DO: Unless you act now, the pressure from this minority may force comics from the American scene. It is members of this minority who threaten the local retailers, who threaten the local wholesalers, who have sent letters to the Senate Subcommittee on Juvenile Delinquency (now investigating the comic industry).

IT IS TIME THAT THE MAJORITY'S VOICE BE HEARD!

It is time that the Senate Subcommittee hears from YOU . . . *each and every one of you!*

If you agree that comics are harmless entertainment, write a letter or a postcard *TODAY* . . . to:

The Senate Subcommittee on Juvenile Delinquency
United States Senate
Washington 25, D. C.

and in your own words, tell them so. Make it a nice, polite letter! In the case of you younger readers, it would be more effective if you could get your parents to write for you, or perhaps add a P.S. to your letter, as the Senate Subcommittee may not have much respect for the opinions of minors.

Of course, if you or your parents *disagree* with us, and believe that comics ARE bad, let your sentiments be known on that too! The important thing is that the Subcommittee hear from actual comic book readers and/or their parents, rather than from people who never read a comic magazine in their lives, but simply want to destroy them.

It is also important that your local newsdealer be encouraged to continue carrying, displaying, and selling *all kinds* of comics. Speak to him. Have him speak to his wholesaler.

Wherever you can, let your voice and the voices of your parents be raised in protest over the campaign against comics.

But first . . . *right now* . . . please write that letter to the Senate Subcommittee.

Sincerely,
Your grateful editors
(for the whole E. C. Gang)

From *Shock SuspenStories* #18

thousands of newsstands and other outlets across the country.

After the dissolution of the monopoly, many comic publishers were left high and dry without a means of distributing their product. Some managed to find other distributors, albeit with smaller networks, or start their own company, such as Dell.

WE HERE AT MAD ARE ALL FOR FIGHTING JUVENILE DELINQUENCY. BUT WE ARE FOR FIGHT-ING THIS PROBLEM INTELLIGENTLY AND SCIENTIFICALLY. WE JUST CAN'T TAKE SERIOUSLY THOSE PSEUDO-EXPERTS WHO COME FORWARD FROM TIME TO TIME WITH ARTICLES PRO-CLAIMING CURE-ALLS FOR THIS VAST AND COMPLICATED PROBLEM. ARTICLES LIKE THIS:

BASEBALL IS RUINING OUR

THE BATTER'S function consists of swinging a lethal weapon, a club, with all of his brute strength, at a defenseless ball, with the sole purpose of smashing it as far as he can. From this act, our impressionable children learn, wrongly, that the stronger you are, the greater will be your reward.

PICTURES BY WALLACE WOOD

THE BUNT is another form of batting the ball. The player, who is expected to swing hard at the ball, suddenly switches his stance in order to tap a pitch lightly down in front of the plate, catching his opponent off-guard. Here, our young people learn that sneaky tactics are also rewarded . . .

S ociety is like a garden, and our children are like flowers that bud, grow, and bloom there. Unfortunately, in today's garden, many of our flowers are going bad. The fact is, they're turning into stinkweeds! When *one* weak flower goes bad in a garden, it is nothing to worry about. But when *many* flowers begin going bad in a garden, that *is* something to worry about. Pretty soon the whole place will be one awful mess!

Today, juvenile delinquency plagues society. Thousands of flowers are going bad in our garden. It's time we exposed the cause. And it is not Japanese Beetles!

The cause can be found right smack in the middle of our garden . . . on the grass . . . where they play "Baseball"!

For many years, I worked closely with "juvenile delin-quents". Then my hair turned gray, and they kicked me out of their gang. But while I was with them, I studied them. I questioned them, probed their minds, uncovered their ids, examined their egos, and rifled their pockets. And in every single case I examined, I repeatedly came up with the same shocking fact: *At one time or another, every one of those poor misguided children had been exposed to the game of "Baseball"!* They had either *played* it themselves, or *watched* it being played . . . not to mention the countless other in-direct exposures such as "*Baseball Magazines*", "*Baseball Record Books*", and the worst offender of all, "*Baseball Bubble-Gum Cards*".

Yes, the game of "Baseball" is souring the soil of society's garden, rotting our flowering youth.

Let me analyze this "game" for you. Let me expose the psychological undertones present in this so-called "sport".

A SHOESTRING CATCH describes the action of a player who runs in and retrieves an otherwise safely-hit ball before it touches the ground, literally catching it at his shoes. Such a feat usually earns a burst of applause, teaching that to deprive another of what is rightfully his is a laudable act.

From *Mad* #34

Still another obstacle was, after the introduction of the code, retailers began refusing titles without the code's "stamp of approval" on the cover, thus preventing any publisher wanting to continue their crime and horror books per usual from reaching the newsstand.

As a direct result of these factors, many publishers were forced out of business: Fiction House, popular for its half-clad

Dr. Frederick Werthless, shown above, gathering material for this article from the "Dodger Yearbook", interviewed hundreds of teen-age delinquents as they left Children's Courts all over the U.S. "The evidence was overwhelming!" states Dr. Werthless. "Almost every delinquent child brought into court had a past record of either playing or watching baseball!"

CHILDREN

by FREDERICK WERTHLESS, M.D.

And I can do this! After all, I'm a *Psychiatrist!*

The very essence of "Baseball" is "hostile aggression"! Take, for example, the act of "Batting". The function of the "batter" is to swing a lethal weapon, a club, with all his brute strength, at a defenseless ball, with the sole purpose of smashing it as hard and as far as he can. The harder and further he smashes it, the greater his reward!

What kind of healthy example is this for our youth?

With his act of brute force successfully completed, the "batter" seeks out safety by running to first base. *Runs*, mind you, like a thief in the night!

Is he so plagued with guilt that he cannot walk?

The opposition, a team of nine equally "hostile" and "aggressive" men, whose purpose is to deprive the "batter" of his desire to reach safety, pounce upon the "violence-inflicted" ball, and attempt to relay it to the protector of a base before the "batter" can arrive.

An arbiter, dressed in a uniform subtly suggestive of a policeman, judges the play and makes his decision. Consequently, only one of the protagonists can be pleased. The other must rebel!

He defies authority as our children watch!

And so it goes through the course of the game . . . one disgraceful exhibition after another . . . deplorable examples for our impressionable youth.

Study the pictures on these pages, and the documented case-histories on the following page . . . and see if you don't conclude that BASEBALL IS RUINING OUR CHILDREN . . . that the "game" should be banned, the players committed to institutions and the stadiums turned into parking lots!

BREAKING UP THE DOUBLE PLAY, a despicable practice, consists of a runner's sliding into a base with spikes high. The base player, in avoiding these lethal blades, cannot get his throw away, and is lucky to get away himself. Here, our younger generation learns *the advantages of dirty tactics* . . .

ARGUING WITH AN UMPIRE is the usual practice in baseball. If a player does not happen to agree with a decision, he enters into heated disagreement with the arbiter, to the point of name-calling and nose-thumbing. From this display, children learn that *rebellion against authority is acceptable.*

THE PITCHER uses many deliveries calculated to cause the batter to miss. These consist of assorted fast balls which curve, drop and even slide. Then, he uses a complete change of pace, the so-called "let-up" pitch, confusing the batter, and implanting in young minds the *evil seeds of deception.*

From *Mad #34*

jungle heroines and violent pulp-adventure stories, published its last comic, *Jungle Comics* #163, with its Summer 1954 issue; Harvey, publishers of *Chamber of Chills*, *Witches Tales*, and *Tomb of Terror*, dis-continued their horror comics and pivoted to children's entertainment, with titles such as *Casper* (the *Friendly* Ghost), *Richie Rich* and *Baby Huey*; Comic Media, publishers of two of most notorious pre-Code horror comics, *Horrific* and *Weird Terror*, summarily folded; Stanley Morse, who famously said: "I don't know what the hell I published. I never knew. I never read the things. I never cared," and published *Mister Mystery* and *Weird Mysteries*, also folded. Star Publications ceased in 1955 when Jerry Kramer died and co-owner L.B. Cole opted to work for

Crime Detective #9

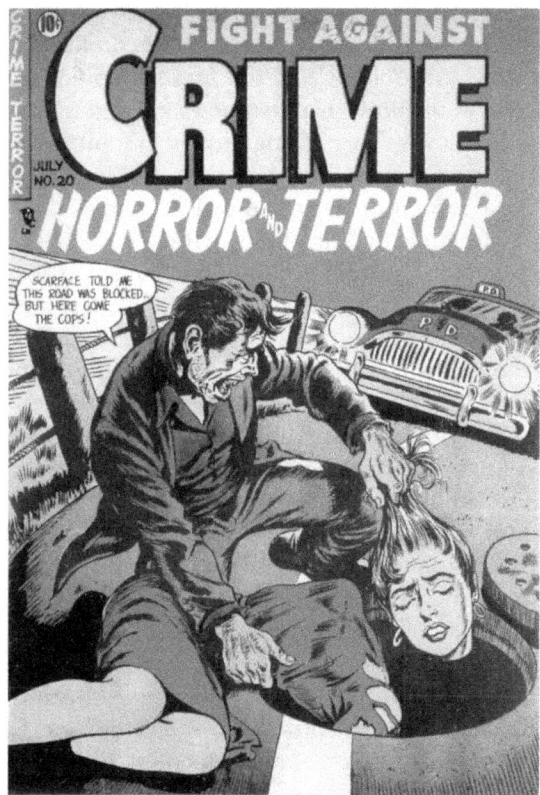

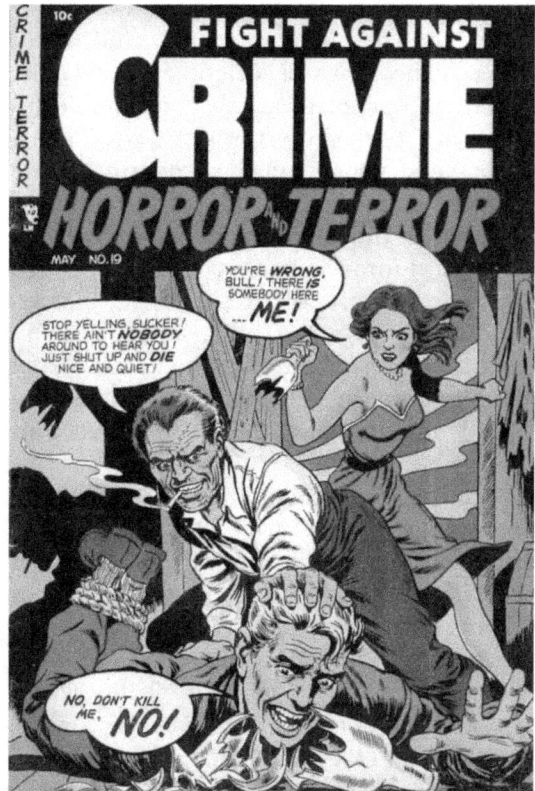

Did these Pre-Code covers go too far? You Decide.

Gilberton's *Classics Illustrated*. Other publishers who shuttered their doors, not necessarily a result of the code, but because of the generally unfriendly climate, included Avon Comics, Ace Magazines and Quality Comics.

Subsequent to entire companies going out of business, hundreds of writers, artists and others involved in the business of comics left the industry, never to return. Some notable names were Matt Baker, Charles Biro, Lou Cameron, Harry "A" Chesler, Jack Cole, Victor Fox, Lev Gleason, Al Hollingsworth, Jerry Iger, Graham Ingels, Jack Kamen, Joe Maneely, Cal Massey, Ben Sangor, and Archer St. John. Included were many others who saw no future in "funny books."

In effect, the halcyon days of the Golden Age of comic books were over.

Looking back, Wertham may have appeared on the surface to be altruistic and ostensibly driven by what he thought were the best intentions, but they might not have equated to authentically representing his viewpoints on the harmful effects of comics. One insight into his motivations was a note found in his archive years later, requesting the subcommittee during the planning stages of the hearings to begin only after publication of *Seduction of the Innocent*. Accordingly, it begs the questions: Was he cleverly disguising his own, self-serving, larger-scale strategy? Was he merely grandstanding for publicity? Was he even being truthful?

In May 2010, Wertham's private papers were released to the public by the Library of Congress's Manuscript Division after having been previously donated by his wife, Florence Hesketh Wertham's estate in 1997 and 1998. The items were processed in 1992 by T. Michael Womack and a staff of assistants.

The collection is comprised of 222 standard storage boxes containing 82,200 documents and totaling 91 linear feet. Although some items date from as early as 1884, the bulk of the material is from a thirty-year period from 1945–1975. The papers include correspondence, memoranda, speeches and lectures, reports, research notes, patient case files, psychiatric tests, transcripts of court proceedings, newspaper clippings, drawings, photographs, and other materials. The range of topics include child abuse, censorship, civil rights, comic books and their psychological aspects, juvenile delinquency, pornography, racism, sex crimes, and others. Also included is a quantity of the comics he examined along with the onion skin paper that he used to write notes on and insert into the books.

Over recent years, a number of historians have drawn critical attention to the veracity of Wertham's claims and supported their assertions with convincing conclusions based on their meticulous research and analysis.

One of the leading challengers to Wertham's claims is Carol Tilley. Tilley is a professor on the faculty of the School of Information Sciences at the University of Illinois, and is a comics historian, librarian educator, and youth advocate. Labelling Wertham's book "hyperbole," Tilley wrote the article, *Seducing the Innocent: Fredric Wertham and the Falsifications That Helped Condemn Comics,* published in *Information & Culture: A Journal of History* (University of Texas Press, Vol. 47, No. 4, 2012), in which she concluded that Wertham "manipulated, overstated, compromised, and fabricated evidence," as well as misrepresented stories and used misrepresentative samples of young comic book readers, all who coincidentally happened to be juvenile delinquents at the time they were interviewed. Tilley has written and lectured extensively on the importance of comics, saying "Comics tell stories, comics communicate ideas, they are an important and valuable and indisputable part of our cultural heritage and they belong to all of us."

Carol Tilley

In the chapter, *Seduction of the Innocent: The Great Comics Scare* from the book *Milestones in Mass Communication Media Research* (New York: Longman, 1983) authors Shearon Lowrey and Melvin L. DeFleur cite the compelling example of Wertham's lack of the use of standard criteria when he chose (or ignored) not to adopt the scientific method to form the basis of his argument. Instead, he relied largely on his case studies and his own conclusions on the relationship between society in general—and children in particular—and mass media. While it sounded convincing, it is not the commonly accepted means for accurately measuring data to present a feasible case. Nevertheless, the public swallowed his assertions hook, line, and sinker.

In a 1988 interview, Stan Lee succinctly stated: "[Wertham] said things that impressed the public, and it was like shouting fire in a theater, but there was little scientific validity to it. And yet because he had the name doctor people took what he said seriously, and it started a whole crusade against comics."

All things considered, the fact is that many comics *were* offensive and distasteful by the consensus moral and social standards of the time, and a fair number of people would agree even today. But the larger question remains: were they *harmful* to children or other readers who might be influenced enough by the violence and sexual innuendo that proliferated in the words and images to compel them to act out the same scenarios they read in comic books?

Wertham would often produce the few instances where he found this was true. On the October 10, 1948 "Meet the Author" radio program, cartoonist Al Capp defended comics against Wertham. Wertham had recently published his article "The Comics... Very Funny" in the August *Reader's Digest* and was fully prepared in anticipation of any challenge to his assertions. However, during the conversation, Capp brought up a startling statistic to counter Wertham: in the previous ten years in New York City alone, over 800 medical doctors had been charged with manslaughter! "Using Dr. Wertham's logic," Capp explained, "the fact that so many

Kids were not the only ones reading comics: Here, GIs serving in the Korean War (circa 1951) find needed escapism in these four-color publications.

doctors have been charged with manslaughter might make us suspect that all doctors could be guilty of manslaughter." The fact remains now as it did then: any significant correlation between comics and crime has yet to be conclusively proven.

We must also remember that, even though many of the traits remain inculcated in today's values, community sentiment had a decidedly more conservative nature in the 1940s and 1950s and reactions to perceived subversions to the status quo were largely more unanimous and less polarized than they are today.

As for Wertham, he was a complicated individual with an expansive social issue to address, and his view on comics was only a small part of his ultimate goal, which was to determine the causes of violence in human nature. That it proliferated in the media made comics an easy target for his acrimony.

In addition, it is hard to resist some degree of presentism when discussing certain aspects of past history and applying what we know now to the context of yesterday's events. Society and the evolution of its concepts of morality and behavior have changed significantly in the last 70 years, and while we may not fully understand the motives behind those prior events, we can reflect on the outcomes and how they have influenced the present-day. For example, the Comics Code Authority was revised several times (1971, 1982, and 1989), in part to reflect changing moral and societal attitudes and behavior.

While it may be difficult to imagine the lengths that were taken in the 1950s to protect children from undesirable comic today, comparable activities are taking place, such as the recent banning from bookstores, libraries, and schools of books deemed offensive by some of the same organizations and individuals who have a similarly resolute mindset. "The stripes have changed, but the animal hasn't" as the saying goes, and it might be only a matter of time when the matter once more falls in the lap of the government to sort the issue out.

Cartoonist Walt Kelley (who, along with Milton Caniff and Joseph Musial testified on behalf of the National Cartoonist Society at the Senate Hearings) may have best summed it up when his comic strip character, Pogo, once famously said: "I have met the enemy and he is us."

Next: "LITTLE SHOPPES OF HORROR: PRE-CODE HORROR COMICS PUBLISHERS"

John Navroth is a four-time Rondo Award-nominated writer and regular contributor to Nightmare Abbey *and* Cryptology *(Two-Morrows Publishing). For readers interested in learning more about horror comics and the Comics Code Authority, visit John's site at: fearinfourcolors.blogspot.com.*

THE CRAFTSMAN'S OTHER COUNTRY

BY CHARLES WILKINSON

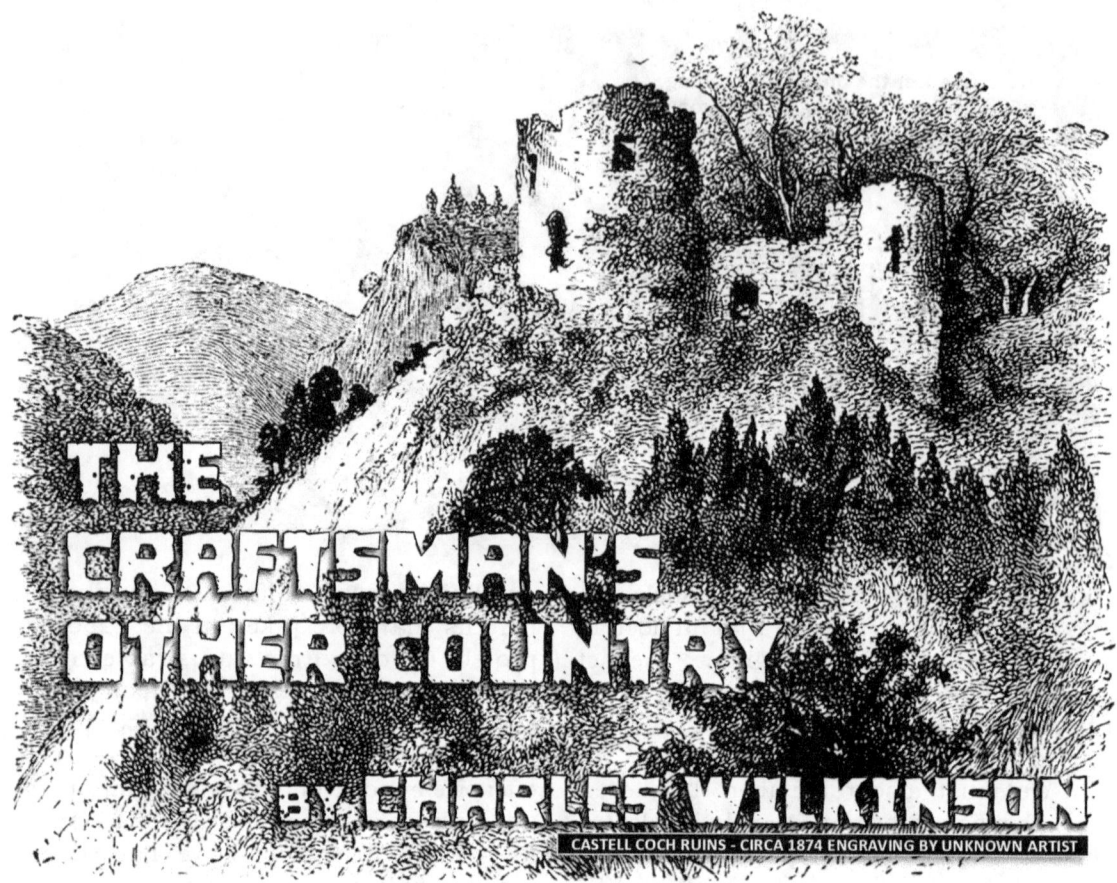

CASTELL COCH RUINS - CIRCA 1874 ENGRAVING BY UNKNOWN ARTIST

AT FIRST LIGHT, I AM AWOKEN BY THE SOUND OF SAWING. IT CEASES AFTER ABOUT A MINUTE. LYING IN BED, WATCHING A COLD, SILVER-GREY SHAFT OF WELSH SUNSHINE CUT MY BLANKET IN HALF, I RECALL TODAY is the beginning of the forty-ninth year since my nativity. By way of marking this event, I last night entreated my host, Edwyn Probert, a friend since our student days at St David's Theological College, to ask his servants to provide me on the morrow with a hot bath, a notion he poo-poohed, being ever an enemy of advanced ideas in hygiene. Surely it would be a most parlous procedure to take a bath at any time in mid-winter, he'd proclaimed, but especially whilst staying on a mountainside in Wales. And was I not aware that washing in warm water opened up the pores, permitting all manner of disease to permeate the flesh? Yet I persisted with my request: I would start my year clean in body if not in anything else, I averred. He laughed, and, being one who never wanted for largesse, said it would be arranged.

And now, to my unfeigned delight, the door is opening and servants carry in a commodious tin bath and tall pitchers from which steam spirals into pale arabesques. A sponge and a most commendable quantity of soaps have been provided. Once the servants have left, with my heartfelt thanks echoing in their ears, I disrobe and commence my lavations. It is then that I notice that the sawing which I remarked upon earlier, has resumed. I am perplexed, for the sound is distinct and yet there are no woods nearby; indeed, not so much as a copse, for the house in which I am a guest, Castell Coch, is situated half way up a foot-hill, a bare, wind-battered place, its surface scoured almost down to the rock beneath a thin layer of soil. It is true that below, adjacent to the stone-strewn track that does duty for a road, there is an ancient well, its site protected by a storm-withered grove. It is, I suppose, not inconceivable that the sound of sawing has been carried on the gale, even now rattling the windowpanes and frolicking in the chimney so that the flames in the grate flicker and dance.

Once my ablutions are complete, and as I stand by the fire to dry myself, I recall my time at college. Edwyn and I were not diligent students; we were more given to drinking than divinity—frequenters of the many inns of the town, and seldom seen in the lecture halls. There at the behest of our fathers, both ministers of religion, we had been bred for the church and yet had no inclination for it. At the end of his second year, Edwin left at the instigation of his tutor. I idled on through my final year and departed with a "gentleman's degree." Determined to avoid ordination, I decamped to Cardiff, where Edwyn had already found the employment that was to form the foundation of his fortune.

I had not seen him for more than a year when I received a summons to visit him at his new property in a far-flung corner of mid-Wales. After purchasing some land, he built a house in red sandstone, which he designed in the mock-Gothic manner now fashionable. To me, it seems as much a folly as a fortress. Although small enough to be affordable and easily maintained, it was perhaps constructed to bolster his conceit of himself as a country gentleman of ancient lineage, the proud proprietor of strong walls, a crenelated tower and a portico with a botched resemblance to a portcullis.

Edwyn is in the dining-room, feeding a newly lit log fire with kindling. His girth is wider than formerly and his stomach strains against his gaudy waistcoat, which is cut too close to his body. His face, ever tending to the florid, is empurpled, his cheeks darned with clotted red threads, although his hair, now freaked with grey about the temples, flows over his collar, its curls lavish and Byronic.

"Ah," he says, giving the fire a final prod with a poker. What a privilege it is to have a learned divine in residence here at Castell Coch!" He smiles, lopsidedly, his eyes brightening at his banter, knowing full well that I but narrowly avoided failing my degree. "But come, we must breakfast, and then I will show you my estate."

As we step out onto the forecourt, wisps of thin white rain, called *glaw isgafyn* in these parts, shivered over the high hills to the west. The sky is clotted with clouds, some grey, others the colour of curds. The vista comprises bare hills with no other habitation in sight; there is hardly a man-made structure apart from the stone covering of the well.

"You are strategically placed for a life of solitude, if that is what you desire. Perhaps now the fires of youth have died down you will return to your theological speculations," I say, by way of responding to his earlier sally. "You will become quite the hermit."

"It is true that I am somewhat less out in society than was once the case. But that is because the quality of conversation in the neighbourhood is not what I require, being almost solely concentrated on agricultural matters."

"And so most days you never speak to anyone, apart from your servants."

Pensive, Edwyn looks down for a moment, as if studying the ground ahead for molehills. "There are a few people of quality on the other side of that hill, and some of the "middling sort" in the town, which is not so difficult a journey in my carriage when the weather is fine. You need not fear that I have become absolutely the solitary. I will introduce you to a few of my more tolerable neighbours before you leave."

As we are walking down an incline in the direction of the well, which is situated in a declivity not far from the path, I catch sight of the figure of a man attired in grey clothes that might have been tailored from the rain-clouds behind him. His step is light, almost airy. He is carrying something, but at this distance it is not easy to discern its nature.

"You're trespassing!" Edwyn says, his tone strident, his features warped with fury. "How many times do I have to tell you people? This is my land."

I have never seen my friend so angry, for he is normally an equable fellow—even when in drink. Meanwhile, the man, apparently oblivious to being the object of so much ire, deposited his burden in the well, and walked quickly down to the wicket gate and onto the path.

"Is there no right of way?" I ask.

"They claim there is; I have informed them there is not."

"Which saint is it dedicated to? I assume it is a holy well."

"Some claim as much, but no one will tell me the name of the saint. In the map of the area, it is identified only as The Chalybeate Well."

"Ah, so they come to take the mineral waters?"

"No, it is undrinkable, reddish-brown, tainted. You would have to boil it first, and no one would take the trouble to do that."

The final yards down to the well are steep, and not having a stick I tread with care. Edwyn, arriving ahead of me, is waiting by the arched door of a turret-like structure built in blocks of grey stone, with machicolations at its summit. One might imagine it as having been fashioned as a fortress for *i telwyth teg*, the mythical race in which some of the local inhabitants still believe, or so my friend assures me.

"If the people aren't visiting the well for its medicinal properties, I assume it's a sacred site for them."

"Yes, it is said they come to bless, but also to…"

As he speaks, the wind whips up from the west, unsettling the last leaves in the grove, as if his unspoken words disturbed them. Before I can respond, Edwyn beckons me through the arch. Inside, there are benches around the edge of a pool, its waters thick, muddy, reddened with iron deposits. As I peer down, I perceive there is a frog at the bottom, which I mistook for a carving until it moved its head.

"I'm told," he continues, "that the well was carefully looked after until around fifty years ago. Why it was no longer maintained, I do not know, for then it had some utility; now it is but the object of their superstitions, and I do not see why I should oblige them in that."

As we walk back to Castell Coch, the wind increases, careening with a sharper edge over the stark hills, its horripilations raising the short, sheep-cropped grass.

"*Tippyn bach ora*," I remark.

Edwin stares straight ahead, his manner more aloof than is normal. "I do not speak our ancient tongue, as you well know. I have a few words—no more. I am a proud Cardiff man now, and I want nothing to do with their old language and legends."

"Spoken like a true Welshman," I retort, although I know he will not care for my rejoinder.

He was silent for a moment, evidently stung. "I am as true a Welshman as any, simply one who is not mired in outmoded manners and ways."

We walk back to the house in silence. The place appears larger than it is when viewed from below. As soon as I follow him through the door, I'm aware of a pervasive scent of sawdust; it is as if I am standing in a joinery. Yet there is no rasp of blade on wood or hammering down of nails nearby, nothing to indicate that men are at work inside.

"This morning," I tell him, "I thought I heard the sound of carpentry and now there is a distinct smell of sawdust. Are you having…"

He swings round, frowning, evidently perplexed. "There were cabinet makers here, but they have been gone many months. For my part, I can detect nothing. And as for the sawing…no, I cannot account for it. But the acoustics in this valley are strange, and the wind carries many sounds from afar."

"And yet there seem to be no other dwellings close by."

"So it might appear, but on my walks I have come across many of these poor men's houses, some little more than a byre, barely distinguishable from the grey rocks around them. Oh yes, they are out there, hidden in the folds of the hills and fields; you may depend upon it."

EDWYN HAS SET OUT for the town on unspecified business. Although he asked if I wished to accompany him, I replied that I have yet to recover fully from my long journey; the hour that he wished us to rise was not agreeable to me. The house is quiet, apart from the storm's orchestra that plays percussion on the windowpanes and sings off key in the chimney like a badly strung violin.

The previous evening the *froideur* between Edwyn and me, brought on by his belittlement of our language and culture, softened and then melted somewhere between the second and third glass of claret, and he was once more his cordial self.

"I have invited a neighbour to dine with us tomorrow evening," he said. "I doubt that you will take to her, certainly I don't, but it will be a diversion for us."

I laughed. "If you dislike her, I cannot imagine why you should wish to give her hospitality. Is her function purely to provide a subject for denigration once she leaves?"

"*Dislike* is too strong, but as you will learn she could never be justly accounted a *likeable* woman. No doubt it will be possible to have some sport at her expense, but no, my motive is rather that she keeps a most excellent table. Should she return our invitation you will not be disappointed."

"And what is this lady's name?"

"Mrs. Roberts-Jones-Evans," he said, uttering every syllable slowly and with parodic solemnity. "There are rumours about her. But they are quite ridiculous."

"In what way?"

"She is an herbalist, a skill that adds not a little piquancy to her cooking. But some would have that she is..."

He paused and turned his attention to the fire. Although I quizzed him, he did not deign to add anything of substance, saying only that I should judge for myself when I met her.

And now, as I peer out of my bedroom window, which overlooks the approach to the house, I observe a fellow, who had appeared to be en route to the well, wending his way up the slope towards the front entrance. Dressed in drab cloth, breeches, heavy boots, and a black, broad-brimmed hat, he is a working man, I've no doubt. Only his red neckerchief adds a gash of colour. Is he seeking employment at Castell Coch? If so, I fear he will be disappointed, for Edwyn disdains a large staff, employing only two women, who come in to clean in the morning and cook in the evening. I run down the stairs, expecting him to knock before I arrive, but there is no sound. When I open the door there is nothing but the wind's fury, an empty forecourt, and the rain-blurred hills beyond.

Edwyn returns from town by the middle of the afternoon. Although damp and mud-splattered from the ride, he is in high good humour, helped, to be sure, by an hour or so in a hostelry, for his trousers are stained with red wine.

"While you were out, you had a caller who did not arrive."

"Come, Mr. Medwyn!" he says, smiling. "Do not test me with your conundrums, for my wit is not at its keenest today."

"I mean that there was a man who walked up to the door, but by the time I arrived he had vanished."

Edwyn frowned and asked me to describe the caller. As I did so, his uneasiness grew, and he was silent for a while before recovering himself. "You are most probably right, Morys. He was but one of those poor fellows who in hard times take to the road and look for work."

As I'm dressing for dinner, I become aware of a faint smell, neither fragrant not foul, but somehow familiar, although it is more than a minute before I can name it. It has transported me back to a time when my father's house was under repair, a time which recalls joiners at work. Then, with an unnatural clarity, I recall a pot of hide glue, kept warm and fluid by the fire, ready for use. I am at a loss as to an explanation for this, for there is nothing in my room to account for it. Nor do I comprehend why since I have come to Castell Coch, I have had such a strong intuition of an invisible realm of carpentry: its planks, saws, pegs, planes, hammers, mallets, augers and awls.

By the time I arrive in the drawing-room, I am late and the guest is there and seated before me. Mrs. Roberts-Evans-Jones, a thin-featured woman with a pendulous nose that seems to hang over her upper lip, is wearing a black chimney hat, but from the fine quality of her silk shawl it is evident that she is no working woman.

"Ah, you're with us at last. This is Mr. Morys Medwyn, a companion of mine since our college days in Llanbedr Pont Steffan."

"Why, Mr. Probert, I did not know you

were intended for the church."

"An interlude of no great significance or duration, aside from the fortunate fact of meeting Mr. Medwyn there."

Mrs. Roberts-Jones-Evans turns towards me, her green eyes bright with sceptical intelligence. "I perceive that you too, Mr. Medwyn, do not appear to be in holy orders." She spoke precisely, with only a little of a Welsh lilt.

"You perceive correctly, Mrs. Roberts-Jones-Evans. I had no vocation for it."

After cook calls us through to the dining-room, we stand for a moment, while Edwyn, greatly to my amusement, garbles a grace, an innovation since my arrival here and no doubt performed, albeit ineptly, to appease our guest. We discourse on the state of the church in Wales and the rise of "The Jumpers" in the locality, those who take their religion from Mr. Wesley and William Williams of Pantycelyn. Is it true, I ask, that they "jump for joy?" Mrs. Roberts-Jones-Evans assures me this is so and that she has seen it. She nurses no inclination to make a Methody of herself, but she believes the people of that persuasion to be strong in the faith and honest. It is then that the conversation touches on Castell Coch.

"This is a fine place you have here," I tell our host, "but how did you gain permission to build on this site?"

"The farmer was easily persuaded to sell me some land. It helped that there was previously a castle on this very spot, although long since destroyed."

"What was it called?"

"Castell Coch."

"Was it also made of red sandstone?"

"No, it was not," the guest says. "It was constructed from the same material as the well. After it was destroyed, the people carried off the stones and used them to fortify their dwellings, but they also improved the enclosure of the well. They were making a point."

"Oh, what point?"

"The lords of the castle were not greatly loved. They had denied access, with some degree of success, to the well, which has been a place of power and healing for the people since before recorded history. When Glyndwr's men stormed the fortress, they made common cause with them."

"Alas, Morys, you have broached a topic of some disagreement between our honoured guest and me."

"Oh?"

Mrs. Roberts-Evans-Jones is most strongly of the opinion that it is wrong of me to try to forbid access to the well..."

"Wrong and foolish," she interjects, with not a little asperity.

"She brooks no opposition on this matter, as you see. But I maintain that there is no legal right of way and never has been. This traipsing around over private territory was not permitted, as has already been conceded, by the lords of the previous property on this site."

"Never allowed by the laws of the *sais*, I grant you. But sanctioned by long custom and in accordance with the laws given to our country by Hywl Dda."

The wind is crying out, seeking every cranny and crevice in the castle, which is far from proof against the weather, in spite of its recent construction. The candles on the long table shudder and paint temporary shadows on our livid hands and faces. The panelled walls recede, draped in darkness, creating the sense that the room is contracting around us, leaving only an island of uncertain light.

"Why our guest would even have it," Edwyn says, turning to me, "that I am in some danger from whatever tutelary spirit guards the well. This is a return to the creed of our pagan forefathers, is it not, Morys? And yet I thought our guest a Christian!"

"The saint guards the well. It is a holy place."

"So you and others have told me often enough, Mrs. Roberts-Jones-Evans. But he has no name does he, this saint, who appears never to have walked on this earth?"

"No name that you will find in any Romish calendar. Yet his spirit is real enough."

A silence, far from companionable, falls. When the conversation resumes, it is comprised of themes of no great moment. Mrs. Roberts-Evans-Jones is adamant in her refusal of more wine, but our host continues to drink freely. It is a relief when the lady bids us a muted farewell. The hour is late and I retire to bed, leaving Edwyn at the fireside to drink whiskey and reflect on the flames fanned by the draughts in the chimney. From my bedside window, I watch the swirl of snowflakes as they whiten then vanish, burnt-out stars taken back by darkness, restored to primordial absence, only to spark again, reignited by the never-fading inferno.

THE NEXT MORNING I awake to vast silence, sensing a world snow-muffled, its rivers chained in ice. I make my way to the window. The well's roof has been thatched in white; not a single footprint on the hill marks the track of man or beast; the sky is blank and birdless, as if it overlooked Lake Avernus. I was to have left after lunch today, but I predict that this will prove impossible. There is no choice but to presume for longer on my host's hospitality.

There is a knock on the door, and the servants enter with hot water. In answer to my enquiry as to whether their master is up, they reply that he is still abed—recovering from last night's libations, I assume. As the water is still too hot, I return to the window. To my surprise, the man that I had seen approaching the house is again walking towards the front door, his attire unaltered in spite of the bitter snow. I should have thought that even the hardiest hill farmer would not have refused to wear a coat in such conditions. This time I will beard the fellow and discover his business. Flinging a coat over my nightgown, I clatter down the stairs and, not waiting for his knock, I un-bolt the lock and open the door wide. Again, there is no one to be seen. At least, this is what I assume, until a sudden wind from the west flurries in, raising feathery streaks of snow. At the edge of my vision, I catch sight of a figure in white fleeing wildly down the slope, with both arms extended, as if about to take off and fly into the hills. As I turn towards it, it seems visible for a moment before a second gust frays its outlines—and then it vanishes.

Edwyn rises at midday, and in a bad humour. I find him once again by the fire, his head in his hands, a remedy for the previous night's intemperance in a tumbler close to hand. No doubt there will be strong liquor in this draft, as well as sugar, rose water, and ambergris.

"I fear I will have to stay with you a few days yet," I inform him. "Later, I will in-vestigate, but doubtless the roads will be impassable unless there is a great thaw."

He waves a hand, in what I take to be a gesture of assent. I decide to disturb him no longer. Shortly afterwards, I borrow a pair of sturdy boots left in the porch, and set out. There are no footprints leading either in the direction of the door or away from it; not even an imprint of a bird's claw. Since no further snow has fallen this morning, I am at a loss to explain how the working man walked over such pristine ground. I perceived him most clearly, and he seemed to have nothing of the phantom about him, no hint of having escaped from the security of the grave.

On the next day, Edwyn is impatient, ill at ease, pacing from room to room and star-ing out of one window after another. I am no longer in good odour, for he barely speaks to me unless I ask him a direct question; even then his answers are either laconic or elliptical. As to whether he is still suffering in the aftermath of his recent carousing, I am uncertain. It is not until evening, after he has taken a small glass of wine, that I tax him further.

"Are you expecting a visitor?" I ask. "One whose arrival is imminent?"

For a moment, I believe that he will not respond, as he continues to push his food around his plate and take sips of wine. Then he says, his manner most curt: "Isn't it clear enough? I'm keeping a look out for them."

"And they are?"

And now at last he relents somewhat, for he has ever been an advocate of plain speaking, and all this making of mysteries suits him ill. "The villagers."

"Are they coming to the well, even in this foul weather?"

"Yes, they are. They never rest. And it is not just to the well. Last night I heard them in the house."

"Surely not!"

"And they are everywhere in the grounds.

It is as if they mean to regain it all, down to the last clod of mud, every inch of grass, every stone and glow-worm."

"What do you mean to do?"

He shrugs, his expression wild, suffused with uncertainty. "I should never have invited that woman into this house. It has been worse since she was here. She is no object for ridicule. I had little idea of the extent she is in league with them. They say she is "a cunning woman"—and more than that it seems. She has a hold on them. I never thought that true till now."

"A *consuwyr*? Why...she seemed harmless enough. And she is of gentle birth, is she not?"

He gives me a black look and does not speak again.

That night I sleep badly, my dreams confused, connected only by grotesques, grinning, spitting, and gurning, their faces twisting, mouths pouring imprecations, as if the gargoyles on a church had deconsecrated themselves and come to life. At midnight, I awake with a start, convinced that demons are running up and down the stairs, laughing and chanting maledictions. In the morning, Edwyn is not to be found.

It is four days before the thaw. The servants find the master of the castle face down at the bottom of the well. On hearing their cries, I go down to join them. Recovering his cadaver brings further discoveries. Near him in the red pool of water are the remains of divers dead frogs, pierced with pins. There is also an abundance of broken slates, many with Edwyn Probert's name etched on them in ragged script. At last, I perceive that the local people come to the unknown saint's well as much to curse as to bless.

IT HAS BEEN over a year since the events that I have recorded took place. My narrative has been set down in a style that I hope will be found consonant with the disquiet that I felt in those days. Now time has placed some little distance between the calamity that befell my friend and the present moment, I am returning to my manuscript to add the information that I obtained over many months, and which may serve as a footnote to the nature of the forces that overwhelmed Castell Coch, although I fear no full explanation will ever be possible.

To my surprise, I discovered that I had been appointed as an executor of Edwyn's will and, in the exercise of my duties, I returned to his estate in the spring, although probate had not yet been granted. I found the place greatly changed. My carriage had reached the town before I realised that I had driven past my destination. Only by paying close attention to the topography, for the well is screened from the road by the grove, was I able to identify the spot. Of Castell Coch, there was no trace, its arched windows and turrets, its portcullis of a portico, gone, not even permitted an afterlife as a ruin; the whole edifice dissolved, leaving only an eerie absence and the outline of its foundations in the grass. The well had been re-roofed and rebuilt in red sandstone. Everything else, I presumed, had been carried off into the hills.

As I stood there, watching the red kites gliding far above me, I recalled how the morning that Edwyn's death was discovered, I heard, as clearly as if the craftsman was in the room with me, the sound of wood being sanded, the screws being turned, and with this came the scent of varnish, the soft music of the final polishing, the percussion of hammering.

That afternoon, a few hours after a servant had gone to the town to contact the undertaker, I saw a man dismounting a horse in the lane and then making his way to the entrance. As soon as I had clear sight of the fellow, I recognised him from his red neckerchief and singular gait: the elusive visitor I had observed on two former occasions. Yet this time there was a pronounced solidity about him; the sound of his footsteps firm on the path, his stark features delineated in the cold light. I understood that he was no deception conjured out air. I went down to meet him. Had he been to Castell Coch before? I asked. No, he replied. He would have had no cause. He was the carpenter, come to measure the corpse—for the coffin. And then I knew I had already heard the making of it from the saw's first rasp on bark to the knocking in of the last nail.

At Edwyn's wake, I told Mrs. Roberts-Jones-Evans this tale. She seemed not a whit surprised. "This is the *tolgeth*, the phantasm of a death foretold," she explained, allowing herself a hint of a smile, "and not uncommon in our part of Wales." Of her own part in my friend's tragedy, I am unsure; although it is said that her grandfather was in the timber trade. No doubt all that I had heard and witnessed came from the carpenter's other workshop, where what is not yet apparent in this world is fashioned and completed, made ready to move from one realm to the next.

Charles Wilkinson's publications include The Pain Tree and Other Stories *(London Magazine Editions, 2000). His stories have appeared in* Best Short Stories 1990 *(Heinemann),* Best English Short Stories 2 *(W.W. Norton, USA),* Best British Short Stories 2015 *(Salt),* Confingo, London Magazine *and in genre magazines and anthologies such as* Black Static, Interzone, The Dark Lane Anthology, Supernatural Tales, Theaker's Quarterly Fiction, Phantom Drift, Bourbon Penn, Shadows & Tall Trees, Nightscript, *and* Best Weird Fiction 2015 *(Undertow Books, Canada). His collections of strange tales and weird fiction,* A Twist in the Eye *(2016),* Splendid in Ash *(2018),* Mills of Silence *(2021) and* The Harmony of the Stares *(2022), appeared from Egaeus Press. Eibonvale Press published his chapbook of weird stories,* The January Estate, *in 2022. He lives in Wales.*

ELLEN K. '84

Out in the Cold

By Steve Rasnic Tem

THE ONLY INDICATION OF A HIGHWAY WAS THE SOILED TRACK UP ITS MIDDLE, AND THE SCATTERED PILES OF FILTH ALONG THE MARGINS LEFT FROM EARLIER PLOWING. IT OCCURRED TO JOSH THERE WAS NOTHING DIRTIER THAN DIRTY SNOW.

He stayed inside in this kind of weather. Now in his seventies, he'd become overly hesitant behind the wheel. He avoided driving when there was the slightest hint of rain. But he'd given himself until the new year to get a few things out of the family cabin before it went up for sale. His three adult children would get the proceeds. It would be a wonderful, if late, Christmas gift.

Josh hadn't told his kids about the sale, not that he imagined they would care. It had been over ten years since any of them visited their mountain retreat. He'd encouraged them to go up and take what they wanted, but they showed no interest, not in the furniture, not in any of the toys they'd loved as kids. He couldn't understand it. Raising those little kids had been among the best days of his life.

Now they had lives and families of their own, and his role was greatly diminished. April would have said that was the way life was supposed to work, but now he had no April to guide him. He had to figure old age out on his own.

They said they'd see him at Christmas, but it was already December twenty-first, and he'd heard no definite plans. Selling the cabin so they wouldn't have to deal with it after he was gone was a big present in itself. He couldn't wait to see their faces when he handed them the money.

He encountered little traffic once he left the city limits. He drove as slowly as he could get away with. He couldn't remember the last time he'd pulled a trailer, certainly not on icy roads. At least it was empty for the trip up. He figured he'd be okay as long as he didn't have to back up. One more thing to fret about. He wasn't sure if that would be necessary at the cabin. He hadn't seen the place himself in years, even though he'd kept paying the bills. A foolish waste of money. The cabin had been April's project, and he was reluctant to let it go. He'd always hoped—he wasn't sure what he'd hoped. More interest from the kids? A new love who would move into the mountains with him? He used to believe there might be a better life available somewhere. Living in grief made for a cold hereafter.

They were expecting more snow in the mountains, or had that already occurred? The sky was heavy with white, and as he drove around the curves and gazed beyond into the valleys below he couldn't always distinguish the white sky from the white ground. The trees were a green so dark they looked like black smears. Most of the landmarks he remembered from previous visits were erased. Those vast stretches of nothing were dangerously mesmerizing. He gripped the wheel, focusing on the vague suggestion of road ahead. Driving had become an act of faith and a strained reach for memory.

Josh was surprised by the lack of development, or maybe the snow obscured the details. The last time he'd been up here he'd seen numerous ongoing construction projects with fanciful names: Paradise Pines, Evergreen Acres, Lost Woods. He could find no signs of them now. Broken shacks and dark, collapsing shells lay tumbled off the hillsides. He imagined additional wreckage crushed beneath the snow.

He had a week's worth of food in the trunk, much more than he needed. Not that he was hungry. He was rarely hungry anymore. There might be some good meat still in the freezer at the cabin. Frozen meat lasts forever, doesn't it? He believed people had eaten mammoth meat in recent years with no reported harm. In the old days, the farmers slaughtered their animals around the solstice to stave off starvation and so they wouldn't have to feed them through the winter.

Today was the solstice, the shortest day and longest night of the year. Josh didn't exactly know what that meant, but he worried about making it to the cabin before nightfall. His eyes were no good anymore in the dark. Already gloom had descended from the ridge tops. All that white was turning into gray.

He hadn't passed another vehicle in some time, an hour or two. This seemed so unlikely he was afraid his trip had gone terribly wrong. It was four days before Christmas, one of the busiest travel days of the year. Families were reuniting. Friends were traveling to see friends. Yet there was no traffic on this mountain road. Perhaps he had taken a wrong turn somewhere. Perhaps he was on the wrong path entirely.

This wouldn't have happened if one of his adult children had agreed to come with him. He felt a sudden flash of anger which he struggled to tamp down. Best not to drive while angry. Best not harbor anger toward your children when all they were doing was trying to live their own lives.

Life should never be reduced to a tedious preparation for death. Josh didn't make New Year's resolutions, but next year he would do better. April would have been so disappointed in him.

He would need to make a rest stop soon. He was surprised he'd lasted this long without one. Another reason Josh didn't like going out. He was always looking for a bathroom. One of the more inconvenient aspects of aging. He hadn't yet experienced any humiliating accidents, but he knew those days were coming.

It had been a mistake to start thinking of such things, because now he had to go badly. Still no signs of a gas station, or of any other commercial establishment. He should pull over to the side of the road, but that seemed unwise since he couldn't tell where the pavement ended. Getting stuck or driving into a ditch seemed a distinct possibility.

Josh slammed on the brakes. There was no traffic and no one around to see him. He kept the engine running, set the emergency brake, unbuckled, and stepped out of the car. He kept the door open as a modesty shield, pulled down his sweatpants, and began urinating on the snow-packed road.

Those faded, mustard-colored sweatpants. He hadn't worn them in years. He wasn't sure why he'd put them on today, or this stained red sweatshirt. He thought they'd be good in the cold, but they weren't, and if he got them wet they'd be unbearable. He wasn't thinking. The decision to go today was a sudden one. He realized he'd left his cell phone at home on the dining room table.

What a foolish thing to do. There was no phone in the cabin.

He was in an area of the mountains which might have been recognizable if the landmarks weren't smothered in white. There was something familiar in the way the slopes came down to the roadbed, and how a particular ridge was thick with trees but with a bald spot in the middle.

The air tasted of cold and a decaying green beneath the snow. They'd scattered April's ashes somewhere near here at her request, and he was ashamed he wasn't sure of the exact location. There had been a particular turn in the road with a spectacular view of the valley beyond. It might have been behind him now, or just ahead.

A cousin tried to comfort him with "things happen for a reason." What a terrible lie. They never spoke again. He and April always understood one of them would die before the other, but he'd always believed he would be the first to go. His lack of control over this one basic element of reality enraged him.

The cold had a peculiar lure. Here he was standing with his ass hanging out and yet he felt no discomfort. A thought came, unbidden, *how far can the dead travel through the still, cold air?* Both his parents died during the winter. He was now older than either of them. He'd read that the mortality rates for the elderly went up significantly during the winter, when it became unexpectantly easy to pass through that dark curtain and leave the life you used to love, not knowing what was waiting on the other side. But it seemed such a shame, stopped from seeing another summer of possibilities.

And now the sun was beginning to enter its grave. Josh glanced up at the wooded ridge, looking for signs of sunset through the clouds, wondering how much time he had before darkness fell and it became dangerous for him to drive. A large animal watched him from the edge of a straggly copse of trees. He knew what it was, but he couldn't find the name for it. This had been happening more frequently. It was worse when it happened in front of the kids. He wanted to say *moose*, even though he knew it wasn't a moose. He'd never even seen a moose except

in pictures. It was an m-something. It knew Josh did not belong here.

He looked down at his feet. There was blood on the snow. He checked himself over. The blood was coming out of his fingertips, from under his nails. He'd had issues with bleeding in the past, but nothing like this. Maybe it was the cold. People sometimes said the cold cut like a knife. Could that be true? He should have worn gloves. Had he even brought gloves?

He pulled his sweatpants up and got back into the car. He'd deal with the bleeding later. He needed to get to the cabin before it was too dark to find the way. He needed to eat something. He didn't feel at all hungry, but he couldn't remember the last time he'd eaten anything.

A few minutes later he was at the intersection where the feeder road leading to their cabin joined the main highway. There used to be a sign, but Josh couldn't find one. It had been knocked down or stolen. They'd had a lot of problems with stolen highway signs in these mountains. He had no idea why. Some people got off on getting other people lost. He recognized the two large trees bracketing the road. They were enormous and scarred from drivers misjudging the angle and striking them. For the first time that day he felt confident he was on the right track. The light was quickly draining out of the afternoon. He drove carefully between the two trees but had to back up and restart when a corner of the trailer caught on one of the trunks. He squeezed by with a soft scraping sound. The cabin was a couple of miles away he thought, more or less.

A battered red post indicated the entrance to the driveway. Nothing had been plowed here. All the neighbors on this lane were also part-time. He'd forgotten how thick the trees grew on either side of the road into the property, so close together they were practically a wall. The limbs from both sides joined overhead, creating a cathedral-like ceiling. So, it wasn't twilight here. There was nothing ambiguous about it. Here it was full dark, full night, and all he could see was what his headlights picked out: dark trunks with shining stripes of snow down their sides, the burning eyes of animals whose bodies blended into the underbrush, the narrow ribbon of brilliant snow unrolling out of the blackness ahead of him, a difficult path back into what had once been a wonderful life. Josh had been skeptical about getting the place, reluctant to spend the money. But April had been so right about this, as she had been about almost everything else.

Eventually the path widened, the trees shying away from the car, and Josh could see the dim outline of walls and roof, porch, and a flickering illumination coming from behind the windows which should not have been there. He knew the drive curved here to make a parking spot in front of the porch, but because of the snow Josh could see no trace of it. There was nothing he could do but hope his memory guided him correctly.

He struck something with his right front bumper, and there was a soft crunch and a bump as he drove over something. But the car was in the right position, so he stopped and turned off the ignition.

He sat for a few moments listening to the soft ticking of the warm engine. He hoped he could get it started again when it came time to leave. That wasn't what he should be worried about, but he'd rather worry about that than how a fire could be burning in the cabin's fireplace, because now he could see and smell the smoke drifting from the chimney.

He rolled down the driver's side window an inch or so to make sure it wasn't the car he was smelling. Wood smoke, the slightly sweet, somewhat spicy scent of cedar. It was what they'd always burned—there was so much of it here. The smoke made his mouth water, and he was thinking he'd fry some meat for dinner. It was the first time he'd felt hungry all day. So, he'd be eating meat, assuming whoever was living in the family cabin did not murder him first.

Josh looked around the front and back seat for a weapon. He didn't own a gun. He did own an axe, but it was somewhere inside the cabin. Groping around the passenger side floor his hand landed on his big heavy flashlight. He doubted he could do much damage with it, and somehow that was a kind of relief, but at least it filled his hand with some weight.

He stared out the window, afraid. If something came for him out of the darkness he might not see it in time.

He climbed out of the car conscious of how ridiculous he must look in his blood-stained yellow sweatpants, old tennis shoes (had he really left his boots at home?), and ratty red sweatshirt. He'd brought along an old jacket, but he wasn't sure where he'd packed it. He glanced at his hands. The bleeding had stopped, but now his fingers were a sticky brown color. He tightened his hand on the flashlight and made a couple of short practice swings, attempting to feel powerful.

A branch encased in ice hung low over the car. It still had its leaves, each preserved as if under glass. A breeze tickled them, eliciting a wind-chime sound. The snow leading up to the steps came to mid-calf. Josh's feet went numb almost immediately. Less snow covered the steps and the porch itself, and he wondered if these had been recently swept. There was a large woodpile on the porch by the door. He couldn't remember if it were similar in size to the one they'd left behind years ago. Several rough-made timber chairs were scattered about the porch, a couple on their sides. Josh could see his kids in them. They loved that rustic furniture when they were small.

He grabbed the doorknob firmly and turned it. It was unlocked, which of course it shouldn't be. He pushed the door open and stepped inside, ducking his head and shoulders protectively.

A frantic look around revealed no one in ambush. The fire in the grate was still going but needed tending. Ashes had spread across the hearth, and it needed a new log. There was a pile of logs on the floor nearby, roughly hewn, and the axe leaned against them. He wondered if he should put down the flashlight and pick that up instead.

He was aware of a fine dust filling the air. He wondered if he might be breathing in bits of dead things. He thought of shaking that nonsense out of his head. The situation required alertness.

"Hello! Anyone here?" Maybe calling out wasn't the right thing to do. Josh had no experience in these matters. He waited for a response, listening for sounds from the bedrooms, maybe a window opening for an escape. The cabin looked as if someone might be nesting here, but he could see no indication any cleaning had occurred. The living room floor was covered with scraps of newspaper and clothing, old toys arranged in flanks and columns before the fireplace. Many of the toys were broken. His little boys sometimes played so rough they resembled a pack of wolves. But they insisted on keeping these broken bits, refusing to throw anything away. Maybe they considered them trophies.

A dead branch leaned against the wall by the front window, the family's abandoned decorations creating dusty Christmas adornment. No attempt had been made to polish or even clean the ornaments before hanging them. The wax figures of Santa and angels were so grimy they appeared furred.

Josh opened the door to the bedroom he and April once shared. The bare mattress was soiled and layered in leaves. Decaying sheets and blankets had been arranged to cover the floor. The kids' room was in similar shape, with the bunkbed mattresses stacked in a corner. The beds themselves were gone. Josh wondered if they might have been used for firewood. More toys made a pile in the center of the room. He hadn't realized they'd left behind so many. Or so many clothes. There was an extensive wardrobe of small children's outfits scattered around the bedroom. He recognized some of them: the matching, red-striped shirts his two boys wore in summer, his daughter's yellow sundresses. Some months all she would wear was yellow.

Some of the clothing had been carefully arranged, laid out on the floor as outfits as if in preparation to get the children dressed for the day. Shoes, socks, and underwear, matching shorts and shirts, sundresses with socks and tights, a little girl's delicate shoes. There was something almost sweet about the gesture, and subtly disturbing.

The bathroom was in awful shape, and he spared it only a quick glance. The kitchen looked greasy. There appeared to have been a range fire at some point (which never happened when they were here as far as he could remember). At least no food had been left out.

The refrigerator was unclean, but empty. He wasn't sure if it was still working.

The only place left to look for an intruder was the back porch. He proceeded with the flashlight held in front of him like a prod. He had no idea why he was holding it that way. The door was stuck—he had to use his shoulder. He wasn't disappointed to find nothing more than the old chest freezer on the other side, which didn't have a fan, so he couldn't tell if it was still running. He managed to force it open. It was iced over, but beneath the ice he could see the shadows of packages lurking.

He looked through the porch's back window. The snow was deeper behind the cabin. It appeared as if some had slid off the roof in a tiny avalanche, effectively blocking the back door. There was little to see from this vantage. A profound blankness covered everything.

Josh had no idea what to do. He should have been paying more attention to the place. He couldn't very well sell the cabin as is. Who would buy it in this condition? He didn't have the expertise, stamina, or funds to get it into sellable shape. More immediately, how was he going to protect himself from his squatter until he could leave again, and alert the police?

Back in the living room he tended to the fire, sweeping up the ashes, moving a couple of new logs around until they had enough air to catch. He stuffed some paper into the gaps. The pieces went up with a satisfying *whump*.

So, his squatter must have gone out. All Josh had to do, he thought, was keep the trespasser out until daybreak. He could barricade the door and block the windows, but he still might have to stay awake all night. But he might not be able to drive out of here safely. He checked his watch. It was almost eight. But he'd been here for only a short time. He had no idea when sunrise was supposed to be. It was the longest night, or was that the night before? The difference was probably only a few minutes.

He felt so foolish. He'd planned to do this for the kids, but clearly, he had let them down. Not that it mattered now. He reminded himself a life can only be lived forward, not back. Grief and regrets were irrelevant to whatever he might do with his time tomorrow.

There was clean bedding, food, other things in the car Josh could really use right now. But he was afraid to venture out. That person might be waiting. Even if the invader didn't carry a weapon, it was doubtful Josh was much of a match for him.

He pushed a cabinet against the door and sat for a time staring into the fire. It felt incredibly relaxing. He could do this at home, so why hadn't he been?

The fire was blazing. He felt the heat in his face and chest but nowhere else. He desperately wanted to close his eyes, but he did not dare.

He caught himself dozing and sat up with a start. This wouldn't do. He stared at his hands. They didn't hurt, and they weren't bleeding anymore, but they looked a horror. At least he could clean himself up. He went to the kitchen sink and turned on the faucet. There was a delay, and he worried the pipes might be frozen, when the water came. He splashed some on both hands. There wasn't any soap, so he rubbed them together vigorously. Muddy-colored water drifted across his fingers, and there was the faintest scent of blood. He felt hungry again, but he wasn't sure what he was hungry for. This had become a problem in recent years. He was often without an appetite, and when he was hungry, nothing sounded good. Many of his meals he left half-eaten. His GP gave him a list of foods he should eat—for his kidneys, for his heart. His children shared nutritional recommendations they'd gathered from the internet. None of it excited him.

Now his hands were wet, and he could find no towels. He ran into the kids' room, grabbed something off the floor, and rubbed his hands in it. He thought he'd washed off all the blood, but the garment stained a deep red. He examined the cloth—one of his daughter's yellow sun dresses. He felt like a fiend.

His hands were wrong. They were sharply bent and ended in long slivers of bone. He ran back into the living room and tried to get a better look at them in front of the fire. His hands appeared spotted in the firelight but were otherwise normal. He looked at his watch. It was after midnight.

He spent a few minutes sorting through the army of toys arranged on the floor. He remembered most of them, cars and planes and anthropomorphized fire trucks, several dolls with key facial features marred or chewed off. He wondered if the cabin might have rats. According to his lying watch it was four AM.

He saw his children playing on the floor with their armies of toys, barking orders at imaginary friends, April cooking in the kitchen, Josh either helping or trying to stay out of her way. How many times had this scene been repeated over the years? He remembered his own childhood, playing with his own brothers, and even when he was little, yearning for a life away from the family which knew everything about him. When it snowed he'd run out in the cold, his mother screaming after him to put on a jacket, just so he could have five minutes alone.

He didn't need to find a way to be alone. Alone would always be with him. His own children would figure that out someday. He could tell them from his own experience, but it was probably something they didn't want to hear.

He heard noises outside, branches breaking under the weight of ice and snow, the sound reverberating for miles as the dark air cracked from the cold. He looked at his watch. It was six AM.

He went to the front window, thinking it might be getting light out again. He didn't know what time sunrise was, but didn't it start getting lighter before then?

A shadow was sitting in one of the chairs on the porch. It turned its head and stared at him: long dirty hair and beard, clothing like rotting leaves, or it might even be his skin, falling off and dirtying the porch. Josh thought of a Santa Claus fallen on hard times.

Was he the one who had been staying here? He didn't look all that dangerous. Sick certainly, dying perhaps. Josh couldn't let him just die out there, could he? When a wandering stranger comes to you seeking food and shelter you need to let him in. April would have.

Not that the man was necessarily seeking. He hadn't bothered to knock on the door. Folks like him, at least in the stories, they always had an important message, or judgement, to deliver. By the time Josh got to the door to open it the shabby man was standing their waiting.

They sat together in the living room without speaking for hours. Seven AM. Eight. Nine. Still with no sunrise. The longest night of the year, but Josh didn't believe this was what everyone meant.

"You should take better care of yourself," Josh finally said to the man. What was he thinking? It seemed a foolish remark to say to a stranger. But April used to say the same thing to him, and April was far from foolish.

When the man spoke it was in an old man's voice, a voice which sounded shockingly familiar. "There are wolves out here, did you know? They're hungry. Hunger will make you desperate and bold."

"I always heard there were bears up here. We warned the kids about them, but we never saw any."

"The bears hibernate. It's their special power, to be able to sleep that long. For the females, it's an especially pregnant dark. They give birth toward the end of their long sleep, did you know? It must be like sinking into a dream of childbirth, then when you wake up in the spring the children are there waiting, begging you to take them outside to smell the flowers."

"That's the young for you," Josh said. "They can hardly wait to get outside. Eventually they don't bother to come back."

He thought the stranger was smiling. It was hard to tell. There was so much caked on dirt, so much wounded flesh. Bits were falling off onto the floor. Josh would have a great deal of cleaning to do after this man left.

The heat of the fire hastened the dissolution of dirt and mud. First the man's battered tennis shoes were revealed, then the mustard-colored sweats, then the ragged red top. He brought out his hands and tapped them playfully on his knees, the fingers no more than bones, long and curled and sharp.

"Waking up every morning still alive, it's a big surprise, isn't it?" Josh said. "Then you have to decide what to do with the day. Sometimes that's a horror too much to bear."

In the old times they believed the lack of sunlight was caused by monsters who stole the sun. Josh went out onto the porch and sat in the dark waiting for the return of the light. It never came.

Steve Rasnic Tem's writing career spans over 45 years, including more than 500 published short stories, 17 collections, 8 novels, miscellaneous poetry and plays. His collaborative novella with his late wife Melanie, The Man on the Ceiling, *won the World Fantasy, Bram Stoker, and International Horror Guild awards in 2001. He has also won the Bram Stoker, International Horror Guild, and British Fantasy Awards for his solo work, including* Blood Kin, *winner of 2014's Bram Stoker for novel. Earlier this year he received the Horror Writers Association Lifetime Achievement Award. Visit his website at:* www.stevetem.com

THE LAST TRAIN
BY SIMON BESTWICK

COMING TO BONE STREET'S ALWAYS A SHOCK TO PEOPLE, ESPECIALLY WHEN THEY REALISE THEY CAN'T GO BACK. Oh, you *can* turn around and go back under the viaduct at the bottom of the street—the only way in or out—but Bone Street's the one place the Closers can't follow you. If you go back, they'll be waiting; no one knows exactly what happens then, but we all knew, the moment we sensed them on our trail, that whatever it was would be terrible.

And so there you are, confined to a cobbled street where half the buildings are boarded up and the sole green space is six feet square with a decidedly manky-looking apple tree in the middle of it, with a bench to eat your sandwiches on. Not everyone can bear it. Some *do* walk back under the viaduct; others hang themselves, cut their wrists, or more often drink themselves to death.

But generally speaking, if you last the first few months, you're here for the long haul. Now and again, though, people get the Bone Street Blues, as we call them: a kind of cabin fever, a yearning for home. Impossible, of course, because the viaduct is strictly one-way, and it's the only way out or in.

Or so we all thought.

I GOT MARRIED, a few months ago, to Sadie, one of the girls from Dahlia's massage parlour. She's only there part-time now; I needed help behind the bar at the Station Hotel, and she was glad of the chance to change careers.

Sadie is, beyond a doubt, the best thing that's happened to me since I came here, perhaps the best ever. She's a genuinely good person, which is a rarity anywhere, but on Bone Street in particular: kind, sweet-natured, gentle. She's also tiny and slender, looking far younger than her thirty years, so she tends to bring out most people's protective side.

Pretty much everyone adores her; I'm not exactly sure why she loves *me*, but I'm very glad she does. So my first question—when she said she was worried about Kerry—was to ask what I could do.

"I don't know, Tim." She curled up against me in bed. "Pretty sure she's got the Blues."

"Oh, Christ."

"She's been bad lately. You not noticed?"

"I *had* thought she was keeping to herself a bit."

Kerry was a dark-haired, dark-eyed woman of about forty. She was tall and leggy, with a proud high-cheekboned face that made her look decidedly forbidding when she wanted to; she was in high demand at Dahlia's as a dominatrix. But under a very hard-nosed front she had a softer, more motherly side, which Sadie (being Sadie) had brought out during her time at the massage parlour.

Usually, when the girls and boys from Dahlia's came to the bar, they'd all gather round a table for a few drinks, cackling ever more raucously over the stories they exchanged. But in recent weeks Kerry had sat in a corner by herself, drinking a succession of neat gins in silence. She'd lost weight, too. I hadn't realised how much until that night: her table had been directly under one of the brighter lamps, which had thrown her gauntness into sharp relief.

"She's been talking about Brandon a lot, when she's pissed," said Sadie. "Her little boy. And you know she's not a big drinker, normally. Not since—you know."

If the Closers come after you, it's because you've taken a life. It doesn't have to be premeditated, or malicious. It can be accidental or even, as in Sadie's case, self-defence. It doesn't happen to everyone with blood on their hands, of course, just some; the lucky ones find their way here.

In Kerry's case, there'd been a drunken scuffle on a girl's night out, at the Printworks in Manchester. She couldn't even remember what had started the altercation, with a blonde woman she'd never even seen before; only the last few seconds of screaming and shoving before the blonde lost her balance, fell off the kerb and cracked her head on the tarmac.

Kerry ran when the police came. Maybe she'd already sensed the Closers drawing near—she wouldn't have stood a chance against them locked in a police cell. And since her son was at home with the baby-sitter, she never got to say goodbye. Not even so much as one last look.

That'll prey on anyone's mind.

"I don't want anything bad to happen to her," Sadie whispered.

I hugged her. "Me neither, love."

"Will you keep an eye on her? I will, too."

We'd both seen the Bone Street Blues before. Sadie knew as well as me there's

very little you can do: it either passes or, one way or another, kills the sufferer. But that's easily said when it's not your friend, or when the woman you love's not asking.

"Course I will, sweetheart."

BONE STREET has a limited list of entertainments, the main ones being booze and whatever pleasures of the flesh you can afford with one or more consenting adults at Dahlia's. But despite its name, the chicken shawarmas at Ahmed's Kebab House of Death are very nice, and don't carry the risk of cirrhosis or an STI, so the next morning I decided to treat myself.

It was a warm spring day; I thought about sitting on the bench at the green to eat, but it was already occupied. I barely recognised Kerry at first; normally immaculately made-up and smartly attired in a trouser suit or little black dress, today she wore jogging pants, trainers, and a baggy, food-stained sweatshirt, face scrubbed and hair scraped back in what we used to call a Salford Facelift.

She was staring fixedly up the street, at old Mr. Polodski's Mini-Mart. She was smoking, and from the pile of ground-out cigarettes between her feet, had been for a while; if I'm honest I hesitated to approach her at first, but having promised Sadie, I headed over. "Hi, Kerry."

"Tim."

She scooted up, motioning to the seat beside her. After a moment, I sat down. "How you doing?"

Kerry shrugged. She looked even more gaunt in daylight, not to mention tired and ill: her skin was patchy, she had deep bags under her eyes, which were badly bloodshot, and she reeked of smoke and gin and stale perfume.

"Sick of this place," she said at last. I couldn't think of any reply, but she went on. "Don't know how anyone stands it. Suppose no one does, really. Kills us all off, this place, one way or the other. Know what I mean?"

Unfortunately, I did. While there were old people here, I couldn't think of anyone who'd actually *grown* old on Bone Street. "Not much you can do about it, though," I said.

"Isn't there?"

Kerry was staring at the Mini-Mart again. "If you're looking for a magic carpet, love," I said, "I don't think he sells them."

"Don't be a bigger twat than you have to," she said, almost absently. "Think about it, Tim. We get food here, don't we? Old Polodski's got it all, and he never runs out. Same with Ahmed." She nodded towards the kebab house. "We can even order stuff, if we want something in particular. But where does it *come* from, Tim? Magic carpet, maybe?"

"Don't be daft."

"Then how?"

"How should I know?"

"No one seems to." She pointed at the Mini-Mart. "Not even old man Polodski, and you'd think he'd have some idea, wouldn't you?"

"They just get left outside, don't they?" I said. "Polodski brings them in every morning."

"But left by *who*? Eh, Tim? Someone's got to bring that stuff in. Someone comes every few nights, when we're all asleep—somehow manages to make sure no one's about when they do. They leave whatever's on order there—meat, veg, fags, booze—then bugger off again. Someone, somehow, comes and goes. *Goes*, Timmy. Which means there's a way out."

"Does it?" I said. "Even if there is, there's still the Closers."

"Sod 'em," she said. "I don't care if they get me. Long as I see Brandon first."

"And if they get *him* when they come for you?"

"They don't do that."

"How do you know?" Although the Closers could only scent people who'd killed, what happened to any bystanders present when they caught up with you was the kind of unanswered question often pondered after too many Scotches in the Station Hotel's bar. Even if the Closers didn't attack them directly, for all we knew the very sight of them was lethal.

"They *don't*," she said. "If they come for me again, I'll run. But I'll see him first. Say goodbye, if nothing else." She nodded towards Polodski's again. "There's a way out, and I'm gonna find it."

• • •

THAT CONVERSATION did nothing for Sadie's peace of mind, and the two brief talks she subsequently managed with Kerry at work were no more help. She became more worried still when Kerry stopped turning up at the massage parlour at all, and couldn't be found at her flat.

I began to wonder if she'd actually found a way out after all, till Mr. Polodski reported she'd come into the Mini-Mart for bottled water, sandwiches, and a bottle of gin at two a.m., looking even more haggard and dishevelled than before. A couple of nights later she ventured into Ahmed's for a burger, but neither of them saw where she slipped away to afterwards.

Sadie tried standing in the middle of the street and shouting for Kerry to come out and talk, but without success. All the rest of us could do was exchange sad, resigned glances. No one remembered anyone with so bad a case of the Bone Street Blues ever recovering: if she wasn't dead already, it was just a matter of time.

But Sadie, being Sadie, wouldn't accept that, which was my big concern. I was sorry about Kerry, but if you let something like that get to you too much, you'll go down the same way. I didn't want to lose Sadie too.

About a fortnight after I met Kerry on the green, I was shaken awake in the middle of the night. Startled, I lashed out reflexively; thankfully Sadie leapt back in time.

I immediately knew things must be bad, or she'd never have woken me like that. My reaction was a nasty legacy from my Army days, one I'd warned her about when we first got together, for her own safety.

At first I thought my worst fears were being realised: she was dressed in trainers, jog-pants and sweatshirt with her hair scraped back and face scrubbed: she could have been Kerry's clone, down to the wild look in her eyes.

"Come on! Fast!" She pointed at the window. "We've got to help her."

"What—?"

"It's Kerry."

Sadie explained, bouncing up and down with frustration as I pulled on my clothes, how, unable to sleep, she'd been watching the street for any sign of Kerry, as on numerous nights before. She'd left her post to pee, and when she'd come back she'd seen the pavement outside Polodski's stacked with boxes of groceries; as she'd stared, several more had been pushed around the corner of the alley beside the shop to join the rest.

All had been still for a few seconds after that; then there'd been fresh movement from an abandoned building opposite the Mini-Mart, as a tall, thin shape had squeezed itself through a boarded-up doorway and dashed across the street. In retrospect, it made perfect sense: what better position could Kerry have found to watch the place she was convinced held the key to her escape? Either way, she'd already disappeared down the alley; I was still lacing my trainers when Sadie, finally out of patience, bolted down the stairs.

I caught up with her outside the Mini-Mart and grabbed her arm, putting my finger to my lips. She nodded, and I moved past her to the alley corner. I doubted whoever was making the deliveries would react well to being discovered, given the lengths they'd gone to conceal themselves; if there was any trouble I'd rather meet it before Sadie. Although chances were it would have gone through Kerry first.

The streetlights and the halogen lamps in the Mini-Mart's back yard glinted off the alley cobbles; there was no sign of Kerry, or anyone else. Motioning to Sadie to stay put, I began picking my way down, gritting my teeth when footsteps from behind announced she'd ignored me completely.

Polodski's yard, bare and brilliantly lit, offered no hiding place; besides, it was surrounded by railings on all sides, with the one gate leading to it locked and chained. Then I heard movement from the far end of the alley: from the footpath beside the beck.

The beck emerges from a culvert beside the viaduct and runs the length of Bone Street before disappearing into another under Bone Square. It's the colour of stewed tea and barely a foot deep, with a bed of rubble, broken glass, and rusty cans. Each embankment is reinforced by a brick wall; the one on our side is level with the street, but the one opposite goes up as high as

you can see. Although that isn't particularly high, as a misty haze always hangs over the beck, rendering everything above a certain height invisible.

Long before my time, two people supposedly tried scaling the wall in search of a way out. One fell and was smashed to pulp; the other climbed on up into the mist and was never heard of again. Unless you counted the screaming. It's generally assumed that even if you get over the wall, the Closers, or something equally bad, are waiting for you.

A narrow footpath with a rusty safety railing runs along the embankment. There are half a dozen lamps; most are broken, but the nearest one to us was working, and in its glow we saw two thin, pale hands release the railings and vanish. Sadie ran forward; I chased after her, and we peered down. A wrought-iron ladder was bolted to the embankment wall; at the bottom, I glimpsed Kerry's dark hair just before she vanished again, this time seemingly under the embankment itself.

At that point, I hesitated. Kerry was clearly on the heels of whoever was making the deliveries, and I was more certain than ever they wouldn't welcome snoopers. We might be too late to do her any good, and only in time to put ourselves in danger. Which I might have risked on my own account, but not on Sadie's too.

Unfortunately, Sadie had already taken that decision out of my hands; before I could say or do anything, she was over the railing and climbing down as well. Gritting my teeth, I followed once more.

Buddleia bushes sprouted from the brickwork, and tall grass and cow parsley at the river's edge. Behind them was an archway; from above, the overgrowth hid it completely, even in winter. Beyond the vegetation, the archway led into a dark, damp tunnel. At the end a light gleamed on tiled walls; I glimpsed a thin running shadow as Kerry reached the far end and disappeared from view yet again.

"Come on," Sadie whispered, pulling me forward. I resisted for a moment, but she glared back at me again with a look that simply said *She's my friend*, which, for Sadie, was the be-all and end-all.

Love makes fools of the best of us, so I nodded. And forward we went.

There was a smell of damp brick, moss, and decay. The roof dripped, and the floor was uneven; Sadie grabbed a tight hold of my arm for support, which ironically saved me from falling when I stood on some broken masonry and nearly turned an ankle. We went as fast as we dared, encouraged by how quickly Kerry had covered the ground, speeding up as we neared the end and the glow from ahead illuminated the floor.

The brick tunnel opened into a square, white-tiled chamber lit by stark fluorescent lights in the walls, with another tunnel—also tiled—leading off. Faint, unplaceable sounds drifted down it.

Sadie's grip shifted from my arm to my hand. For the first time since she'd dashed out in pursuit of Kerry, she looked uneasy; if she could ever have been persuaded to turn back, it was then. But if Sadie cared about someone, she'd do anything for them; she'd never forgive herself if I talked her into pulling back now. Or, probably, me.

The tunnel walls were lined with yellowed posters from half a dozen different decades: *An American Werewolf In London. Royal Vinolia Tooth Paste. The Beatles' Yellow Submarine. Omo Adds Brightness To Whiteness. Cinzano Does. Dig For Victory Now.* The sounds from up ahead became louder: a hum of power, a hiss of compressed air or steam.

We emerged from the tunnel onto an underground railway platform. There were no logos or insignia on the walls, just more old posters and a large plaque bearing the words BONE STREET. There was a black tunnel entrance at either end, and standing at the platform itself, a train.

It gave off a faint electric hum, along with the hissing sounds we'd heard; curls of steam rose from underneath it as it did. The lead-grey, unmarked carriages were tubular and flat-ended, the gaps between them sealed with concertinaed bands of black, rubberised material. The train's windows were lit, but opaque with dust; inside the driver's cab, something blurred and shadowy moved.

When someone grabbed my arm and pulled, I almost yelled aloud, but managed not to; nor did Sadie, although she did say "Kes?" before another voice hissed: "Sh! In here!"

The platform had two alcoves with benches set into them; what I hadn't noticed —as we'd been staring in completely the wrong direction—had been the doorway we were standing next to. It seemed, in the light from the platform, to lead into a small office of some kind—I made out a desk and chairs, covered in dust, just before Kerry shut the door behind us, whispering "Down."

We crouched in silence, while the train hissed and hummed. It still wasn't completely dark: there was a window in the door, reinforced with wire-mesh. Like those on the train it was filthy, but it let enough light through to show Kerry's hollow face and wetly glistening eyes; I wasn't sure if she was crying or oyster-eyed from all the gin.

"Nearly made it," she whispered. "All the doors were open. But they shut as I got there. But now I know. Next time, I'll—"

Another, much louder hiss came from the platform, accompanied by a series of whirrs and clunks. Kerry's hand tightened on my arm. "The doors."

There was a loud clang, then a heavy thump as someone dropped down onto the platform.

"The Driver," whispered Kerry.

Then the clang again—the cab door, maybe, slamming shut?—followed by what sounded to me like footsteps, albeit very strange ones. Next, a thump of heavy objects, and a scuffing, scraping sound as they were pushed along the platform.

As the noise approached the office, Kerry let out a little gasp. "He's got more boxes to drop off—we can—"

The sound abruptly stopped. Kerry released my arm to clap her hands over her mouth; now Sadie clutched me instead, her small fingers digging in like claws. Seconds ticked by, as we waited for the Driver—for some reason, I automatically put the name in capitals—to open the office door. And then? When I tried to contemplate it, my mind turned grey and blank. As Kerry knew well, any kind of physical confrontation can all too easily get fatally out of hand, and the one law on Bone Street is *thou shalt not kill,* no matter what the circumstances. It revokes your sanctuary from the Closers: you either go back under the viaduct or they come and get you. To say nothing of what might become of our much-needed supplies.

There was a long, heavy exhalation, and then the Driver began moving again—across the platform, down the tunnel and back towards the surface.

Silence returned. Kerry straightened up, peering through the window, then grabbed the handle and pushed the door wide.

"Kes—" Sadie began.

But Kerry wasn't listening; before we could stop her, she'd rushed across the platform, towards an open carriage door.

Sadie plunged after her: with her long legs Kerry reached the train in seconds, but Sadie wasn't far behind. I caught them both up, and the three of us went through the doors so close together that when Kerry abruptly stopped to avoid a collision with something hanging from the ceiling, Sadie and I piled into her, and the three of us went sprawling.

The carriage floor was thick with dust, which sent us all into coughing fits and made our eyes stream, but there was more solid detritus there too: tatters of some thin, cottony fabric that clung unpleasantly to my fingers, and hard, yellowish-white objects that were smooth in some places and porous in others. Different pieces, in different shapes.

I'd seen such things before, but it took a couple of seconds to remember where. Just as it dawned, Kerry let out a hollow, despairing moan.

When I looked up, I saw heavy sacks made from some white material suspended from the ceiling; my first thought was that this was how goods for Bone Street were stored in transit. But then I saw they weren't hanging from hooks but stuck directly to the ceiling. And then I saw what the sacks contained.

Some had been hanging there so long they'd begun to unravel, exposing their contents. The remains inside the one directly above us were wholly skeletonised, only held together by the remaining webbing. Older ones had come apart completely, hence the

bone fragments littering the floor. Another cocoon, newer and cleaner-looking than the rest, was unbroken except where a mummified hand, the colour and texture of wood, protruded, hooked into an agonised claw.

"No." Kerry was crying openly now, staring up at the nearest cocoon as though it contained her own son—which I suppose that, from her own point of view, it might as well have. "No, no, no."

Sadie slipped her arm around Kerry's shoulders. "We need to get back in the office, sweetheart. Before that thing comes back."

Kerry shook her head, still sobbing. I was tempted to drag her out forcibly, but she'd almost certainly fight if I did, which would most likely get one of us injured or worse, and then there was the noise to consider. Best to let Sadie persuade her. I turned to check the platform for any sign of the Driver's return; as I did, there was a loud pneumatic hiss. I had a split-second of the worst kind of realisation, where you simultaneously know what's going to happen and that it's too late to do anything about it. And then every set of carriage doors slammed shut.

"Oh *shit*," said Sadie, summing up the situation perfectly. Kerry moaned again.

"Easy," I said. There'd been no sign of the Driver; chances were the doors must close automatically after a certain time. I couldn't see a button to reopen them by the doors themselves, which meant there must be a central control. There might be one on the outside of the train, but that would be no use to us. Or there might be one in the Driver's cab.

I shouldered my way through the hanging bodies. The handle of the cabin door turned, but it was securely locked. There was a glass panel in it, as impenetrably dirty as the windows; I thumped on it, but it was thick and solid, unyielding. I ran back to the doors and the three of us tried digging our fingers into the join to prise them apart, but they wouldn't budge.

"Now what?" whispered Sadie.

I crouched and studied the door mechanism. Each door was driven shut by a piston running from a sleeve on the carriage wall, and each sleeve had a metal housing at its far end, apparently seamless but connected to several thin copper pipes running up from the floor.

"Okay," I said. "Air or steam must get pumped through these, to drive the piston. If the pressure from those is holding the door shut, then if we break one or more of them—"

Sadie grabbed my shoulder, so hard it hurt, and put her hand over my mouth. Kerry had covered her own mouth with both hands; in the hush, I heard something moving across the platform, back towards the train.

No wonder the footsteps we'd heard before had sounded strange. When I looked again at the hanging corpses, I realised my mistake: I'd assumed the Driver must be human.

The cabin's outer door opened, then slammed shut again. Any second now the train would be in motion, leaving Bone Street behind. *Now or never*, I thought, and grabbed one of the copper pipes, to try and wrench it loose. Which turned out to be a mistake.

Compressed air or steam, I'd said; if I hadn't panicked, I'd have thought to check which one first. As it was, I learned the hard way: the pipe was scalding hot, and I couldn't hold back a bellow of agony as I let go.

Sadie clapped her hand back over my mouth, but the sounds from the Driver's cabin had already stopped. A moment later, a shadow loomed up behind the grimy window.

"Oh *shit*," said Sadie, once more summarising things to perfection.

"Oh God." Kerry sounded terrified, but at least she'd snapped out of her previous despair. "What do we do?"

Before I could answer, there was a *clunk* from the cabin door, and the handle began to turn. As it swung open, a limb of some kind reached out from inside: black, chitinous and serrated, and ending in a thin, curved claw.

Sadie and Kerry were already in flight; I had to go full tilt to catch them up. When we reached the end of the carriage, I was sure that door would be locked as well, but Kerry pulled it open.

All we could do was keep moving: perhaps we could have cut through the rubbery material between the carriages, but I doubt my old Swiss Army knife would have done so in time, not with the Driver right behind us. I didn't allow myself to consider what would happen when we ran out of train.

There were even more corpses in the next carriage, so closely packed we could barely squeeze through. Two cocoons fell apart as we squeezed past, bones clattering over the floor, which was even thicker with dust. It billowed up in choking clouds, reducing visibility to almost nil; when I looked back the only sign of our pursuer was renewed movement among the swinging cocoons we'd already disturbed, as another, frighteningly bulky, shape forced its way through them.

If we could just open a big enough lead on the Driver, we might stand a chance. It shouldn't take long to break one of the copper pipes, then force the doors. Even then, of course, the Driver might pursue us back through the tunnels. Or up the embankment wall. I'd only the vaguest idea of its appearance, and would quite happily go to my grave with nothing more, but I kept thinking how fast spiders could climb with their thin, scuttling legs, and how pitifully slow we three would be in comparison, trying to get up a ladder in single file. God help whoever was Tail-End Charlie there.

But first we had to get off the train, and no matter how fast we went, how frantically we shoved or tore through the hanging, swaddled corpses in that carriage, or the next, or the next, the Driver was never any further behind, moving with the terrible, relentless speed of a machine.

I hadn't counted how many carriages the train had, and soon lost count of how many we'd already negotiated. I only knew we'd reached the last one when I heard Kerry scream and saw her wrenching desperately at the door at the end, which remained steadfastly shut. The window in the end door was cleaner than the others; beyond it were the empty tracks, leading into the tunnel behind.

"Oh shit," said Sadie, once again. "Oh *shit*."

I crouched beside the platform doors, pulling my sweatshirt sleeves over my hands for protection; even through the material, the pipes were searingly hot. I yanked with all my strength, but nothing shifted.

"Oh, Christ," said Kerry. "It's *here*."

Fresh clouds of dust billowed up and the dangling cocoons swung and shifted as the Driver closed in. Its jagged, spiky shadow was vast in the hazy light; it hissed, and a sickly sweetish smell, like the seepage at the bottom of a bin, washed over us.

I wrenched at the pipes again. Nothing.

"Please." Kerry pressed herself back against the end door, sliding slowly down. "I only wanted to see my little boy."

The Driver hissed again, almost dismissively, and kept coming. Kerry covered her face with her hands.

"Come on, then!" Sadie screamed, so suddenly I jumped. She stepped forward, a yellowed femur clutched in both hands, like a baseball bat. "Come on, you bastard! Come on!"

I wanted to drag her back, but at best that would only buy us a couple more seconds. Instead I kept yanking on the pipes. I felt something give, but still the thing came on, while Sadie screamed and brandished her makeshift club. It would be upon us long before I'd any chance to force the doors.

But then it stopped.

Sadie had the thighbone cocked back over her shoulder for a swing, face white. Her eyes, always big, were wider than I'd ever seen them, as if the insanity of what she was doing had finally sunk in. Then she rallied. "Well? Come on if you're coming, you bastard!"

The Driver gave a final hiss, louder than the rest; a fresh reek of wastebin-seepage crashed over us. It could have been amusement at the tiny, defiant figure at the end of the carriage, or it could have been fear: spiders are spindly creatures, after all, and those thin legs are very breakable. Whatever the reason, a moment later it began moving again—but this time away from us, scuttling ever faster as it went.

Of course, once the Driver was once more sealed safely in its cabin, the train would start moving, and then we'd never get off—not till the end of the line, and I never wanted to see where this train terminated. I hauled on the pipes again, and finally something cracked; when I gave one final pull, a pipe at last snapped free of the housing, letting out a jet of steam that would have boiled my face if I hadn't thrown myself backwards in time.

The train's engines thrummed and vibrated. By the time I got up Sadie was already at the doors, digging her fingers into the join. I did the same, and we pulled in opposite directions; the doors resisted for a long—a *very* long—moment, but finally slid apart.

I pushed Sadie out onto the platform, then stumbled after her before turning back, remembering Kerry. As I did, she ran for the doors, but just as she reached them, they flew shut again, and then the train rolled forward. She scrabbled at the doors, but they refused to budge; then the train accelerated, and we last saw her through the window at the end, pounding on the glass and screaming, before it entered the tunnel beyond the platform, and carried her into the dark.

Simon Bestwick is the author of nine novels, seven under his own byline, and two as "Daniel Church." His short fiction has appeared in numerous venues—foremost among them Nightmare Abbey—*and been reprinted in* The Best Horror of The Year. *His novel* The Ravening *has been shortlisted for The August Derleth Award; his third "Daniel Church" novel,* The Sound of the Dark, *will be published by Angry Robot in October. He lives on the Wirral with fellow author Cate Gardner. He loves dogs, tea, Pepsi Max, and to his editors' continuing dismay, far too many semicolons.*

Thanks for dropping by the Abbey. See you next time, dear friend.

www.ingramcontent.com/pod-product-compliance
Lightning Source LLC
Chambersburg PA
CBHW080744250626
47162CB00010B/3020